Praise for William Hazelgrove's Novels

"If somebody doesn't make a movie out of this book, there's something wrong with the world. George Kronenfeldt is an engineer who is, again, out of a job (he's a good engineer but not a good employee)—and this time it's right around Christmas. Faced with a bleak financial future, George seizes on a new project to keep him occupied: to convince his nine-year-old daughter that Santa is real. That sounds nice enough, until you realize it means Bob intends to dress up in a Santa suit, rent himself some reindeer and a sleigh, build ramps to get them on his roof, hire a movie director to whomp up some special-effects footage of the reindeer and sleigh landing and taking off, and generally tear his house (not to mention his family) apart. This could have been played as an out-and-out slapstick comedy, but instead the author approaches the story like a character study: a portrait of a man with the best intentions in the world watching those intentions collide with reality. It's a steamroller of a story, starting small, with George's idea, and getting bigger and bigger as George tries to put the elements together, as his obsession takes him further and further away from reality. Beautifully done."

—Starred Review ALA Booklist

"Hazelgrove has a natural grace as a storyteller that is matched by his compassion for his characters."

—Chicago Sun-Times

"An exemplary novel dealing with the death of the American Dream."

—Southern Review of Books

"Hazelgrove's writing has the natural arc of a baseball game."

Junior —Library Guild

"The funniest serious novel since Richard Russo's *Straight Man*, rich with the epic levity of John Irving and salted with the perversion of Updike."

—Chicago Sun Times

"The rollicking story of a writer whose piece of the American Dream falls apart."

—Chicago Tribune

Real Santa
by William Hazelgrove

ISBN 978-1-940192-96-3

Published by
köehlerbooks™

210 60th Street
Virginia Beach, VA 23451
212-574-7939
www.koehlerbooks.com

Cover design by Dalitopia Media

A **$1.99 (or less)** eBook is available
with the purchase of this print book.

CLEARLY PRINT YOUR NAME ABOVE IN UPPER CASE

Instructions to claim your eBook edition:
1. Download the BitLit app for Android or iOS
2. Write your name in UPPER CASE on the line
3. Use the BitLit app to submit a photo
4. Download your eBook to any device

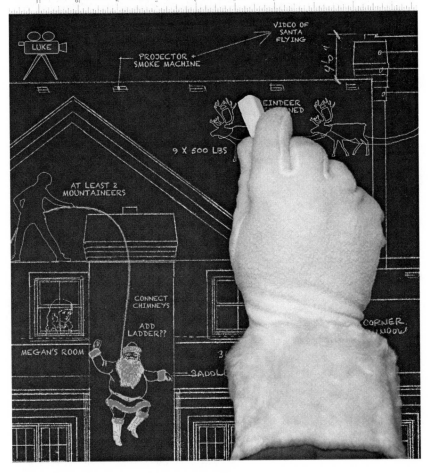

VIRGINIA BEACH
CAPE CHARLES

For Kitty, Clay, Callie, and Careen

And Believers Everywhere

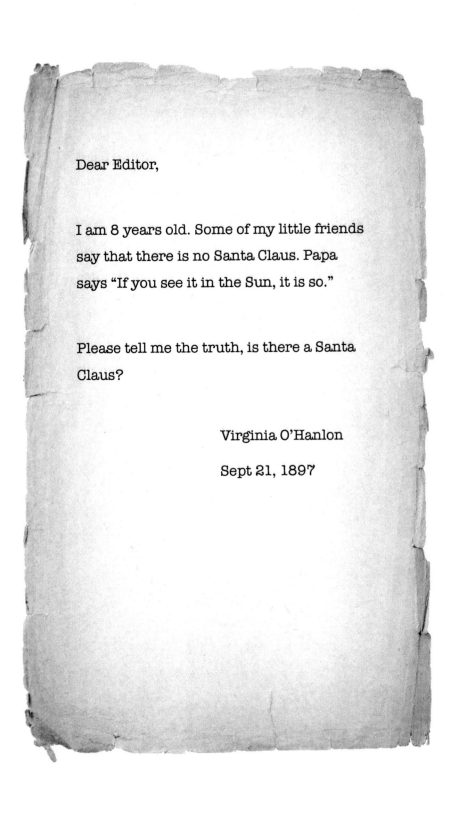

Dear Editor,

I am 8 years old. Some of my little friends say that there is no Santa Claus. Papa says "If you see it in the Sun, it is so."

Please tell me the truth, is there a Santa Claus?

Virginia O'Hanlon

Sept 21, 1897

1

The Question

"SO, IF ALL the icecaps are melting, where will Santa Claus go to build his toys?"

Barbara Worthington frowned at the boy in the back row. Leave it to Josh Pataki to throw the class into a tailspin. The fourth graders had been sedate, even bored; now their little hands were shooting up all over the classroom.

"Well, Josh, think about it. How cold do you think it is in the North Pole? Those are incredibly hostile conditions. How long do you think a man with a beard and a red suit could survive up there?"

Mrs. Worthington looked at her class, and Josh Pataki in particular. She was at the long end of her tether. Next year she would retire after forty years of teaching. *Forty years.* And for forty years she had been fielding questions about Santa Claus.

"I don't understand what you mean," Josh said through his coke-bottle glasses and stoppered nose. He had been a walking plague all year, and now he was doing the wrist roll with his nose. Mrs. Worthington handed him a Kleenex, walking in front of the twenty-five sets of eyes of Ridgeland Elementary.

"Well, Josh, Santa Claus supposedly lives in the North Pole in brutal subzero temperatures with an ice pack surrounding the pole and unbelievable snowstorms. Not much lives up in the North Pole even with global warming, which by the way has not been proven. So my question is simply, how would Santa Claus survive up there?"

Josh rolled his shoulders. "He would live in his complex built by elves like in *Santa Clause 2.*"

"Hmm ... and how do these elves build this complex up there? Where do they get their funding? Where do they get their skill set to create this mythical complex? Where would they get building materials, electricity?"

More hands shot up.

"Children, we are not going to stop our science hour to talk about Santa Claus."

The hands started to fall until there was only one arm still up in the back. Mrs. Worthington motioned her hand down, but the kid's hand stayed up there anyway. This was all Megan Kronenfeldt. The girl was bright, independent, and as literal as an accountant. She had a habit of calling out points that contradicted what Mrs. Worthington had mentioned a week before. She was almost a savant.

"Yes, Megan," Mrs. Worthington said wearily.

"Then what I understand you to be saying, Mrs. Worthington, is there is no Santa Claus in the North Pole because no one could survive without a facility and you don't believe there are the elves or anybody else to build that facility."

Mrs. Worthington stood with a faint blush coming to her cheeks. She saw the e-mails raining down from above. Parents would crash the school server with their onslaught of indignation that she dared to destroy the myth of Santa Claus. Deloris Ketchum had been forced into early retirement for saying that Santa Claus was a myth. The parents had e-mailed the district, the superintendent, even the mayor. Deloris retired five years early with just half of her pension.

And now Mrs. Worthington was standing in the same crosshairs.

"Well, Megan, I'm just saying that weather conditions are harsh in the North Pole and that people must be prepared to meet those conditions ... including Santa Claus."

Megan stared at her, and Mrs. Worthington had a sudden image of Natalie Wood in *Miracle on 34th Street* staring down her mother and saying, "He's just a nice old man with whiskers, but he's not really Santa Claus." Megan's eyes stared at her in the same disbelief as that young child star.

"That is not what you said, Mrs. Worthington," she countered, shaking her head. "You told us to *think about it* and inferred it was too cold for Santa Claus to survive and that elves could not really build a facility for him to build his toys, therefore, ergo, there is no Santa Claus."

Ergo! Ergo! Where do these children get their words? Maybe it was better she was retiring. These were not the same children she started with in 1975. These children surfed, texted, tweeted, Skyped, downloaded, and used words like *ergo.*

"Now, Megan, I did not say that," she replied, smiling icily. "Let's not put words in my mouth."

"Yes you did. You said that, Mrs. Worthington," Josh chimed in.

She glared at Josh Pataki, and he slumped down in his chair. She turned to Megan sitting at her desk with her hands clasped and her two pigtails sprouting like antenna. "Now, Megan, *of course* there is a Santa Claus. I was just pointing out that there are certain conditions we must be cognizant of and with global warming—"

"You didn't say that, Mrs. Worthington. You said that elves couldn't build the type of facility that Santa Claus required. I think what you are really saying is that you believe there is no Santa Claus."

Mrs. Worthington stared at the child. This was the same one who corrected her explanation of the Internet, saying the Department of Defense had this capability much longer than people knew and the network had been in place for a long time except they didn't want to release the technology to the general public. This walking science book was now boring down with her hard twenty-first century logic.

"Megan, that is not what I said."

"Mrs. Worthington, you said, *think about it,* there are very hostile conditions in the North Pole and that a man in a red suit and a beard really couldn't survive—"

"Megan, that is not what I said! There is a Santa Claus! He lives in the North Pole with his elves in a facility built by elves! I am retiring at the end of this year! *There is a Santa Claus, and he will give me my pension and I WILL RETIRE!"*

The fourth grade of Ridgeland Elementary stared at her. Megan tilted her head and squinted.

"I didn't think Santa Claus gave financial products, Mrs. Worthington."

Mrs. Worthington stared at Megan as the bell rang. She sat down behind her desk while the children put on their hats and gloves. She closed her eyes and felt the stare. Megan Kronenfeldt stood by her desk.

"Yes, Megan."

"Mrs. Worthington, I thought pensions were regulated by the state. I'm not sure Santa Claus could provide you with one of those."

"Believe me, Megan," she said wearily, "he's bringing me a pension."

Megan rolled her small shoulders fitted to her purple backpack.

"Oh, well. He must have filed an exception then to state laws."

2

The Gift

MEGAN'S FATHER STARED at the man behind the glass desk. "What are you saying, Mike?"

Mike Soros leaned toward his laptop, an antique sextant, a cell phone, a modular sleek office phone, and the picture of his three kids and trophy wife. He flashed a smile of bleached teeth. "What Jim and I are saying is that maybe we would all be better off if *a change* occurred."

"A *change*?"

Mike clasped his hands. "We have been friends a long time, George. We go way back. We sailed together. We have had dinner parties together—your kids my kids, your wife, my wife."

"We established we are friends, Mike. Get to the point."

Mike smiled. George should have known something was brewing when both partners came in wearing suits. Mike's suit looked like something James Bond would wear, while Jim sported the used-car variety, complete with epaulets of dust on the shoulders. Suits meant they were either pitching a client or someone was getting canned.

"I'm just not sure the fit has been there between you and S& G."

"What? My work hasn't been up to your standards?"

Mike chuckled and looked at Jim. "Nobody is questioning your work, George … it's more, well, your approach. S&G is going through a lot of changes in these lean times, and we really now have to be a lean, mean cyber-fighting machine."

George saw Clive Randall look in through the glass wall. The whole damn office was glass conference rooms. Clive and George locked eyes. Clive's twenty-nine-year-old blushing expression told him all he wanted to know. His hire had raised suspicions. Why hire someone when business was in the toilet, unless of course someone was getting fired?

"I can sue you, Mike."

"I'm sorry."

"You obviously hired that little shit Clive to take my spot, and it is a clear case of age discrimination."

Jim and Mike exchanged glances, then Mike smiled.

"We are the same age, buddy!"

"No, I'm fifty. You are forty-nine. "

Mike laughed. "C'mon, big fella. This is not about age. Hell, you are a young man!"

George saw himself in the glass, a man with a bushy grey beard and thinning grey hair in a checkered shirt and khakis. He didn't feel like a young man. He felt like an old man getting his ass handed to him.

"If you fire me, then I will sue."

Mike leaned back with his hands clasped. "Well, there have been some issues with your work."

"Name it."

"The bike bridge over Breckham Road."

George shifted. "Alright. What about it?"

Mike dropped the Byronic pose and came forward. "What about it? What about the million-dollar price tag? What about the railroad bridge you built that had the mayor calling and asking what the hell we were doing putting a railroad bridge through the middle of town?"

"I did it to specs, anticipating stressors for the next one hundred years. There could well be railroad traffic one day going across that bridge."

"It was supposed to be a bicycle path, not a bridge over the Erie Canal!"

George smoothed his beard. "I designed the bridge with a single span so—"

"That girder looks hideous, George! Do you know other firms come and look at that thing and laugh their ass off?"

"No."

Mike looked down and breathed heavily. "Look. I didn't want it to come to this, but you just don't play ball. You fight us on every design. You think you know better, and maybe you do, but I need a team that can play ball together. You are a one-man show, George. You probably should have your own firm again."

"I did that once before. I don't have that kind of capital."

"Then I am sure you will find a position very quickly."

George snorted. "Give me a break. We are in a depression, Mike!"

His employer shook his head. "There you go again. This is a recession that is ending. But you call it *a depression*. Maybe *you* are in a depression, did you ever think of that?"

"No."

"The point is, you just have to contradict everyone, George."

"That's not true."

"Really? Then why aren't you working on the bridge over the Crimson River anymore?"

"Because Frank Gifford doesn't know his ass from a hole in the ground when it comes to design," George muttered.

Mike laughed again, shaking his head. "You see. You are your own worst enemy! Frank offered to leave the project, but I said no way, because I know he will get it *done* while you sit there and fight over some design flaw that only matters to you."

Jim cleared his throat. "All we are saying is that we think you would be happier somewhere else. Our image is changing, and I don't think you are going to ... well, change with us. You are the old-time engineer, and that is good, but we need a different image now."

He turned and looked at the older heavyset man.

"An image?"

Jim rolled his shoulders. "Yes, we are becoming, like Mike said, a lean, mean cyber-fighting machine."

George held up his phone. "I have a BlackBerry."

Mike stared at him.

"Do you remember when we went sailing?" Mike asked.

"Of course."

"And do you remember we were up in the harbor and we had to pull the boat out?"

George felt his skin warming. "Yes. Get to the point."

"And the man who owned that forty-five-foot sailboat said the wind is so strong that you have to really give it a lot of power or you will be blown back into the dock?"

"And?"

"And you said, 'No.' You said that the wind would pull the boat forward and you didn't think giving it a lot of power was a good idea."

George cleared his throat. "What is your point, Mike?"

His boss leaned over his desk. "My point is that *wasn't your boat.* We were renting the man's boat for a day, and he told you how to get out of the dock and you wouldn't listen to the owner. You had to do it your way and what happened then?"

George frowned. "I'm sorry."

"What happened when you tried to take the boat out of the harbor?"

George paused, feeling his pants bunching up his crack. "The boat hit the dock," he murmured.

"And what happened?"

"It wasn't my fault that bumper wheel didn't hold," he protested.

"What happened, George?"

He looked down at the glass desk, pulling on his beard.

"Tore a gash in the side of the boat."

Mike held up his hand.

"You see. We own this firm, Jim and I. We are the owners of *this boat,* and we can't afford you to tear a gash in the side of our boat."

George stared at him.

"So what … you are firing me twelve days before Christmas?"

Mike dipped his head, opening his hands. "I would look at it like a gift. You get to spend more time with your family over the holidays, and you can hit the ground running in the New Year. I envy you really. We'll be slaving away right up to Christmas Eve, and you'll get some quality time with your family."

George stared at the owner of S&G Engineering.

"Oh, really, Mike? Then why don't *you* go home for the holidays, and I'll stay here and work."

Mike smiled tightly. "Because I'm the owner."

"No, really, Mike. If I'm *so lucky,* I'll stay here and you and Jim can go home and be Mr. Mom. Go ahead. I'll cover you."

Mike paused, two pink blushes on his cheek.

"You know, I did you a favor by hiring you, George. I knew your history. I knew you had bounced around from firm to firm for this very reason. But I was willing to take a chance because we were friends."

"You were a man short, and you got me for a song," George scoffed.

Mike rolled his shoulders. "If that's the way you want to see it."

"That's the way it was, *Mike.*"

Mike made a sound through his teeth.

"This is probably why you and Cynthia didn't make it. You just can't get along with people."

"She ran off with her high school boyfriend after she connected on Facebook," George replied dully. "It had nothing to do with me."

"But why was she interested in a high school boyfriend?"

"Recyclables."

"What?"

"Recyclables. She said I didn't clean the recyclables enough before I put them in the container."

"And you think that's why she left you?"

George shrugged again. "It became an issue. She started leaving them on the front steps when I came home from work."

Mike snorted. "I don't think that is why she left you."

"You seem to have all the answers, Mike. Why don't you ask her?"

"And your relationship with your kids is not so great either."

"As if it's any of your business, but Megan and I are fine."

"I meant your other kids."

George shrugged. "Jeremy and Jamie are adults now."

Mike laughed lightly. "Right. Well, listen. We are willing to be fair. I'll give you a month's severance."

"*Woof woof.*"

Mike stared at him. "I'm sorry ..."

George put out his tongue, panting quickly.

"*Woof woof.*"

"I'm sorry. Are you *barking* at me?"

"Dogs always bark when you throw them a bone, Mike."

Mike shook his head, throwing up his hands. "Fine. You get a month's severance. We'd like you to have your desk cleaned out by the end of the day."

George panted again with his big tongue toward Mike.

"Woof woof."

Mike stood up and nodded coldly. "I think this meeting is at an end."

George turned around, grabbing the arms of the shiny chair. He pushed up his rear to Mike and howled, *"ARROOOOOOOH!"*

"What are you doing?"

George stuck his rear up higher and wiggled it around.

"ARRRRRRRRROOOOH!"

"STOP IT!"

The entire office had stopped to watch an engineer shaking his ass in the air. George raised his head and howled again.

Mike turned bright red and pointed to the door.

"GET OUT OF MY OFFICE!"

George shook his ass again.

"ARRRRRROOOOOH!"

3

YouTube Santa

MEGAN AND JACKIE listened to the *Eminem* song her brother had loaded on her mother's defunct iPhone. Jackie stared at the phone while lying on the floor in front of a plastic corral and plastic horses. Megan continued feeding her horse on her Nintendo DSi.

"My brother loaded me with five hundred songs."

Megan was humming *Joy to the World* and thought Eminem yelled a lot. She was asking for an iPod for Christmas she would load with Taylor Swift and Katy Perry, and Hannah Montana. She didn't really care for the rappers that Jackie said were really cool.

"My brother told me something."

"What's that?" Megan murmured, waiting for Gumballs to tap his hoof.

Jackie looked to the door they had closed with the NO TRES-PASSING SIGN taped outside. Jackie flicked her long hair back. She had just turned ten and had pierced ears and wore makeup, although the makeup smudged her eyes and the lipstick made her look like a clown. She leaned in. "Nathan says that Santa Claus isn't real."

Megan put down her DSi and looked at her friend. "Who leaves the presents then?"

"My brother says it's *our parents.*"

Megan returned to her horse and began giving him water. "I don't see how they could buy all those presents without anyone seeing them."

"My brother says they hide them, and he found his iPod before Santa even brought it!"

Megan continued feeding. She had been thinking about Mrs. Worthington's declaration that the North Pole was too harsh for Santa Claus.

"I don't think that is true. My father doesn't believe in myths or even religion. He says he always will tell me the truth. Besides, they don't have enough money for all the presents."

"Oh, well, that's fine," Jackie said, shrugging, holding up Kanye West and singing along to an unintelligible lyric.

"You'd think he would be on YouTube if he was real," Megan continued, and then a thought occurred to her. "Does your phone have a video camera?"

"Sure."

Megan paused. "Then this is what I'm going to do! I'm going to stay up and wait for Santa and videotape him and put him on YouTube for the whole world to see!"

Jackie looked doubtful.

"My mom would kill me if I tried to stay up late."

"I'll bet my parents will even let me use their video camera, and I'll set my alarm so I wake every hour and I'll check downstairs until I catch him!"

Jackie was bobbing again to the music.

"Cool!"

Megan tapped her DSi pointer against her teeth.

"But first I'll ask my mom."

"You mean if you can stay up?"

"No. I'll ask her if she and Dad are Santa Claus."

4

A Christmas Panzer

GEORGE TURNED INTO his neighborhood, with the box of his belongings on the seat next to him. He drove past inflated Christmas globes that looked like incubators. There was a giant Frosty the Snowman, St. Nick, and a few penguins. George didn't care for the inflatables with the pneumatic pumps and the flaccid plastic on the snow like giant rubbers.

He had come to accept the smiling pumpkins lolling on their tethers and even a few turkeys during Thanksgiving after they had moved out of the neighborhood bordering the city five years ago. His country home with the wraparound porch swung into view. It was a Victorian built around the turn of the century, and the Realtor had almost not shown it to him. It's too old, she had told him. George reminded her they were moving from Park Ridge, a community of old homes, and she had stubbed her cigarette and shrugged. "It's your nickel."

George slowed to look at his lights. Two weeks ago he had lined the entire roofline with fat Christmas bulbs like his dad used to do when he was a kid. Most people in the neighborhood had their homes professionally decorated, but George took pride in the multicolored lights running up to the peak, the icicle lights bordering his porch, the swirled twinkles around his pines. He put a wreath on every window and an electric candle in the center. His house *was* Christmas, and he felt the hurt of the day subside.

George breathed deeply. He loved the Christmas rituals. They had to buy their tree right after Thanksgiving and decorate it that weekend, complete with the old G-Gauge Lionel train from when he was kid. Then over the next three weeks they would go downtown to Chicago and see the windows at Macy's and then Santa. After that they went ice skating on Michigan Avenue or had lunch at the Walnut Room on the top of Macy's. At some point they would go see the big tree at the State of Illinois Center and catch *Scrooge* at the Goodman Theatre or watch *It's a Wonderful Life* on the big screen at the Music Box Theatre on the North side with the sing-along Santa Claus.

Then they would catch the lights at the Lincoln Park Zoo and have a Christmas Eve dinner of fondue with chocolate. During all of this, George made sure they watched the prerequisite Christmas movies, *Miracle on 34th Street* (old version, noncolorized), *White Christmas, Holiday Inn, Christmas in Connecticut, Scrooge* (1941 version with Alastair Sim), then the newer additions—*Elf,* National Lampoon's *Christmas Vacation* and then the final movie, his all-time favorite: *A Christmas Story.* George loved Christmas because it was the only time he felt like a kid again. The rest of the year he felt like an overburdened adult getting older with each passing year. But at Christmas, he was young again.

George turned from his house to find a Panzer cannon pointed at him. The cannon wobbled slightly in the wind and bobbed up and down, then continued its sweep of the neighborhood. He watched George Shanti's inflatable warn all comers that Christmas would be brought in with a Panzer. It was the inflatable that made you wonder about the man. Why would anyone purchase a tank with a turret that rotated and flashed *Merry Christmas* when it shot you?

He and George were neighbors in the classic Midwestern sense. They waved and talked occasionally. They had found little to connect on after mowers and rakes and grass seed. The inflatable Christmas tank made its debut the year before, and George had vowed to take it down. He had purchased a Daisy BB gun,(the same kind in the movie *A Christmas Story*) and one night, after Mary and Megan were snug in their bed, he had slipped out the back door and snuck down to the three pines in his front yard.

From there George could see the tank very clearly. The night was bitter cold and the electric pump worked to keep the tank inflated and turning on its axis. The turret wobbled and jolted along as George lay down in the snow like a GI in the Battle of the Bulge and extended his BB gun out of the pines. He watched as the turret rotated around and pointed directly at his house. Sometimes it got stuck and bumped up and down as if taunting George.

George cocked his gun and lowered his eye to the site. He aimed dead center on the tank and squeezed the trigger and heard the soft thunk of the BB. The tank continued on its merry rotation, flashing *Merry Christmas* with each shot. George listened and heard no hiss of pressurized air. He cocked his rifle again and aimed at the center of the tank . The soft thud of the BB hitting the polyethylene reached him like a defeat. He then stood, like John Wayne with a Winchester, and began to unload a volley of BBs, trying to find a weak spot where the inflatable might give way. But the cold had turned the plastic into *a tank,* rendering the BBs as harmless as summer gnats. George emptied his gun and contemplated attacking the tank like a crazed soldier who has run out of bullets, but realized Shanti would press charges if he caught him. So the tank remained.

George sighed and pulled into his driveway, feeling his phone vibrating in his chest. He glanced at the number and considered not answering. "Yeah, Dad."

"You're a hard guy to get hold of."

George put his Prius in park and settled back into his parka.

"Yeah, well, a job and kids and Christmas will do that."

"Kids! I thought you only had one kid."

"Well, I do have another family."

"Oh, well I don't count them."

"That's great, Dad."

"How's the job?"

George paused. "Not so good ... I got fired today."

"Jesus! *Fired!* You got fired before Christmas! How the hell did you manage that?!"

George shut his eyes and rubbed his brow. Leave it to his father to put getting canned into the category of a choice. *You opted to get fired before Christmas?*

"I didn't manage anything, Dad, but yes I got fired before Christmas."

"How the hell did that happen?"

"They just pulled me in and told me I was fired."

"But what happened? Were you drinking on the job? Were you banging some broad in the office?"

George stared out of his fogged up windows. In his father's world, people only got canned for being a drunk or banging Betty the floozy secretary. No one ever got canned for a bad economy, performance, or because they just didn't like you anymore.

"There's a depression on, Dad."

"This ain't no depression! Let me tell you, I was a kid when there was a depression and this ain't no depression. You still got your house, don't you?"

"Yes, I still have my house, Dad," George said dully.

"Then it ain't no depression, but seriously, son, what the hell happened? This is your third job in six years!"

"Fourth in six years, Dad."

"Fourth or fifth, does it matter?"

George really didn't want to go down this road again. He felt kind of stupid and silly for waving his ass in the air and barking. He had to clean out his desk and office, with his coworkers staring at him. He should have just flipped Mike Soros the bird and walked out.

"There were some political issues, Dad."

"*Political?* What, they fired you because you were a Democrat?"

"Yeah, Dad. They fired me because I was a Democrat. Jesus!"

"Those dirty bastards!"

"There were performance issues, Dad."

"Performance issues? What do you mean? When I worked for the railroad, you just did the work. There was no *performance* involved. When I was in that caboose testing the bridges after WWII, Floyd Habersham and I were out there in the middle of nowhere and—"

George sighed. The story of his father going all over the country in a railroad car with Floyd Habersham was legend. He had heard many times how he tested *every bridge* in the country and big steam locomotives backed onto the bridges to see if the steel would give way. He was glad to hear the familiar beep in his ear of another call.

"And Floyd and I went all over the damn country—"

"Hold on, Dad. Hold on. I have another call."

"Dad?"

"Yes, hello, Jeremy," George said, feeling the good tidings of his only son.

"Dad! Everyone at college has a new car, and I just have that old clunker you gave me."

"I see. Is that a problem?"

His twenty-year-old son made a sound in his throat. "Yes, it's a problem, Dad. My car sucks! And Mom says it's your fault that I don't have a good car because you won't let her sell the house!"

George rubbed his eyes behind his glasses. "Now, that's not true, son. We can't sell the house until the economy comes back."

"Mom says you are a liar. That you live in a big house in the country while we are in this shitbox!"

"She shouldn't say that—"

"Hold on. Jamie wants to talk to you."

"Dad! Dad!"

George sat up in the car.

"Hello, sweetie."

"Dad, I want an iPhone!"

George breathed heavily in his fogged over Prius. "Well, now, you have a phone. I gave you my old BlackBerry and—"

"I don't want your shitty old-man BlackBerry! I want an iPhone!"

"Now, Jamie—"

"Mom says you have to get me one because you don't pay her child support!"

"Well now, you are eighteen, and by law, I don't have to pay that anymore, but I do and your mother—"

"Dad, I'm a senior in high school!"

"I know honey, but—"

"It's embarrassing not to have an iPhone and be a senior!"

George breathed heavily. His Prius was a steamed up capsule, and he really wanted to forget about this day. "I'll see what I can do—"

"Mom wants to talk to you."

"George!"

"Yes, Cynthia," he said wearily.

"I didn't get the check! It's Christmas. I need money!"

"I sent it to you. You should have it today or tomorrow," he replied calmly.

"It better be here or so help me we are going back to court. It's bad enough you won't let me get out of this *shithole*, but now you stiff me on support!"

"Shithole," George murmured. "So, that's where Jeremy gets that."

"He knows a shithole when he sees one. I could move on with my life if you would let me sell this shithole!"

George rubbed his forehead.

"Cynthia, if you sold now you couldn't pay off the note."

"That's your opinion! And I got a kid driving a beater and a daughter who needs a phone while you're out there in your perfect home with your perfect family while we get screwed!"

George drew a small circle on his fogged over windshield.

"I'll see what I can do for the kids."

"That check better be here tomorrow, George, or I'm going to file again!"

The phone went dead and George paused, remembering his dad was on the line still. He sighed and clicked over.

"What the hell? Did you forget about me? I would think you need family now that you got canned."

"Dad, I'll call you later."

"But—"

George turned off his phone and got out of his car into the clear, cold night. He stood in the drive, staring at the lights winking in his pines. He felt some of the stress leaving. It was Christmas again. He heard a slight whirr, a sliding of cold plastic, and turned. The Panzer pointed at him and fired.

5

Holiday Inn

THE HOT FUDGE sundae was perfect. The cherry tip sat on the hardened chocolate like a beacon and the chopped nuts littered the landscape. The vanilla ice cream was two concave half-moons perched in the silver dish. The whipped cream swirled like fluffy snow setting off the lighthouse cherry. George ate his warmed chicken and stared at the sundae. The kitchen was littered with dishes of ice cream with five different bottles of hot fudge, five cans of whipped cream, three jars of cherries, a glazing spray, and four jars of assorted crushed peanuts.

"I think it is your best yet, Mary."

His wife pulled her Christmas sweater closer together. "I don't know. I think the ice cream is a little off … the scooper just didn't melt it correctly."

George gnawed on a chicken wing. Since they had moved, Mary's profession as a food preparer had become very part time. People just weren't spending much on ad budgets anymore.

George sighed, staring at the sundae.

"I'm now one of these marginalized old white males you read about in the paper. I have been thrown into the dust heap of failed white men."

Mary looked at him, her eyes hard behind the rounded lenses. "Nonsense. People move around with jobs all the time. You are a very good engineer, George. Your work speaks for you."

"We should have never moved," he moaned. " Now we have this big house. We should have stayed in your townhome with the small mortgage."

"Don't be ridiculous. The best thing we did was move. This is a lovely house, and we will manage. You are a resourceful man."

George looked at his wife. That's what he loved about her. She was practical. Yes, she looked like a librarian. That's what his dad had called her when George first brought her over. "Where did you get that damn librarian," he had asked.

George had met his wife online at Match.com.

"Online? Online? What the hell kind of a way is that to meet a woman?"

"Maybe you should try it, Dad. Mom's been gone five years."

"I would never go on a computer to find a woman. You don't know what kind of disease you could get. Are you wearing a goddamn condom?"

But he had gone online and found Mary, who had lived in Park Ridge all her life and never married. She did wear button-up sweaters, hard, flat shoes, granny glasses, and Mary Tyler Moore hair, but what his father didn't know was that Mary was great in bed. They had become engaged within six months.

"That Mike Soros is a real prick. Telling me how lucky I was to be getting fired."

Mary listened while George finished his wine.

"I'm going to tell that Shanti that I don't want his Panzer turret pointed at my house."

"I'm sure he will reposition his tank if you ask him," Mary said brightly.

George chewed on this then swung back to Mike Soros. "I'm not a *team* player?! I'm the biggest team player there is!"

"I know you are, dear."

"I'm not a cyber-man? I have a BlackBerry!"

"Of course you do, dear."

"I may not use it for everything ... but I have one."

"I'm sure he didn't mean it," Mary murmured, raising her camera and flashing five quick shots of the melting sundae.

"And he criticized my bike bridge, saying other engineers laugh at it!"

"I'm sure no one laughs at your bridge, dear."

"Asshole," he grumbled. "He's just jealous because I built that bridge to last for the next hundred years!"

"Of course he is," she continued, shooting five more from the top down.

George finished his meal and looked at his reflection in the kitchen window. His flat grey hair and beard were not familiar to him. This other older man without a job had snuck in and eaten his dinner and drunk his wine. What this other man really wanted to know was, *Now what?*

"Where's Megan?"

"She's in her room." Mary put down her camera and slid the sundae to George.

"You sure?"

"Go ahead. I'm done with it."

Joy to the World floated down the stairs. Megan was singing in her bedroom. Mary glanced toward the stairs then motioned George into the laundry room. He followed his wife into the room, which smelled like detergent. She shut the door and pulled a piece of paper from her pocket.

"Megan gave me this right before you came home."

George looked at his wife and began to read the perfectly typed note.

> *Mom,*
>
> *I have doubts about the existence of Santa Claus. Mrs. Worthington pointed out in class today that conditions in the North Pole are very harsh (thirty below) and that Santa Claus really could not survive up there. Also, she seemed to doubt that elves were capable of building the facility needed to build toys and provide shelter to the big man. When I questioned her, she seemed to contradict herself and violated Dad's basic rule: Data should prove to be a coherent thesis. Also, several of my friends (Jackie) have told me that there is no Santa Claus and that parents actually purchase the presents. I have some doubts about this, as I don't see parents being able to pay for all those presents!*
>
> *Finally, I have surfed on the Internet in search of eyewitness accounts of Santa and found none. The few I did find were amateur videos of some man dressed up like Santa. Dad always said empirical data is needed to verify any thesis. I*

have thought it over, and I don't physically see how Santa could pull off landing his sled on our roof, climbing down the chimney, distributing multiple gifts, then going back up the chimney and taking off again. Also, a minor point: How do all the letters get to him with no zip code if they are just addressed to Santa in the North Pole? Does he have a special arrangement with the post office?

So I have decided to use a video camera (if you'll let me) and wait for Santa on Christmas Eve, setting my alarm to go off every hour, and then if I do catch him on video, I will post it on YouTube and settle it once and for all. I promise I won't be tired the next day. By the way, can I sleep over at Jackie's tomorrow night? And can you get some more milk that is not skim?

Sincerely,

Megan

Love you. Love you. Love you.
Kisses XXXX

"That Jackie!" George fumed. "I always knew she was a bad influence. She'll be getting high and giving her pot next!"

Mary raised her eyebrows. "How about Mrs. Worthington telling her Santa couldn't make it in the North Pole?"

"She should be fired!" George fumed. "I'm going to call the principal tomorrow morning!"

Mary shrugged. "It won't do any good. She's retiring. I guess she just figured she'd let that little grenade roll before she left."

George stared at the letter again and shook his head.

"Great. I lose my job, and now my daughter doesn't believe in Santa Claus anymore."

Mary crossed her arms, glancing toward the closed door.

"I think she still believes. But she is your child and wants proof that he exists. She is nine. She's getting to the age where they stop believing."

George leaned back against the washer, deflated. Megan had been his second chance at fatherhood. He had screwed up with Jeremy and Jamie. He had put too much time into his career and probably brought on the divorce, although he really believed Cynthia was chemically unbalanced. But Megan was the daughter where he would do everything right. They were very close, and he went to every school function, every Girl Scouts function, everything! And now he had blinked, and she was growing up.

George looked at his wife. "She should still believe in Santa. I remember the best moments of my life were when my mom and dad tucked me into bed on Christmas Eve and I had those electric candles in my window. I was just so excited, and the room was in a dull-yellow glow from the candle, and I was just waiting for Santa ..." He shook his head. "I can't have her lose that."

Mary pursed up her mouth, the small wrinkles appearing on her upper lip. "She believes in logic, facts, proof. I have been doing magic elves with her for the last week, having them mess up her room, and I think she believes in them, but ..." Mary paused, looking down. "But kids talk and text and check out everything online. It's harder to keep secrets. I remember when I realized there was no Santa. I was probably Megan's age. And I cried and cried."

Mary put her hands on the dryer and moved some folded clothes. "It is sad when they stop believing, but they grow up."

"It was even worse with my other kids," George muttered. "Jeremy asked Cynthia if there was a Santa Claus. She told him, and I quote, 'There is no stupid Santa Claus. We buy all the gifts.' "

"That is so sad."

"I think they blame me for that too. I ruined their life, and I told them there was no Santa Claus. They forget it was their mother who wanted to go to Florida for Christmas and swim at a hotel pool on Christmas day. No tree ... nothing. I tried to give the kids gifts, and she was lying out by the pool."

George held up the letter. "So what do we do about this?"

"I'm going to leave that to you, George. She respects your opinion, but you have to explain to her how Santa delivers the gifts." Mary looked at her husband sadly. "After that, we just have to accept that our little girl is growing up."

6

Santa's Relativity Cloud

GEORGE CLIMBED THE stairs to his daughter's room and stood outside, listening to her hum *Rudolf the Red-Nosed Reindeer*. He felt the day lift from his shoulders again. Just the sound of Megan's voice had the power to cure ills, aches, and pains.

"Hi, Daddy!"

"Hey there, pumpkin."

She was in her bed behind a fortress of stuffed animals. He walked over and hugged her, breathing in the faint scent of soap and feeling her wet hair. "How was your day, Daddy?"

"Oh, fair to middling," he replied, sitting on the bed and looking around her room. There was a Hannah Montana poster along with several posters of Cinderella, one of puppies, and an old *Gone with the Wind* poster he had rescued from a video store. There was also a bulletin board of softball pictures, Girl Scouts pictures, drawings from school, and a pair of tickets from Wrigley Field when they saw the Cubs last summer.

"I heard you lost your job," she whispered, setting down her DSi.

George stared at his daughter, with her spreading blond hair. Megan had Janis Joplin hair. Where did such a thicket come from? No one on his side had the wild curly hair of his daughter and her saucer-size brown eyes.

"Really? How did you know?"

"I heard Mom on the phone. Don't worry, you'll get another one,

Dad. You always do."

"I'm not worried, pumpkin."

"I'm not either, Daddy," she continued, putting down her DSi and picking up a book.

"What are you reading?"

"Ramona Feeds Her Puppy."

"Hmm, is it good?"

"I just started."

George nodded, staring outside at the snow piled up on her windows. Farther on he could see the large double chimney of the old house. The fireplace hearth was so large, a man could climb into it. "So I heard you were playing with Jackie today."

"Uh huh."

George stroked his beard and shifted on the bed.

"I heard you gave your mother a letter."

Megan put down her book and stared at her father.

"She wasn't supposed to show you that."

"Why not?"

"Because it was *private.*"

"Oh." George shrugged. "I think questioning the existence of Santa Claus is something you need two parents involved in."

Megan put down her book and sat up next to a large stuffed giraffe. "I'm sorry, Daddy. I just don't see the data to support Santa Claus."

"Just because Jackie says there isn't a Santa Claus doesn't mean it is so, Megan."

She shook her head. "It's not Jackie. I frankly don't see how parents could afford all those presents."

"Exactly!"

Her brow furrowed. "But I have done research on the Web, and I know all about the history of Santa Claus. How he started as a Dutch legend of Sinterklaas, which was brought by settlers to New York in the seventeenth century."

"Okay."

"And how he started to appear in the American press as St. Claus, but it was really the popular author Washington Irving who gave Americans information about the Dutch version of St. Nicholas and then the more Americanized version appeared around 1823 in the poem *'Twas the Night Before Christmas* by writer Clement Moore, which included details about elves and the names of his reindeer and the method of going down the chimney and all that."

George stared at his daughter. "You really did your research."

"And, it was the American illustrator Thomas Nast who gave us a fat Santa Claus when he drew his picture in *Harper's* and the whole thing of good children and bad children came about and the workshop at the North Pole, which as Mrs. Worthington points out is a very hostile environment."

"Let's hear it for Mrs. Worthington,"George murmured.

"But it was really the Coca-Cola Company in the 1930s that gave us the red-suited Santa we know today."

"That is quite a history."

Megan frowned and scrunched up her brow. "Yes, but really, Daddy, I just don't see the proof. I have gone all over the Internet looking for actual footage of Santa landing on the roof with his sled, climbing up to the chimney." Megan gestured out to the darkness. "Going down the chimney and delivering the gifts, then going back up the chimney, getting into his sled, and then flying off into the sky."

George squinted at his daughter.

"There is no YouTube video of that, huh?" he asked.

"No. Just some guy in his backyard going *HO HO HO*. It was really pathetic." Megan formed a small fist. "I want empirical *evidence*, Dad. And to be honest, I really just don't see how the physics makes sense."

"You don't, huh?"

"No. Reindeer, Daddy, cannot fly."

George nodded slowly. "Hmm … well I see how you arrived at your hypothesis, but I must point out there are three hundred thousand species of living organisms we have yet to discover, and we can't rule out the existence of flying reindeer."

Megan scrunched up her mouth, her eyes narrowing. "Then how can he get to all the children of the world?"

"Speed of sound," he replied, shrugging. "There are probably two billion children, and that gives him thirty-one hours." George pulled out his BlackBerry. "So maybe … mmm, 822.6 visits per second, maybe a total trip of 75,500,00 miles around the world, 650 miles per second, speed of light. It's doable."

"What about payload? How can he carry all those toys?"

George punched the calculator on his phone.

"Well, let's give it two pounds for each kid, two billion kids, then the sled is carrying three hundred tons of cargo, not including Santa. Yes, it's doable."

"Daddy!"

"What?"

"We are talking here about a man in a sled!"

George put away his phone.

"Megan, Santa is magic, and he *does* exist. You just have to believe it."

"Then how does he know what I'm thinking?"

"Elaborate underground antenna collects electromagnetic waves from the thought waves of children."

"Uh huh … what about the elves? What proof is there of that?"

George leaned over. "You know those tiny screws in your DS there?"

"Yes."

"You know that tiny Phillips head screwdriver we have to use to get them out?"

"Yes"

"Well, that's an elf screwdriver."

Megan squinted at him. "I think you are fibbing."

George crossed his chest. "It's true."

"How can he make it to every house, and why don't I ever see him?"

"Relativity cloud. That allows him to control space, time, and distance. The relativity cloud moves so fast, you can't see him—a lot like the way a bee buzzes by."

Megan pointed out the window. "And the chimney?"

"Same relativity cloud. He can shrink and expand the cloud."

"What about finding his way?"

"GPS," he answered.

Megan sat back and stared at her father, one eyebrow raised. "Really? I need hard evidence, Daddy," she stated flatly. "That is why I am going to stay up with a video camera if you guys let me use ours, and I will videotape Santa, and then I will put it on YouTube to prove his existence forever."

"I don't think that is really necessary, Megan."

His daughter raised her hands over her head. "You are the one who told me to not trust my senses and to look for fact! Well, I am looking for fact."

"I said that?"

"Yes."

George puckered his lips and stood up. He walked across the room and stared at the nearly flat roof covered in snow. He then stared at the wide chimney outside her window. The second roof was a skirt that ran around the house and protected the lower porches. The chimney in the back of the house was oddly short.

"So, you are determined to do this?" he murmured.

"Yes!"

George pulled on his beard and stared at the three letters from the North Pole on her bulletin board. A cutout reindeer head was posted on the top. "What's this?"

"That's my reindeer head I made in class. Did you know a reindeer's head can be anywhere from one hundred and twenty millimeters to three hundred millimeters big?"

"I didn't know that." George touched the letters tacked to the wall. "And who are these from?"

"One is from Santa, and the other one is from those pesky elves I locked up in the closet so they don't mess up my room. That's another thing, Dad—no one puts an address on the letters to Santa, so how does he get them? They don't even have a zip code."

George turned from the bulletin board. "Special dispensation with the post office."

"Oh ..." She nodded. "I guess I could see that."

He turned back to the roof and stared at the old chimney again.

"So you are determined to videotape Santa?"

"Yes. I will have proof once and for all. I want to see the *real* Santa."

"But you sent him a letter telling him what you want."

Megan held out her hands.

"Of course. I can't take a chance."

"Wise thinking." George stared out the window again at the chimney. "How many reindeer are there?"

"Daddy, there's nine including Rudolf—Dasher, Dancer, Prancer, Vixen, Comet, Cupid, Donner, and Blitzen."

"Nine," he muttered staring at the roof. "And do you know how much a reindeer weighs?"

"Between two hundred and six hundred pounds."

"Hmmmm."

George picked at his beard as he took out his phone and did some quick calculations.

"What are you doing, Daddy?"

"Hmm … nothing."

He turned around and smiled. "I think you have a good plan."

Megan's eyebrows went up. "You do?"

"Yes. And you can use our video camera."

Megan threw her hands up.

"Thank you, Daddy!"

He walked over and gave her a kiss.

"Now, let's get some sleep, little girl."

"Alright."

George turned out her light and walked toward the door.

"Daddy?"

"Yes, pumpkin."

She had snuggled down among her animals, her hair fanning out over the pillow.

"I hope I'm wrong. I hope Santa Claus comes."

"Trust me. You are wrong. And Santa Claus will come. Now get some sleep, precious."

"Good night, Daddy."

George slowly walked down the stairs, grappling his beard. He paused at the bottom then went to get his laptop.

7

Combustible Santa

GEORGE GRUNTED AND picked at his beard, tapping on his computer, his calculator, scribbling notes to himself, balling up the paper, and littering the floor with snowballs. He ate Hershey's Kisses as he worked. He had started with the glass bowl, then he just grabbed the bag from the pantry. Snow blew outside the kitchen window, showing a man under a yellow light with a grey beard and spectacles low on his nose. Some would say he looked like Santa Claus doing his taxes.

George sat back in his chair and stared at the screen of his laptop. He chewed the inside of his mouth. It might all work without too much alteration, depending on where the roof joists were reinforced. He could get up in the attic and check on that. The load-bearing wall should handle the weight, which he put at about three thousand pounds, give or take a little. Now of course—

"George?"

He turned and looked at his wife, clutching her robe. "Oh, hi."

Mary frowned.

"What are you doing up? It's nearly four in the morning."

"Is it?" George looked at his watch. "I guess time got away from me."

His wife walked up and stared at the paper all over the table. "What are you working on?"

George paused. Mary was already fingering his drawings, trying to understand the pictures of reindeer and sleds next to calculations of payload and stress, with the blueprints of the house showing joist locations, the exact run of the roof, the pitch—the critical data for a man trying to place nine reindeer and a sled.

Mary picked up one of the drawings, her eyes bunching. "What are you doing, George?"

He breathed heavily and set his pencil down. "Megan doesn't believe in Santa unless she can see proof that he exists."

"Okay."

"She is going to stay up all night to videotape him when he comes. If he doesn't come, then she'll know he isn't for real."

Mary waved him away. "Kids say things like that all the time."

He paused. "I lied to you when I told you how Jeremy found out there wasn't a Santa. I told you it was my wife who told him, but it wasn't. He came to me and asked me how Santa Claus could do it. He asked how Santa could deliver all those presents in one night to kids all over the world. And I said, *let's figure it out.*"

Mary nodded slowly. "Okay."

"So I took out my calculator and started figuring out miles per hour and payload, and basically I came up with a sled weighing three hundred and fifty-three thousand tons, traveling at six hundred and fifty miles per second, creates an enormous amount of air resistance in the form of friction. So I explained that with this heat, the reindeer will be much the same as a spacecraft re-entering the earth's atmosphere. The lead reindeer would have to absorb fourteen quintillion joules of energy. Per second. Each!"

Mary shook her head. "George, you're losing me."

He breathed heavy, shaking his head.

"Then I told my son that in short, the first pair of flying reindeer would burst into flames almost instantaneously, exposing the next pair of flying reindeer. This would create a deafening sonic boom in their wake, and the entire reindeer team would be vaporized in less than five seconds. Santa meanwhile would be subjected to g-forces equivalent to seventeen thousand times greater than the force of earth's gravity. A two-hundred-and-fifty-pound Santa would be pinned to the back of the sled by more than four million pounds of force and would spontaneously combust. In short, he would be fried beyond all recognition."

Mary stared at him. "You told your son that?"

George nodded. "He was nine."

"Oh, George!"

"I know. I thought in the name of science and deductive reasoning it was better to work it out with him." He looked at Mary. "You know what's worse? I almost did it again with Megan."

Mary stared down for a moment.

"I'm sure Jeremy didn't follow all those calculations."

"No, but he remembered that I told him that Santa would spontaneously combust. It was horrible. He has held that against me ever since." George nodded to the table. "I'm fifty years old. I probably just destroyed my career, and I have two kids who hate me and one who still believes in me."

"They don't hate you."

"Oh, yes they do," he replied, nodding. "I don't blame them. I was always working when they were growing up. I was always lost in my own world."

Mary took his hand. "You were a good father."

"That's not what they would say. Anyway, I determined I wasn't going to let the same thing happen to Megan. I want her to have dreams. I want her to have a great childhood. I want her to believe in Santa until she's ready to give it up. I don't want the world to take it from her. Not yet."

Mary stared at her husband. "So what are you saying?"

George looked at his computer and the pages of calculations. "I'm saying I'm going to be the *Real* Santa. She said she wants to see Santa land on the roof, go up the chimney and down it, deliver the presents, and go back up the chimney and fly away on his sled. That's what she wants to see, and I'm going to make sure she sees a real Santa."

Mary didn't move. She stared at the man with his arms crossed. "But how will you do that?"

"Well, I've worked out a lot of it. I was thinking Dean could help me with the special effects. Obviously, the only real way to pull it off would be a relativity cloud, but since we don't have the technology to produce that, I will have to settle for smoke and mirrors."

George spun around his laptop. "I initially thought getting the reindeer on the roof would be the hardest part. But it really is just a matter of preparation. I'll have a ramp built here. The reindeer can be herded up onto the roof and put into line. Fortunately the pitch of the roof is so slight the reindeer will be able to stand. It is a question of how much the roof can take. I'm thinking three thousand pounds at a minimum with the sled and payload. Obviously the sled will have to be custom, and I'm thinking it will run on rails much the same way a train does and—"

"*George!*"

He looked at his wife, who was now standing.

"Tell me you aren't really thinking of being the *Real* Santa!"

He shrugged. "Who else? There will be a certain amount of risk, and I couldn't ask anyone else to do it. Scaling a chimney in the middle of the night could be considered hazardous work by some, but with proper precautions, I think the risk will be minimal."

Mary felt her face growing warm. "You are kidding."

"No." George picked at his beard. "No. I'm going to do this. I want to keep my little girl's dreams intact, and this is the only way. For one night I will be the Real Santa, and Megan will be able to videotape it, and if she puts it out on the net, who knows, maybe other kids who have doubts will see it."

"But kids just stop believing, George … it's inevitable."

He looked at up at his wife.

"I've been an engineer who has built bridges and screwed up his family. That's all I can say for my life so far. Here is my chance to do something good. I want to do something I can believe in, Mary. I want to do this for Megan. I don't want her to be knocked down by the Mrs. Worthingtons of the world."

His wife sat back down at the table.

"But … won't this be expensive?"

George shifted in his chair.

"There will be costs. But it shouldn't be too bad. Basically I'm going to rent some reindeer for a night and hopefully a sled, and then I'm going to put them on the roof and go up the chimney and down it. There will be alterations to the chimney and ramps will have to be built to get the reindeer up and down, but after that I don't see a lot of costs."

Mary looked at her husband.

"There are only eleven days to Christmas."

He nodded grimly and looked at her. "I need to talk to Dean for the technical problems. Can you call him for me?"

Mary sat quiet at the table. She remembered the night she walked home from the library and saw an old woman walking alone with a cane. At that moment, Mary had seen herself, and she wondered what would she have to show for her life. She had registered on three dating sites the next day and ended up marrying into a family of eccentric Swiss men who engineered cannons for armies and bridges spanning rivers all over the world.

She looked at her husband and nodded.

"I'll call him tomorrow."

8

Don't Mess with Santa

GEORGE DROVE HIS daughter to school through the snow-covered quiet countryside. It was the benefit of moving into the middle of nowhere. You got to see a lot of nature, and it was very pretty with the heavy snow in the pines and the homes looking like something out of Currier & Ives. *Jingle Bells* was on his satellite radio, and George drove with his coffee cooling in the console and his daughter humming along with the Christmas music.

"Well, I don't get to do this every day."

"Why don't you never go back to work, Daddy, then you can drive me every day?"

Megan smiled at him with her two large front teeth.

"I might just do that," he murmured.

"I like it when you take me. Mom always goes over my homework in the car but you just play music."

"That's why dads are more fun."

He pulled into Ridgeland Elementary's parking lot. George looked over at his daughter and had a momentary pang of sadness. She had been turning to him, and her hair fanned over one eye. She looked like a young woman. It pained him to think that next month she would break into the double digits.

"Dad, you are supposed to drop me off in front of the school."

He turned off the car. "I just wanted to speak to Mrs. Worthington about your Christmas party and see if she needs any more helpers."

Megan hoisted her backpack with the small duck clipped to the zipper. The duck gave him heart. She was still a little girl. There was still time.

"That's all set I think, Dad. I think they have enough moms."

"Well, maybe they can squeeze in a dad," he said gingerly. "Come on, you can show me your classroom."

George and Megan squished through the snow and walked into the heated lobby of her school. The smell of institutional food took him back to when he was a boy. Where did that smell come from anyway? It seemed every school in the world was sprayed with cologne of warm caramels. He followed his daughter down through the hallway crammed with teachers, mothers, students and the occasional dad.

George and his daughter walked into her classroom, where kids were dismantling their cold-weather gear. Boots, coats, hats, scarves, melted snow, and gloves were all over the place. The American flag hung on one wall with the ABCs running over the board. Posters about being a good writer, a good citizen, and a good speller broke up the cinder block walls. Children squealed with excitement. George remembered his own moment of bliss in sixth grade when he had walked home from school with a small rubber basketball. It had been a gift from the Christmas party, and he bounced it the whole way, knowing that only good things were ahead.

"Dad, there's Mrs. Worthington, if you want to ask her about the party," Megan whispered.

His daughter had already hung her coat, scarf, and gloves in her cubbyhole. She was very efficient, and George marveled at how different she was from his other children. Everything seemed a struggle with his prior family, whereas Megan seemed preprogrammed. So far, she had been a parent's dream.

"Alright, I'll go ask her," he said, approaching the woman with the silver globe of hair.

George cleared his throat. "Ah, Mrs. Worthington?"

Cold grey eyes turned on him. He smiled at the dowager in the print dress with the cold, thin lips.

"Yes. May I help you?"

"I am Megan's father, George Kronenfeldt."

Mrs. Worthington put down her pencil and clasped her hands.

"Children take your seats!" Her eyes returned. "What can I do for you, Mr. Kronenfeldt?"

"Ah, well, Megan came home and told us about the conversation you had about ..." George leaned down and whispered, "about Santa at the North Pole and how it's too cold for him there."

Mrs. Worthington's eyes frosted over. *"And?"*

George smiled again, tweaking his beard. "Well, I was thinking." He leaned in closer. "If you could just go easy on the whole Santa couldn't survive up in the North Pole stuff, I would appreciate it. Megan is starting to doubt the existence of Santa, and we'd like to keep that illusion in place as long as we can."

Mrs. Worthington's eyes dulled, her mouth turned down.

"It is my job to teach these children, Mr. Kronenfeldt, not perpetuate *myths*."

George stared at the woman, who had crossed her arms. He suddenly remembered Mrs. Gary in first grade who hit him with a pencil because he couldn't make his eights properly. Mrs. Gary hit him on the skull. *No, no, no, no. How stupid are you? You make them like this!* Then he made another snowman. *NO, NO, NO. LIKE THIS!* Whack, whack, whack! Mrs. Gary had broken several pencils before he drew an eight.

"Well, I am just requesting you stay away from Santa discussions then. These children don't really need to hear that the climate in the North Pole is too harsh for Santa and his elves," he continued gingerly.

Mrs. Worthington raised her pencil like a jousting pole.

"Mr. Kronenfeldt, *nobody* tells me how to teach. I will teach as I see fit, and if you have a problem with that, then I suggest you take it up with the principal. I knew I would get one of you parents coming in here whining about Santa Claus."

George felt his face turning red, watching the pencil in her hand.

"Whining about Santa Claus?"

"That's right. Every year it's the same thing. I get some bleeding heart parent who thinks I have damaged their child." Mrs. Worthington beat the pencil in her hand. "Life is hard, Mr. Kronenfeldt, and it is getting harder. The last thing these children need are more *myths*."

George laughed lightly.

"Ah ... well with all due respect, Mrs. Worthington, that is not for you to decide."

Mrs. Worthington stood up in her floral dress with the pencil in her right hand. She batted the pencil toward George like a piston. "This conversation is over. Please leave my classroom."

George stared at her.

You going to hit me with that pencil?"

"*What?*"

"Weren't you ever a little girl, Mrs. Worthington?"

"*Goodbye, Mr. Kronenfeldt.*"

George stared at her.

"You were never a little girl who believed in Santa?"

Mrs. Worthington shook her head.

"We did not have myths in the home I grew up in!"

George frowned.

"What ... were you raised in a Conestoga wagon by nuns?"

"*Goodbye,* Mr. Kronenfeldt!"

"Look, just leave Santa Claus out of the classroom. Okay? And there will be no problem."

Mrs. Worthington's eyes narrowed, the pencil probing toward his face.

"Are you threatening me, Mr. Kronenfeldt?"

George grabbed the pencil from her hand and snapped it, throwing the two pieces on her desk. He leaned in close to the old teacher staring at him like a rapist.

"Don't friggin' mess with Santa."

9

Old Santa

GEORGE'S FATHER WAS studying the Berghoff menu in his floppy hat and long coat, looking more like a bag person than a man who had retired after forty years working for the railroad. The menu framed inside the front door of Berghoff's was from 1931.

"Look at this! This is how much things used to cost! This was when a man could afford to eat! Look, a dinner for a quarter! Shrimp for fifteen cents! None of this bullshit now where you can spend a hundred bucks and still get a shitty meal!"

His father turned.

"Can you believe how good things used to be?"

"Yes, I can," George replied dully, brushing off the snow.

"How did everything get so screwed up," his father muttered.

"You want to get a table, Dad?"

His father shrugged wearily. "Yeah, let's get a table."

They sat down, and his father started looking for a waiter.

"So, you get a job yet?" he asked, dropping his floppy hat on the table. The shiny dome of Kronenfeldt Sr. caught the light.

"No, Dad. I didn't get a job," George muttered.

"Well, coming down to have dinner with me won't get you one."

"I know, Dad." George paused and brought up his notes from the night before. "I wanted you to go over some drawings I made and tell me what you think about my calculations."

His father pulled on his glasses.

"What the hell is this?"

"It's calculations I did on the load-bearing capabilities of the roof of my house."

"Santa Claus . . ." His father squinted. "What the hell?"

"I'm doing a project at home, and I've been working out the numbers, but I wanted to get your thoughts on some of my calculations—"

"What, you're building a bridge over your home? What is this thing?"

George leaned over and tapped the drawing. "That's a ramp."

"*A ramp?* A ramp for what? You driving a car onto your roof?"

"Not exactly. I'm going to be driving nine reindeer on my roof. I figure at about three thousand pounds . . ."

His father looked up.

"Son, have you lost your mind?"

George sat back as the waitress approached.

"What can I get you gentlemen?"

"Double order of sauerbraten extra cabbage, extra spinach, coffee, and a big piece of apple pie."

"And you, sir?"

"I'll take an iced tea and the same," George replied, handing the waitress the menus.

She left, and he stared at his father.

"Seriously, son. I think you should talk to someone."

"I'm doing a project for Megan, Dad."

His father frowned. "What kind of project—a zoo on your roof?"

George clasped his hands and breathed heavily.

"No, I'm going to be Santa Claus. The *Real* Santa Claus."

His dad leaned back against the upholstered booth.

"Oh, good. I thought you might have gone nuts. You're going to just be the *Real* Santa Claus. That's a relief."

George stared down at his plate. "Dad, do you remember what you said to me when I asked you if there was a Santa Claus?"

"No."

George paused. "You said that the only way there could really be a Santa Claus was if he went the speed of light. And that if he went the speed of light, the g-forces would tear him to pieces, and he would be fried like an egg. You said he would combust and splat all over the place."

His father shook his head. "I never said that."

"Yes you did, Dad. You were working and in one of your moods, and I asked you at the wrong time. That's what Mom said."

"Nope. I don't remember that."

George paused. "It doesn't matter, because I said the same thing to my son, Jeremy."

His father shrugged. "He's a grown man now."

"I know that. But I still screwed him by telling him that when he was just a kid."

His father waved his hand. "Ahhh, kids find out sooner or later."

"I never did, Dad."

"Well, you're different. You've always been a little off, son."

"Thanks. Anyway, Megan is starting to question Santa Claus, and I almost told her the same thing. I almost did it again! She is starting to now believe in Santa and won't believe unless she sees the Real Santa Claus."

Kronenfeldt Sr. shrugged. "So that's it. There is no real Santa. Just tell her that."

"I can't do that. I want her to believe in Santa, Dad."

"But why?" his father cried out.

"Because you only have a short time before life turns to shit."

"Yeah ... so?"

"And I want to extend the magical part for her."

"Son, you can't stop life. That's just reality."

George looked at his father. "Dad, I am going to do this thing. I'm going to be the Real Santa. I'm going to land a sled on the roof, go up the chimney, go down it, deliver the gifts, and then I'm going to get back in the sled and take off into the sky. I would like your help, but I will do it with or without you."

"I think this last job fried your brain, son."

George smiled and looked down at the table. "I need your help, Dad. I need someone who can tell me what will work and won't. I'm good on bridges, but this is everything. You were a civil engineer and a mechanical engineer. I need someone I can trust. But if you don't want to help me, that is fine."

"What in the hell are you talking about?"

"Dad, I have it all laid out. Here." George pointed to the drawing. "I'm going to have nine reindeer go up this ramp, but I think the pitch might be too steep. Anyway, they will go onto the roof here. Then they will line up and be attached to a sled and go a few feet on the roof. The sled will never really take off or land. That will be done with digital projectors and smoke machines. So the real physical part I need your help on is reinforcing the roof for the extra load, maybe three thousand to thirty-five hundred pounds. There will be two ramps, one for the reindeer to get on and one for them to get off, here and here. They will have to be fairly long and not too steep."

George's father stared at him. "You're going to put reindeer on your roof?"

"Yes."

"Son." He shook his head. "You have really lost your marbles."

"Dad, I'm doing this. I am going to let Megan keep her childhood."

His father chewed on his lower lip then shook his head. "I knew you should have never gone to that summer camp. You never were the same when you came back." He put on his glasses and looked at the drawing. "How are you going to go down the chimney?"

"Same way mountaineers climb—with a rope-and-pulley system."

His father looked up. "There's not enough room in the chimney."

"There are two chimneys. I'm going to have the adjoining wall knocked out, and I will have a ladder or rungs on one side that will allow me to climb up and down the chimney."

His father closed his eyes then held his hands over his face.

"You're going to kill yourself, son."

"Not if I'm careful."

"Son, this is nuts."

George leaned in. "Dad. I have spent my life working and not being with my family. I screwed up Jeremy and Jamie. I'm not going to mess up Megan."

His father leaned back against the booth.

"Son, give her a trip or a car or something, but this, this is a disaster!"

"Then you won't help me?"

His father rubbed his forehead and didn't speak. He took off his glasses and rubbed his eyes. "Jesus!" He shook his head again. "Where will you get the reindeer?" he asked through his hands.

"I have a man I am going to see tomorrow."

His father put back on his glasses and stared at the drawing again.

"Your ramp is all wrong. It has to be a lot longer than this if you want these animals to go on a roof. Do you have a calculator?"

George handed him his calculator. "Thanks, Dad."

"Just don't tell your mother," he muttered.

George looked at his father. His mother had died five years before.

10

The Plan

GEORGE'S FATHER WAS all about the plan. He roughed out the scenario, made to-do lists then commandeered George's calculator and worked out the length of the ramps, pitch, slope, and load capability. Then he designed a track system for the sled that would distribute the weight and give the reindeer something to follow. George knew how to do the calculations, but his father was a man who could create something out of nothing. His plate of sauerbraten was long gone when he read off a list for his son.

"Here is what we have to do immediately," he said, holding up the spiral notebook. "We have to strengthen the roof. I figure nine reindeer at five hundred pounds a piece with a sled and a man and whatever else ... we need a seven-thousand-pound-load limit. I won't know until I get up in your attic what we are dealing with. We have to make sure the roof is level enough so these reindeer don't fall off. The ramps have to be constructed to the specifications I lay out. You need to talk to a chimney guy who can make it big enough to get down. You got to get your pulley system set up so you can go down and back up. You need to find somebody who will give you reindeer on Christmas Eve. You need a sled, a Santa suit. And somehow you got to make your sled and reindeer land and take off."

His father dropped the notebook and raised his eyebrows. "Other than that, it should be a piece of cake, like flying to the moon. Oh, and you got ten days to do it in."

George sat back in the booth and nodded slowly.

"I have a call into a man in Hampshire for the reindeer, and I'm meeting the chimney guy tomorrow and a director who can handle the special effects for landing the sled and taking off."

"George, how the hell you going to do that?"

"Do what?"

"Make a goddamn sled land on your roof and take off with nine live reindeer."

George pointed to the drawing.

"Look, we can project an image of Santa landing with a digital projector. You can project it on smoke, Dad. We have smoke machines at both ends and some snow machines, and we basically will shoot this image into the darkness and then through the smoke and snow. I'll come out with the reindeer."

"You'll come down out of the air? Son, you aren't on drugs, are you?"

"Dad, I won't really come out of the air, but it will *look like it*. I will be waiting behind the smoke and snow, hidden, and then I will go forward, say twenty feet, and come to a stop, give off a couple of *HO HO HOs*, pull up the sack of presents, go to the chimney and down, and deliver the gifts. Then I come back up, get on the sled, and disappear into smoke and snow again and actually go down the ramp on the other side while the digital image of me flies away."

His father stared at the drawing then at his son. "And how do you know how to do this?"

"The Internet, Dad."

"*The Internet?* You got this whole idea from the goddamn Internet?"

"Yes. Parts."

"But you don't know anyone who has ever actually done this before?"

"No, but this should work."

His father rubbed his eyes. "Do you know what this will cost you?"

"I have a fifty thousand dollar line of credit secured by the house."

"And you'll need every cent! These ramps alone are going to be huge! They are like small bridges! We can't have them collapse with these animals, and, I assume, men driving them up to your roof and getting them back down. They will have to be built like that bicycle bridge you built for a locomotive."

"I didn't build it for a locomotive, Dad," he replied dully.

"Sure could have fooled me. Look, son, this is no small project. This is a big project that could really go badly if something doesn't work the way it is supposed to. In other words, you could get killed. Now, is your little girl's belief in Santa Claus worth that?"

"Yes, it is."

"You have lost your mind, son." Kronenfeldt Sr. closed his eyes, speaking down to the table. "And how in the hell are you going to get the ramps to your house? They have to be constructed somewhere and brought in. You going to tell Megan you're building a barn in your backyard?"

"Not a bad idea. But I have a carpenter in mind."

"A carpenter. One? You're going to need an *army* of carpenters to build this thing, take it apart, then put it back together ... and these reindeer, how much is that going to cost you?"

"I'm talking to the reindeer man tomorrow."

"The reindeer man," his father scoffed. "And what if these reindeer don't stop? What if you goose them, and they run off the roof with you in the sled?"

"I won't let that happen," George replied calmly.

"Have you ever driven reindeer before? What are you, Jack London now?"

"No."

"And all this movie equipment, snow machines, smoke machines, digital projectors ... this sounds like a lot of money for these things, and you'll need people who know what they are doing to run them."

George breathed heavy. "I told you, I'm meeting with a movie director tomorrow as well."

"Oh, that guy is going to cost you some bucks. He'll see you coming a mile away."

"He's a friend of Mary's."

His father shook his head.

"Don't you think there is an easier way to do this, son? Give her a car. Give her a trip to Disney World, but this, this is nuts!"

George powered down his laptop and closed it.

"No. I'm going to do this, Dad, whatever the cost."

"Jesus! You are so goddamn stubborn!"

"Takes one to know one."

Kronenfeldt Sr. picked up his hat and breathed heavy.

"Alright, when do we meet the chimney guy and the carpenter for these goddamn ramps and the movie guy?"

"We?"

His father frowned. "I'm not going to let you do this stupid-ass Santa Claus thing alone. It's too big, and you'll need an engineer who can keep all these bozos in line and on spec."

"I have thought this through, Dad. I am an engineer."

"Yeah, well a lot of engineers get themselves killed," his father muttered.

11

Chicago Christmas

SNOW SWIRLED DOWN on State Street and landed on coats and scarves and hats as people moved along Macy's windows. "Look how real she looks, Mom," Megan exclaimed, staring at the small girl asleep in the Victorian room.

"I am so glad they picked this theme," her mother replied, looking at George.

The next window had a man sitting at a desk. It was an old-time newspaper room, and the detail was amazing. George felt his heart open as Megan jumped up and down in her white muff and hat. The people, the traffic, the L going overhead, all added up to Christmas in Chicago. They would finish with the windows then go to the Walnut Room and have dinner, buy some Frango mints, then head for the Christmas tree in front of the State of Illinois building. It had worked out perfectly after the dinner with his father.

George's phone vibrated in his pocket, and he walked away from the windows.

"Mate! Mate, it's Dean!"

"Dean, thanks for calling me back."

"Oh, no problem, mate! Mary said you had a little project going that maybe I could help you on. She was pretty mum, so I really don't know what you are looking for, but I'll be glad to help."

George lowered his voice. "Yes, do you think we could meet? I have some pretty technical questions."

"Oh, no problem, mate! How about tomorrow morning? I'm fairly wide open holidays and all."

"Sure how about nine"

"Yeah sure, mate. At my studio."

"I'm going to bring my dad if that's alright. He's helping me on this project."

"Well, you got my curiosity up, I will have to say, mate. But yeah, bring your pap along, and I'll see you at nine AM sharp."

"Great."

George saw his wife and daughter were already three windows up. He had been coming down to see the Christmas windows ever since he was a kid, when Marshall Field's still ruled State Street. Macy's had taken over, and George felt the windows were just not as good. Still, it was as much a part of Christmas as seeing Santa.

"Sorry, that was Dean," he murmured as Mary read another window for Megan.

George's phone buzzed again. He stepped away.

"This is George."

"Yeah, this is Joe Gionelli. You called about some work on your chimney."

"Right. Right." George watched Megan and his wife walk to the next window. "Yes, I have a very old chimney, over a hundred years old, and it is actually a double chimney with a small wall separating the two. And what I'm looking to do is knock out the adjoining wall between them and make one big chimney."

The phone was quiet.

"You want to knock out the wall separating the two chimneys?"

"Yes."

"Ain't none of my business, but why would you want to do that?"

"Well, I have my reasons."

"I see."

"Can you come out tomorrow, say in the afternoon? I have a morning appointment."

"Yeah, I can do that."

George paused. "Is this something you think you can do?"

"Well, I tell you. In these times I don't say there's nothing I can't do. But I gotta see what I'm dealing with."

"Fine. Say noon?"

"See you then."

George pocketed his phone and felt it buzz in his hand again. "Hello."

"Yes this is Big Bill McGruff of *Reindeers.com.* You the man who e-mailed me about nine reindeer?"

"Yes, yes, thanks for calling," George replied, watching his wife lean toward the windows again.

"Well, I don't normally get no requests for nine reindeer!"

"Well, that's what I'm looking for," George replied, turning, watching his family go down to the next window. "Do you have them?"

"Well, I have them. I might have to bring some over from another farm. When did you want them?"

"I need them for Christmas Eve. Probably all day and night."

"Well, that might be a little tricky. There are handlers that go with them, and I don't know who is willing to work on Christmas Eve ... how late?"

"I will need them probably all night."

The phone aired silence.

"Hmm ... now that might be a little difficult to pull off. I wouldn't even know what to charge for special circumstances like this and—"

"I'm willing to pay. I need nine reindeer and whoever comes with them."

"Hmm ... alright. Well, we should probably meet. I have an opening tomorrow afternoon. Say about three?"

"Yep. That should work. And, oh." George turned, picking out his daughter by the last window. "Do you know where I can get a sled?"

"What kind of sled?"

"A Santa's sled."

"I might have an idea."

"Great."

George closed the phone and joined his family by the last window. Megan took his hand while they stared at the Victorian Christmas in a turn of the century living room. A little girl was opening her gifts under the tree while a mother and father looked on.

12

Hollywood Santa

GEORGE HAD RENTED these type of apartments for years before his first marriage. They were dismal brownstones with moldering wood and damp stairwells with copper buzzers that never worked and mailboxes that rarely closed. Dean had been a master of ceremony when he and his father appeared in his apartment stuffed with computers and posters of Fellini films and, of course, that famous Welles poster of *Citizen Kane*.

"This is my master work," he told George and his father, taking a seat in a director's chair dead center in the apartment.

For the next hour they were treated to a low-budget *Die Hard*. Dean stopped the frame several times to explain shots, techniques, and special effects. Kronenfeldt Sr. yawned and watched with his arms crossed and his floppy hat still on. Dean sped them along, replaying the films nexus with the summation of human motivation: drugs, pussy, and money.

George had to nudge his father awake by the end as Dean turned on the lights. He was a wiry Australian with a helmet of short black hair painted on his skull. He moved things around in his apartment, gesturing to posters and directors of famous movies.

"I tell you, mate, the Cohens really knocked it out of the park with that one. I think Ethan was particularly proud of *Fargo* more than his brother. Parts of the movie reminded me of Australia." George remembered then that Dean had left his wife and four kids in Australia to find opportunity in America. Mary said his family had been waiting for ten years to come to the land of milk and honey.

"So, what can I help you boys with? Mary said you had a hot project, and I am the man for hot projects! By the way, tell Mary sorry about the job falling through for the hot fudge sundaes. The bastards ended up going with some B roll."

George sat up on the couch that felt like something from college. "Dean, I have a project that maybe you can help me with," he began. "I want to land a sled with reindeer on my roof, go up and down the chimney, then have the sled take off. My daughter is beginning to doubt the existence of Santa, and I want to prove to her there really is a Santa."

Dean's face had turned dark red, and his cheeks filled with air. He jumped out of his director's chair. "STUPENDOUS!"

George's father jumped up. "What the hell!"

"BLOODY STUPENDOUS, MATE!"

Dean began pacing back and forth, cigarette fuming.

"Let me get this straight. Your daughter is doubting Santy Claus, and you are going to be the real old boy himself and go down the chimney and all that, and you want me to help with the illusion of Santa's sleigh and reindeer taking off into the sky?"

George nodded. "Exactly."

"STUPENDOUS!" Dean began pacing again. "This could be big, this could be *really big* ..." He stopped and swung around. "What do you call this bugger?"

"You mean, what I'm doing? Well, I have been calling it Real Santa, I guess."

Dean's face flowered again.

"BLOODY BRILLIANT!"

"So really, I just need some assistance on the special effects and—"

"Mate, you don't have to sell it to me anymore! I'll do the movie! The special effects, mate, are a snap!"

His father cleared his throat.

"Dean, maybe George didn't explain it clearly. This isn't a movie. He just wants to make his little girl think there is really a Santa Claus."

Dean's mouth deflated as he sat back down on his director's chair.

"No movie?"

George shook his head.

"No, we are really going to put Santa on the roof. I have reindeer that will be up there with a real sled, and I really am going down the chimney." George laid out the *The Plan* on the table. "What I am thinking though is for the image of Santa flying, we use digital projectors and maybe an image projected on smoke."

Dean stared at the drawing, his face turning fire-engine red. "STUPENDOUS!"

His father leaned over. "I think he left his brains in Australia," he murmured.

"Mate, this is even better! You are actually going to do this!"

George nodded. "Right."

Dean began pacing again, another cigarette in his hand, muttering, nodding. "Okay, this could be big. BIG! You are actually going to be the big man yourself. Actually going to do it. Okay. Okay!"

George watched as Dean stopped, closed his eyes then clasped his hand.

"I'll do it for you, mate! For the girl … ah, what's her name?"

"Megan."

"Right! I'm a father too you know, mate." Dean's eyes filled. "I really miss Danny, Diane, Dewy, and … and …" He shrugged. "I can never remember the last little bugger's name, accident child you know. But for your daughter, yes, of course I will do it!"

"Then you think my idea with the projectors and smoke will work?"

He waved his cigarette.

"Oh, no problem, mate! The way I see it, we could shoot on smoke or a scrim. You say you're going to have the reindeer up there and you want to make it look like they are flying, right?"

"Yes, you see we will have ramps on both sides of the roof and—"

"Piece of cake, mate! PIECE OF CAKE!" Dean sat down and looked at the diagram. "Right. We generate smoke and snow and shoot the image of Santy and the reindeer in the sky, maybe a few pyros, then you come out of the smoke and snow in your sled here. You get out and go down the chimney and deliver the presents to the mite, then you come back and into the smoke and snow again. We shoot Santy into the sky, and your daughter goes back to sleep with sugar plums in her head."

George looked at his father, who was studying Dean intently.

"My FX guys can handle this, no problem. I don't ask for pay, mate, but I do require that I am the director on the set, and that I am able to film this as a promo reel for my next upcoming movie."

George rolled his shoulders and looked at his father. "I don't see a problem with that."

"Now, what's our deadline here?"

"Ah, well Christmas Eve, obviously."

Dean pulled down his cigarette. "Wow, ten days, mate! Okay, I was thinking and going to see the kiddies in the land down under, but this takes precedent!"

"Oh ..." George shook his head. "I don't want to keep you from your kids."

Dean clapped his shoulder.

"Career has to come first, mate, and this is a STUPENDOUS opportunity, and, like I say, a perfect teaser reel for pitching the studios on my upcoming film!"

"I didn't know you had an upcoming film, Dean."

"I didn't, mate, until you came in. Now I do. Here's the title ... *Real Santa!*"

Kronenfeldt Sr. raised his eyebrows. "Catchy."

"Why, this could be the next *It's a Wonderful Life*! Or a bloody *White Christmas* or that other bloody movie with the elf."

George nodded. "Elf?"

"Right! Right! We could have *a classic* on our hands here, mate!"

"I just want to make sure my daughter believes in Santa Claus. I don't care what you do after that."

Dean jumped to his feet.

"You haven't talked to anyone else, mate?"

"No ... I have appointments today but—"

"Any other directors?"

"No, just the reindeer guy and the chimney guy."

"Good, good. Mum's the word, boys. We don't want anyone horning in on our idea. So let's zip those mouths, eh?"

George looked at his father and shrugged. "No problem."

"Good, let's shake then on our deal and my new movie—*Real*

Santa!"

They shook hands all around. Dean stared at the two men, his face filling with blood like a plasma balloon. He threw his hands toward the ceiling.

"STUPENDOUS!"

13

Rudolf

"THIS BROAD DOESN'T know where she's going!"

"It's a computer, Dad, hooked into Global Positioning Satellites."

"I don't give a damn if it's hooked into a donkey's ass, it still doesn't know where the hell it's going! Only a moron would follow this English lady into the middle of nowhere." He gestured to the GPS box on the dashboard. "She has no goddamn idea where she is going, and she won't admit it!"

George looked at his father in his floppy hat. The last comment belonged to when his mother would be driving and his dad would turn to him. *She has no goddamn idea where's she going, and she won't admit it.*

"Dad, it is Global Positioning Satellite technology. The woman has nothing to do with it."

"Then why are you listening to her?"

"Because she—"

Turn Right on McGruff Road.

George looked at the little blue car on the screen mounted on his dashboard as McGruff Road swung into view.

YOUR DESTINATION IS ON THE RIGHT.

"There, you see, Dad. We aren't lost."

"Ah, she lucked out," he muttered.

George started to slow down and saw a driveway peeking out of frosted pines. He turned into the trees and entered Santa's village.

Reindeer antlers poked out from tree trunks with flashing Christmas trees and large red and green ornaments shining on Austrian firs. George continued on to a house that looked like a place Santa Claus might reside—a Swiss chalet made from logs with snow piled up on the porch. A big F-150 truck was parked in the drive with RENDEER plates.

"This must be the place," George murmured.

His father frowned. "What is he, some kind of Mountain Man?"

MAKE A U-TURN.

"See, she still doesn't know what in hell she is talking about!"

George silenced his GPS.

"Well, I better go see about some reindeer."

His father slouched down in the car.

"Leave the engine on."

"You aren't coming?"

"I'm going to get a little nap in," his father murmured. "You handle the reindeer."

George emerged into the winter quiet of a Midwestern snow-storm. "Reindeer should be coming around the side of the cabin any minute," he said to himself.

He trudged to the porch and stared at the antlers mounted to the railing. A barrel of Jack Daniels had a Christmas wreath around the top. George looked for a doorbell but settled for the knocker in the shape of a German beer mug. Heavy footsteps pounded toward him as the door pulled back to a roaring fire and a man with a large bear on his head. That's what his furry black hat looked like to George. His beard mixed with the buffalo robe, that spread out like a king.

"You George?"

"Ah yes, you must be Big Bill McGruff."

He spat off the porch and nodded.

"That I am. You be wanting to see the reindeer."

"Yes."

He charged out of the cabin and plunged into the snow in knee-high boots with woolly mammoth fur. George followed the large man through the heavy snow around to the back of the cabin. A clump of brown reindeer turned and stared at the two men approaching the slatted fence.

"Well, here they are! You'll find Bill McGruff's reindeer are top of the line and will fit any need yer have. My reindeer have been used all over the country for movies and such. They are a fine breed of reindeer ilk, and I put them against anyone anywhere."

George felt his face numb from the wind squalling through the pines. "Are there nine there?"

McGruff poked a large finger to the reindeer that seemed larger than the ones George had seen in the movies and television. One of the reindeer relieved himself with a sizzling steam and another one defecated cannonballs. This was something that had not occurred to him. *What if the reindeer crap all over the roof? But wouldn't that make it more realistic? Didn't Santa have to deal with the same thing?*

"Yep. Nine on the button," McGruff said, nodding.

"Good. I'll take them all."

McGruff motioned to the cabin. "Let's go parley around the fire."

They tramped back through the heavy snow and onto the porch. McGruff walked into the cabin with snow falling off his leggings in a trail of slushy ice. George stomped his own hiking boots on the porch then walked in. The fireplace staged the room with antlers on either side like totem poles. A large reindeer head was mounted over the mantel.

"Pull up a chair and warm yer bones there, pilgrim."

George pulled an old recliner up to the fire and sat down. The cabin was plain and simple, except for a plasma television mounted to the stacked logs that reminded George of Lincoln Logs from his childhood. He looked around the room and felt the coziness of the shelter against the flurrying storm.

"This is quite a place you have here."

McGruff picked up his pipe and regarded him with cold grey eyes. He flamed a small jet engine and puffed smoke. George noticed a laptop on the kitchen table and an iPhone.

"It fits me needs." He leaned back, motioning with the pipe. "Now, what do yer want nine reindeer for?"

"I am going to be Santa for my daughter on Christmas, and I obviously need reindeer if I'm going to be Santa."

McGruff puffed away, watching him closely.

"Yer going to put the reindeer in yer backyard?"

"Well," George sat back in his recliner, "not exactly. Actually, I'm going to put the reindeer on the roof of my house."

McGruff's furry eyebrows drew together. He took the pipe from his mouth. "No yer aren't. Not my reindeer!"

George took out the folded diagram from his pocket.

"I would say the same thing, but I can assure you my father and I are engineers and we know what we are doing. Dad is asleep in the car or I would have him explain it to you." He handed McGruff the diagram. "As you can see, we are going to have two large ramps going up to the roof. One for the reindeer to go up and one for them to go down. In between these two points they will be harnessed to a sled with me as Santa. They will pull the sled a short distance and stop. They will wait for me while I go up the chimney and down and deliver the presents. Then I will come back and take them down the ramp on the other side."

McGruff puffed and studied the diagram with the fire crackling. His phone rang, and he didn't move. He finally looked up and gestured with the pipe. "Why?"

"I have a nine-year-old daughter who is questioning Santa. She has friends and teachers telling her that Santa isn't real, and I want her to still believe in the magic of Christmas. So I am going to be the Real Santa for her."

McGruff closed one eye. "Mister, it is no business of mine, but yer liable to kill yourself on that roof."

"I can assure you every safety precaution will be taken for animals and humans."

"It's going to cost you a pretty penny. I don't even know if I can get anyone to handle the reindeer on Christmas Eve."

"I am willing to pay."

"They have to be transported to the site. I need at least three handlers for all these animals, then clean up, working on a holiday. Aye, this will be an expensive venture for you."

George crossed his arms. "How much?"

"I can't charge you an hourly rate. There is too many of them. Most people rent two or three at most, and they aren't putting them up on a roof. I'd say four thousand dollars at the minimum for the night, and if you need them longer—"

"Fine."

McGruff teethed his pipe then shook his head.

"I don't know. The whole thing sounds crazy. I don't know if I can risk me reindeer. What if they fall off the roof, then what?"

"I would pay you for them."

He breathed heavily. "Aye, you say that now but I will be the one with dead reindeer. Hmm. I am sorry, mister, but I think the risk is too great."

George stared down at the hearth. "Five thousand."

"I would have to handle them myself and that is me Christmas," McGruff mused, puffing away.

"Six thousand."

McGruff shook his head again.

"Hmm, I am sorry. The risk is too much."

George breathed heavy. If he had no reindeer, then there really could be no Real Santa. He stared at the large man.

"I know it sounds crazy, and I understand your concern, but I want to keep my daughter's belief in magic. I want her to believe there is something good in this world as long as I can."

McGruff puffed on his pipe and didn't move.

George waited then stood up. "Well, thank you for your time."

He began to walk toward the door of the cabin.

"What is your daughter's name?"

George stopped and turned around. "I'm sorry."

"Her name. I said, what is your daughter's name?"

"Megan," he answered.

McGruff stared at the fire, his woolly boots steaming from the heat. "I had a daughter once."

George paused. "Oh … what was her name?"

"Julie … She died of cancer."

George stood with his hands in his coat.

"I'm very sorry to hear that."

"Aye," he said tiredly.

The fire crackled in the silence. George didn't know if he should stay or go. McGruff didn't move, but sat with the pipe in his mouth, his eyes on the fire.

"Well, thank you for your time again." George turned to the door.

"I'll do it for five."

He turned and saw McGruff still hadn't moved. George rolled his shoulders.

"I'll pay six if that will make it any easier."

McGruff turned and pinned him with his good eye.

"I'm not doing it for the money, pilgrim."

14

Green Santa

EVERY TWELFTH MONTH he came to her classroom and raised hell. The big man with the white beard and ridiculous suit interrupted Mrs. Worthington's carefully planned schedule with his *HO HO HOs* and *MERRY CHRISTMAS!* He threw the class into a tizzy with his promise of gifts and goodies, and the children couldn't concentrate on anything except Christmas and *Santa, Santa, Santa!* By the end, Mrs. Worthington felt like the Grinch in the famous Dr. Seuss story, holding her head, screaming out in agony, finally, *Oh the noise, the noise, the noise!*

And now that maniac Kronenfeldt, who Mrs. Worthington seriously believed had several screws loose ...now his daughter had brought the class to a screeching halt with all the kids laughing. Mrs. Worthington wanted to help her, but what Megan had just promised to the class was a bomb waiting to go off. And it had started out so well.

They had been moving along nicely all morning, slipping into science. It was when they were talking about the giant iceberg that had broken off from Iceland that Megan raised her hand and brought the class to a halt.

"But Mrs.Worthington, you said the climate was too inhospitable for Santa. If global warming is heating up the poles and the ice is melting, wouldn't that be better for Santa and the elves?"

The class had turned as one to Mrs. Worthington.

"Well, global warming is a theory, Megan," she began, judiciously, "the way Santa is a theory."

The kids broke into campfires of chatter.

"Children! Children! Please!"

"But Mrs. Worthington , you said it was too inhospitable for Santa and his elves, and now it's warming up. Wouldn't that make it a more viable climate?"

Megan sat with her hands clasped. And there was that hope in her eyes. Mrs. Worthington knew she should just give Megan the bone and move on, but Megan's psycho father telling her not to mess with Santa had really racked her off. *Why shouldn't she debunk Santa?* The myth antagonized her every year and ruined the last weeks of her year. Why shouldn't she poke a few holes in the old guy's red suit?

"Megan, as I said before, the North Pole is a hostile climate. Think about it. Let's keep science in mind, children. Santa Claus would need very expensive equipment to survive in those conditions, and global warming is a theory that some people believe and others don't."

"My father said it's big business ruining the planet, and that only morons don't believe in global warming."

The class turned as if at a tennis match, and it was Mrs. Worthington's serve. She smiled icily.

"Your father is wrong, Megan. Global warming has not been *proven*, and there are natural cycles the earth goes through that could explain the melting of the icebergs."

Megan frowned. "Then if it has warmed up, maybe Santa had a chance to build a factory to build the toys."

Mrs. Worthington rubbed her brow.

"Santa Claus has nothing to do with our discussion, Megan! Santa Claus is a myth! *Myths* cannot be proven! They are generally not true, and I don't want any of your parents coming in here and saying that I said there wasn't a Santa Claus! The idea of Santa Claus is a *myth*, children and, at best, a theory … like global warming."

The children stared at the teacher breathing hard. Mrs. Worthington had hoped they could return to the subject at hand, but the silence, the round eyes, the quivering lips, told her the jolly man in the suit was coming for his due.

"Well, I am going to prove there is a Santa once and for all. My father is going to let me use his video camera and stay up all night and videotape Santa, and then I'll put it on YouTube and bring it to class, and I can prove to the world there really is a Santa Claus!"

The class erupted into a riot with voices on top of each other. This was the equivalent of splitting the atom for children. They said it could be done, but no one had ever seen an atom or Santa. Proof was what Megan Kronenfeldt was offering.

"Children. Quiet! Please!'"

The voices came down, and Mrs. Worthington stared at the child in the middle row. "Your father approved of this plan, Megan?"

"Yes. He's going to let me use the video camera."

The man had rocks for brains. What parent would set themselves up for something like this? Already there were snickers around the room.

"You're lying. Your parents won't let you do that," Johnny Brandis said from the front row, turning his head toward the back to face Megan.

The other kids began to nod knowingly.

"Johnny that will be enough!"

"All you're going to see are your parents putting the presents under the tree," Jackie Spagelli scoffed.

The cat was out of the bag. The room broke down into factions of those who believed it was parents and those who didn't. At the center was Megan Kronenfeldt, who everyone had decided was telling a lie.

"Children, I have had enough of this!"

And that's where they had come to. Megan's eyes had welled up, and she was staring at the top of her desk. Mrs. Worthington was never very good in these moments. Other teachers could handle children crying. She had never been able to cry as a child with her father, and she had to resist telling kids to buck up.

"Megan, we believe you," Mrs. Worthington said, glaring at the other children, daring anyone to snicker.

Megan shook her head and wiped her eyes. "No, you don't." She lifted her head and turned and faced the class. "I'm going to prove to all of you that there is a Santa Claus," she declared. "My dad says there is one, and I'm going to bring you the proof. I'm going to videotape Santa and prove it to the world!"

Mrs. Worthington popped the two aspirin by her desk, drinking the dry capsules down with water. She looked at Megan Kronenfeldt, staring defiantly at the class.

"Oh, shit," Mrs. Worthington said.

15

Santa's Chimney

GEORGE STARED AT the countryside with the Christmas lights twinkling red and green and blue and the distant homes across the wetlands with their porch lights. He could see low-flying planes rumbling overhead toward O'Hare airport and an early moon rising over the trees. The wiry man with the short beard and squinty eyes stood like he was on the ground and not straddling two ladders on the lower roof.

"Well, you got two chimneys here and pretty creosoted up I might add," Joe of Joe Williams Chimney Repair said with his voice hollowing down the blackened sleeve. "When was the last time you cleaned this baby?" Joe pulled his head out from the chimney.

"I never did," George replied, grasping the chimney like a man hugging a life preserver .

"You know, usually homeowners don't come up on the ladder."

George looked down at the roof below. "No ... No, I have to get used to this," he muttered.

"You do, huh?"

George swallowed and took a deep breath.

"Yes. So how feasible is it to widen these chimneys?"

Joe stared back down into the snout.

"Well, looks wide enough for the smoke to go up, but you said you are looking to make it bigger?"

George kept his hands on the roughened brick. He was beginning to get used to the height. This was good. He would have to learn to be calm this high up. The thought that he would lift himself to the top of the chimney and go down it seemed unbelievable.

"Yes. I want to make it as large as possible."

Joe leaned over further.

"Like I said, I don't really see the need for making it bigger, friend."

"I need to make it bigger so I can go down the chimney."

Joe shut one eye, pulling himself high above the chimney.

"You want to go down the chimney, you mean like Santa Claus?"

George nodded to the man plastered against the star-filled night.

"I want to go down the chimney with gifts and then come back up."

Joe spat some of the Skoal swelling his lip.

"Are you joking me?"

George shook his head.

"No. What will it take to make this chimney big enough for me go down it with a sack of presents and then come back up?"

Joe stuck his head back into the dark maul of the chimney.

"Well, now ... have to get rid of this wall here," he echoed into the sooty cavern. "Have to break up the wall of the chimney ... yep, probably best thing to do would be to break down the adjoining wall between the two chimneys."

"Okay."

Joe looked up.

"But I never done nothin' like that before."

"Are you saying you can't?"

"I ain't saying that. Times being what they are, I'll do anything."

"I need this ready to go by Christmas Eve."

"Nine days?"

"That's right."

Joe put his head back in the chimney. "Well," his voice hollowed out. "Best thing to do would be to jackhammer the chimney and just work your way down. Hell of a mess, but once I got the wall out I could chip the walls to make sure you had enough room, 'course you couldn't use it. It would have to be repaired and put back together." Joe popped back out. "Going to cost you some."

"How much to make it big enough for me go down this chimney?"

"Well, unless you gain a bunch of weight ... hmm. I figure it's going to take a full week of hitting it every day … hell, I don't know. I hate to peg it, but if you push me, I reckon I could do it for five thousand dollars."

George felt his breath leave. In the space of one day he had blown fifteen thousand dollars. Dean had asked for seed money to get the digital projectors ("They are two thousand a piece, mate, just to rent them.") and let him know it could be more. He nodded. "Done."

Joe stuck his head back down the chimney and sneezed. "You don't use them too much do you?"

"Not too much."

Joe shook his head. "It's going to be noisy as hell and one hell of a mess."

George thought of Mary. Things were escalating, and the fifty-thousand-dollar equity line could be sucked dry quickly. It wasn't so different from working with contractors on projects he designed. There were always problems and cost overruns. Mary would just have to trust his judgment on this.

"Fine." He nodded. "Let's just get it done."

Joe rolled his tongue against his cheek.

"You mind if I ask yer something?"

"It's my daughter. She's nine and is questioning Santa Claus. I want to prove to her there is a real Santa Claus."

Joe nodded slowly. "So yer going to be Santa Claus and go on down this chimney?"

"That's right."

Joe belched and moved the wad in his mouth.

"My daddy would have never done that for me, I can tell you."

"Nor mine, but that's why I need you to get this chimney ready."

"How you fixing on going down?"

"Rope-and-pulley system. Much the same as a mountain climber. I'll rappel down."

"What about coming back up?"

"I'm going to have two men pull me up."

Joe shoved his head down in the opening again. "You know, I might be able to put some rungs in there for you to hang on to if I have space or maybe some footholds in the brick."

"If it works, that would be great."

Joe popped up with a cigarette in his mouth. George marveled at the way he cupped his lighter, not hanging on to anything. He looked out over the snow-darkened landscape.

"This will be a first for me."

George nodded and felt snow spray from the brick flashing. "Me too," he muttered.

"What happens if you get stuck in there?"

"I hope it won't happen."

"Chimneys ain't straight. They move around, but I'll give you enough room so you won't get stuck in there."

"I appreciate it."

Joe looked out over the countryside, elbows on the chimney. The winter night suddenly froze around them and a half-moon creased the darkness like a pearl.

"Santa Claus," he said, looking across the top of the world. "Don't that beat all."

16

The Grinch

ONE CHILD A few years back had written on his paper *Mrs. Worthington is the Grinch*. She had read the Dr. Seuss book many years ago and the Grinch was not likeable, but he did have an avenue for revenge—and Mrs. Worthington envied him for that. Take these papers she was grading at six PM while the snow swirled outside. They were supposed to be essays on what they would do over Christmas break, but had become polemics on how Santa could survive in polar temperatures.

Mrs. Worthington looked up from a paper with a Santa penciled in the corner and looked at the clock. What did she expect? A man who would say, "Don't friggin' mess with Santa," could not be expected to be on time for anything. He was one of those males so different from her father, who had worked hard and expected his kids to work hard too. These kids with their beliefs in Santa Claus had no idea what real work was.

Mrs. Worthington saw in the window a snow-haired woman with a beehive and a sweater draped over her shoulders. She wouldn't see that woman much anymore. She would walk out of the building at the end of the year and never return. Some thought she was silly to stay on so long. She was seventy, but teaching was her life, and she liked being busy, getting things done. She had never understood leisure, never understood when other people talked about retiring and doing what they want. *She was doing what she wanted.*

Mrs. Worthington bent down to the paper and saw a Santa with *HO HO HO* scrawled beneath him. Mrs. Worthington scrawled beneath Santa: *DID NOT FOLLOW INSTRUCTIONS.* Christmas was something to be endured, but things had gone too far with the Kronenfeldt girl. Mrs. Worthington would use one of his own against Santa this time. And her idiot father would be a perfect foil.

He would be her Grinch.

George and Mary knocked lightly on the door of the classroom. They had received the e-mail requesting a conference about Megan, and George suspected it had something to do with his parting words. But as they walked into the classroom, he felt a warm nostalgic glow. Here was the classroom of his youth; the alphabet going across the blackboard and the vowels and the flag drooping beneath the loudspeaker along with the institutional clock with the hour hand that never seemed to move. He inhaled the sanctum of learning, so safe and nurturing after thirty years in the business world. Then he saw Mrs. Worthington.

"Hello Mr. and Mrs. Kronenfeldt. Please come in."

George walked in feeling the cold blast of the schoolmarm. Even the damn apple was on the corner of her desk. To George she was Mrs. Gary, the cranky old bird in Virginia who flew around the room smacking him on the head again with her pencil. *"No, no, no ...that is not how you make an eight!"* The pencils broke and fell on his desk like spent cartridge shells. He bent to his work, a grimy, sweating boy who no one wanted to sit next to. *"You are the stupidest boy I have ever had in the first grade!"*

"I wanted you to come down here to discuss Megan," Mrs. Worthington began.

George tried to focus on the thin-lipped woman with the bifocals. She had glanced at him as if he were a roach and then talked to his wife.

"We have a ... *Santa issue,* if you will," Mrs. Worthington continued.

Mary was sitting with her hands in her lap. Mrs. Worthington had given up even glancing at George and was speaking directly to his wife.

"Megan is a very smart child, and I enjoy her in class very much. But we had a discussion the other day about global warming ..." Mrs. Worthington pulled the sleeves of her sweater in closer. "Well ... which spun out of control when Santa entered our discussion."

"I heard you told the kids that it was too cold for Santa's elves to build his workshop," George grumbled.

Mrs. Worthington's mouth had turned into a small circle, her eyes over the glasses. "There was some unfortunate discussion of the Santa topic. Yes." She turned back to Mary. "But what I am concerned about is that Megan promised the class something she cannot possibly deliver on, and I fear she might be the laughing stock of the class."

His wife leaned forward. "What happened?"

Mrs. Worthington moved her pencil next to a magnifying glass.

"I am used to Santa entering our classroom at this time of year, but I have to rein the children in and get them to focus, of course."

"You mean by telling them there is no global warming when of course all science points the other way," George muttered.

Mary turned to him and stared.

He shrugged. "Just saying ..."

Mrs. Worthington cleared her throat.

"Megan, unfortunately, promised the class she would prove the existence of Santa Claus by *videotaping him* and putting it on You-Tube." The old teacher paused, sitting back in her chair. "Obviously, she cannot possibly do this, and I fear she will be embarrassed when it comes out that she lied to the class."

"She didn't lie to anybody," George snorted.

Mrs. Worthington blinked twice and leaned forward. Another bad student and, of course, it was a boy. They were always so naughty, going to the washroom, squeezing themselves, talking about bathroom functions. And then they grew up into *men*.

"I don't think I understand what you are saying, Mr. Kronenfeldt."

George crossed his arms and sat back.

"I said she will videotape Santa, and she will put it on YouTube."

"I don't think furthering the child's delusions at this point will help her."

"Oh, you're right. Let's just tell her there is no Santa Claus and life sucks, and while we're at it, let's have her get a job at McDonald's."

His wife and his daughter's teacher stared at him as if he had just farted. To George that was their expression. Mary was squeezing his arm, imploring him with her eyes, but it was too late. Mrs. Worthington was the type of woman he had battled all his life—humorless, cold, the nun who would gladly put him in the corner on a permanent time-out.

George leaned forward, putting a hand on her desk.

"Let me ask you a question: Did you ever believe in Santa Claus?"

"I don't think what I believe is the issue."

"No, really. Did you ever, *ever* believe in Santa Claus?"

Mrs. Worthington stared at this bearded man with the crooked glasses and pens in his top shirt.

"No. We were working too hard to indulge in such foolishness."

"So, you had a lousy childhood."

"I had *a very good* childhood. My father was a man whom children *respected*!"

George rolled his eyes. "Have you ever watched *Miracle on 34th Street*?"

"I don't remember."

"What about *It's a Wonderful Life* or *White Christmas* or *Holiday Inn*?"

"I don't think Christmas movies are the topic here."

George held out his hand, looking at his wife.

"I rest my case. She doesn't have any Christmas spirit! I'll bet she doesn't believe in the Easter Bunny either."

Megan's teacher turned to Mary.

"I have spoken with the principal on this matter, and he concurs. We really need Megan to tell the children she will not be filming Santa Claus and putting it on YouTube. The children are so excited by this, they can barely pay attention, and we need them to concentrate on their studies—"

"Not going to happen," George said flatly.

"I beg your pardon!"

"No." George shook his head. "I don't think I will give you my pardon or anything else." He pumped his finger at the old teacher. "My daughter still believes in Santa Claus, and I intend to keep that belief alive as long as I can."

Mrs. Worthington leaned forward. "You are setting her up for failure, Mr. Kronenfeldt."

"No, I'm not. I'm setting her up so she won't become a jaded old teacher who pisses on children's fantasies."

The room became quiet.

"Then you will not do anything?"

"If it involves telling my daughter there is not a Santa Claus, then hell no! Megan will get her video of Santa and that's final."

"And how is that going to happen?"

"Santa is going to come, that's how."

Megan's teacher eyed the crazy homeless man who had come to her classroom.

"Dressing up in a suit will not solve your problem."

"No one is dressing up in a suit."

"I don't understand."

George spread his arms. "The Real Santa Claus will appear with reindeer and go down the chimney and deliver the presents then fly away into the night. And Megan will get it all on video."

"You are crazy."

George shrugged. "I'd say the inmates are running the asylum."

Mrs. Worthington sat up straight and pulled her sweater close. "You cannot lie to these children but for so long!"

George stood up from the small chair with his wife.

"Santa exists." He pounded his chest. "He exists in the hearts of children!"

"You are a deranged man, Mr. Kronenfeldt," Mrs. Worthington said gravely. She looked at his wife. "You have my sympathies."

The Kronenfeldts left, and Mrs. Worthington sat back down in her chair and listened to their steps fade. She pulled her sweater and stared at the apple on her desk. Santa Claus had harassed her for fifty years with Christmas parties, spacy children, candy-cane jazzed children, class presents, and the interminable discussions of the existence of Santa Claus. She stared at her reflection in the window and nodded slowly.

"I will kick Santa squarely in the nuts once and for all," she murmured to the schoolmarm in the black window.

17

Busted Santa

GEORGE WAS HAPPY to feel the warmth of his coffee cup after the warehouse he met the carpenters in. They had assured him they could build the ramps to his father's specifications and would transport them to his home on December 24th. Dean had found the carpenters and said he used them for many "shoots," but George had to write another five thousand dollar check. He felt like a man who had been on a binge only to wake up and feel the hammerhead of remorse banging away.

Mary drew a finger through the sheen of dust on the kitchen table. Everything was coated with the fine grit of cement. The day had been filled with the sound of giant guns firing down from the roof. Joe had started with jackhammers, and the cement rained down into the hearth and rolled out into the house in a dust cloud. They had sealed the fireplace with plastic, but somehow this dust seeped out, and now the house was coasted with the fine ash of grey particles.

"I hope your project is going well because we now need a Real Santa for Megan to videotape," Mary said wearily.

George felt heat rising up from his neck. He had driven home totaling up the costs, and he figured he had spent thirty grand and Dean told him the digital projectors were now three grand to rent. *Three thousand!* That was when he considered shutting the whole thing down. Maybe he was having a midlife crisis.

The mornings in the mirror examining his teeth, his skin, his very thin grey hair, had taken on another dimension. He had lived a lot of years, and he didn't have a lot to show for it. His savings were meager after the divorce. His kids were not stellar examples of parenting. He and his ex-wife traded insults for Jeremy being a pothead and Jamie becoming a Goth chick covered with tattoos and piercings.

But more than that, George had lately questioned his profession. All he had done was design bridges for thirty years! Sure, there had been other projects, but he was a bridge man and that just seemed trivial in the cosmological scheme of human endeavor. When he kicked the bucket there would be no plaques, no books, no paintings, no buildings to mark his passage. Even the bridges he designed were usually named for some dead president or senator. The *George Kronenfeldt* Bridge simply would not exist.

Maybe that was why he had gone crazy on the bike bridge. He knew it was overkill with the single girder across the highway, but *dammit,* he wanted something to stand for all time that would have his mark, and that bicycle bridge surely did. So it had come down to Megan. He wanted her to become his legacy. He wanted his daughter to tell everyone one day that her dad had kept her belief in Santa Claus alive. He was going to be the Real Santa if it put him right in the poorhouse. And it looked like he was heading there quickly.

"George ..." Mary was looking down at her hands. They were chapped and red from the dishes she insisted on washing by hand. "It is your business what you spend, but how much have you given Dean to help you?"

"Five thousand so far," he muttered.

Mary adjusted her glasses, pulling her sweater together. "It's not that I don't trust, Dean, it's just he is a bit of a dreamer and has some very crazy ideas sometimes."

George stared down at his coffee and nodded.

"Yeah, I picked that up. He wants to film this himself, and I think he is trying to create a movie set."

"Just don't let him put you in the poorhouse, George."

"I won't."

Mary paused again, looking across the table.

"How much have you spent so far?"

"You don't want to know."

She blinked, her arms creating a trail in the dusty covered table. "You're right. I don't want to know. Do you really think this is something we should be taking on right around Christmas?"

"No." George stared at the taped up plastic over the fireplace. "But I can't let Megan down. She promised her class she will bring in a video of the Real Santa."

Mary clasped his hand. "Just promise me you won't lose the house."

George shook his head. "I may be nuts, but I'm not crazy."

She held his hand and nodded. "I trust you."

He felt a strange ripple of fear inside. He always thought of himself as being in control, but lately a madman had taken over who could do just about anything.

"By the way, Mrs. Worthington requested that I go to the Christmas party," Mary continued.

George looked up.

"Apparently you two had some words before the conference."

"All I did was tell her that we were trying to protect Megan and keep her belief in Santa alive."

"She said you threatened her, George."

"I got a little worked up when she said she wouldn't perpetuate myths."

"Well ... maybe I *should* go to the party instead."

"No, no. I promised Megan I would be at the Christmas party, and I'm going to be there."

Mary stared at him.

"I'll be good. I promise I won't say anything else to the bitch ... I mean, Mrs. Worthington," George muttered.

His wife stared at him.

"What?"

" 'Don't friggin' mess with Santa?' Really, George?"

18

Little Cindy Lou Who

MEGAN LOOKED LIKE little Cindy Lou Who among her stuffed animals with her frilly nightgown and two saucer blue eyes blinking up. George walked into her room with the toys all over the floor and heard *Here comes Santa Claus, here comes Santa Claus* floating out of her MP3 player.

"Guess what, Daddy?"

"What?" he asked, moving a giraffe and a tiger on her bed.

"Mrs. Worthington said a bad word the other day in class."

"She did?"

Megan nodded, her eyes getting bigger.

"We were talking about Santa, and I told the whole class that I was going to bring a video of Santa and prove that he's real, and then Mrs. Worthington said it ..." Megan leaned down, putting her hand to her mouth. "It was the one that rhymes with hit but starts with an *s*."

George nodded slowly. "Ah, yes. I know which one that is."

"Everyone started laughing, and she got really mad."

"I'll bet."

Megan held down her pink DSi and put the pointer into the slot. "Maybe she was mad because I questioned her about global warming, because she said that a lot of the icebergs are melting at the North Pole, and I said that would be good for Santa if it's getting warmer at the North Pole."

George felt his pulse quicken, a visceral tensing up.

"And what did Mrs. Worthington say then?"

Megan tilted her head, scribbling again on the small screen.

"She said that Santa was a myth and had no bearing on our conversation about global warming, and that global warming had not been proven to be caused by humans, and that the earth had natural cycles of heating and cooling."

"Bull," George muttered.

"That's what I said. I told her it was big oil and corporations that have been polluting the environment and creating a hole in the ozone layer and the greenhouse gas buildup, but she said that was opinion and not based in fact."

George shook his head. "Unbelievable."

Megan eyes filled with tears, and she looked back down. The Christmas magic seemed as if it might blow away like the snow scurrying across the roof.

"What's the matter, Megan?"

She shrugged and brushed her eyes.

"Will you tell me if I guess it?"

She shrugged again. George moved his glasses on his nose.

"Does it have to do with Christmas?"

"Maybe," she murmured, brushing her eyes.

"Does it have to do with Santa Claus?"

"Maybe."

"Did someone say something?"

"Yes … everyone says it's not true," she mumbled.

"What is not true?"

"Santa … they all say it's just parents."

"Who says that?"

"Everyone, Dad. They won't leave me alone. And I tell them all that I'm going to prove them wrong with my video."

"And you are!"

Megan looked up with teary eyes.

"But what if Santa doesn't come? Then everyone will call me a liar."

"Santa will come," he declared, looking at the chimney outside her window.

"But what if he doesn't, Dad, or I miss him?"

"You will not miss him. I won't let that happen."

Megan stared at him, her eyes sparkling. "Really?"

"Absolutely. You will videotape Santa Claus. I promise."

Megan hugged him and did the little pat on his back she had done as a baby.

"Thank you, Daddy. I was so worried."

"Well, quit worrying. We will make sure we get a good video of Santa to show your classmates."

Megan brushed her eyes and nodded.

"You're still coming to the party, right, Daddy?"

"Absolutely."

"Oh, good. Because Mrs. Worthington turned red when I said you were going to be one of the helpers."

"I wouldn't miss it for the world."

"I can't wait to prove to everyone Santa landed on the roof and went down the chimney and delivered the gifts and then went back up and took off from the roof!"

"Don't you think maybe just having a video of Santa on the roof would suffice?"

Megan shook her head. "Nope. I want to have the *whole thing* on film ..." Megan looked up in alarm. "You're still going to let me use the camera, right, Daddy?"

"Oh ... sure ... sure. I said I would."

"Good, because I told Mrs. Worthington that you were, and she didn't really believe me. But I'm going to prove to her and everyone else that Santa is real!"

Megan looked out the window and frowned.

"Daddy, why is that man working on our chimney? What if Santa can't get down the chimney?"

George stared at the window.

"He's not still there, is he?"

"No. He left today. Mom said he was repairing the chimney so Santa could get down it."

"Well, that's exactly what he's doing. He's making the chimney just right for Santa."

Megan looked at her father and raised her eyebrows.

"Well he better hurry up. He only has eight days left. That's not much time."

"Oh, I know. Believe me, I know."

"Because Santa has to fit all the way down our chimney with all our gifts. I can't wait to see the way he squeezes everything down."

"Me too," he murmured. "That reminds me, have you finished your list for Santa?"

"I mailed that off, remember?"

"Oh, right. What was the biggest thing on your list?"

"A trampoline."

George rubbed his whiskers and nodded slowly.

"A trampoline?"

"Yep." Megan frowned. "I wonder how he will get that down the chimney?"

George stared out the window at the brick column.

"I have no idea."

19

Christmas with the Kids

PARK RIDGE WAS festive with Christmas trees and wreaths in store windows and people dashing here and there as the elevated rambled overhead. George was to meet Jeremy and Jamie for their annual Christmas dinner before his ex-wife took them to Florida on Christmas day. Every year George would suggest they spend Christmas with his family, and every year they declined, citing early flights and logistics and their mother's intransigence against anything concerning George.

So it had all come down to a Christmas dinner with his two children at Winterbeans. George walked into the dim light and was greeted by the hostess, who said his kids were waiting for him at a table. His former town had the small town quality of people actually knowing you. George could still walk in, and the bartender would bring him his ice tea and chopped salad while he caught up on the local papers. It was really what George had craved. A nestled home in a community of people who knew your name and cared that you existed. So why in the hell did he move out to the country?

George couldn't quite answer that except to say he wanted a fresh start with Mary. Shortly after Megan was born they had decided Mary's condominium was too small, and George drove out and saw the rambling white farmhouse and a life among the cornfields of his new family. An *American Gothic* existence appealed to him, and the bonus was the bridge project over the nearby river was a three-year gig.

Then of course the economy tanked, and George's house along with everyone else's lost forty percent in value. Not that he was considering moving back, but it was strange to not even have that option. And now his former life was staring him in the face with the twin eyes of filial accusation. *You always worked. You were never there for us. You and mom always fought. You left. Mom left. You left us in that shitty house with no money.*

"Hey, guys," he said gingerly, sliding into the booth.

Neither texting head rose from their collective laps. George pulled off his coat and scarf and watched his son and daughter stare down under the table. He noticed his daughter's hair was flaming red with one side shorn up like the old group A Flock of Seagulls. His son looked like a mountain man with shaggy hair down to his shoulders and a beard approaching a Civil War general.

"And what can I get you to drink?"

George looked up at the pretty waitress.

"I'll take a Boddington … kids?"

"Miller," came from his son.

"Same," came from his daughter.

George held his hand up to the waitress.

"Ah, Jamie, I think you are a little young to be drinking beer."

She shook her head and rolled her eyes.

"Whatever, Dad. I drink all the time."

George laughed and winked at the blonde twentysomething.

"How about a Coke?"

"Fine," Jamie grumbled.

George nodded. "A Miller and a Coke then."

She left, and George looked at his kids. Jamie laughed at something on the screen, and George noticed several more studs on her right eyebrow along with freshly minted tattoos rolling up both arms. *Goth. Biker chick.* It was strange to think of his own daughter with her ripped black fishnet shirt hiding a black lacy bra in terms of one of those Goth girls he had seen at Depeche Mode concerts.

"So … how is school, Jamie?"

"It blows," she muttered.

"Well, there must be some classes you like in your senior year."

"It all sucks dick."

George stroked his beard and turned to Jeremy.

"So, son ... how is college?"

"Same. It sucks," he murmured, fast-action thumbs not slowing.

George sighed and leaned in.

"Hey, guys, this is our Christmas dinner. Why don't we put the phones away?"

Jamie looked up at him as if he had just hit her.

"You make me come down to this lame dinner, and now I can't even use my phone. I'm seventeen you know, Dad!"

"I know, I know. I just thought we could ... talk while we are in our company."

"Talking is so lame," Jamie muttered, but she shut down her phone.

Jeremy put his phone in his coat and stared at his father.

"So how is everything out in *Bedford Falls?*"

George watched the drinks come.

"Just a wonderful life," he murmured.

Jeremy drank his Miller and frowned.

"I'll bet ... after you leave us in the shithole."

George put down his beer.

"You have a nice house."

"Not as nice as the one you live in," Jamie sneered, sulking with her Coke.

"We don't live in a mansion, Dad. We live in the *shithole* you left Mom in."

George held his beer between his hands.

"I didn't leave your mother. She left me. Remember, guys?"

"That's not what she said," Jamie muttered.

George didn't want to go down this path because it only led to *Dad is an asshole.* He picked up the menu and tried to steer away from the village of filial discontent.

"So, what are we going to have?"

"I'm not hungry," Jeremy growled.

"Me neither."

George looked over his menu at his two sulking kids.

"C'mon, guys, it's on me."

"Yeah, it's the only thing we get out of you," Jamie said, scowling.

"Now that's not true—"

"I want a new car, Dad," she declared.

"Talk to your mother."

"That's what you always say, but you don't pay her anything!"

George put down the menu.

"That's not true, Jamie. I have paid your mother on time every month, but she blows it on vacations."

"Bullshit!"

George stared at the two hot eyes of sooty mascara.

"You left her without a penny," she cried out. "And now everybody has cars, and I have to drive that old shitty station wagon you left Mom with while you moved out to *your estate* with your perfect daughter and perfect wife and left us to rot here!"

George breathed wearily. "I don't have a perfect daughter or perfect wife," he said quietly.

"*Oh, really?* Megan is so smart. Megan is so sweet. Megan is so cute," his daughter mimicked in a high-pitched screech. She jammed her finger in her mouth. "It makes me want to barf!"

"I never treated you any different than I treat her, Jamie."

"Yeah ... Right."

Jeremy raised his beer.

"I think Jamie's got a point, Dad. I mean, what's this Santa you're going to be or whatever?"

George stared at his son.

"Who told you?"

"Mary did. I called her, and she said you were out seeing some guy about reindeer. *Reindeer, Dad?* You never got us reindeer."

"Yeah," Jamie sobbed. "You never got us any reindeer!"

George paused then leaned forward on his elbows.

"Megan is at the age where she is beginning to question Santa ... so I decided I would be Santa for her."

Jeremy squinted. "But you are getting real reindeer?"

"Well, yes. You see, she wants to videotape Santa, so I'm going to have the reindeer and a sled and I'll be in it on the roof—"

"Wait a minute." Jeremy sat up in his army jacket and stared at him. "You mean you're going to put reindeer on the roof for your kid?"

"Yes—"

His son slammed back against the booth. "Great! What ... are you going down the chimney too?"

George paused. "Yes."

"Dad ..." Jamie's face resembled prison bars with her inky tears. *"You never went down the chimney for us!"*

Jeremy shook his head.

"Yeah, I mean, what the hell, Dad? What's this costing you?"

"Well, the reindeer are hefty but the digital projectors are really setting me back."

"WHAT?!" His son glared at him and slammed his beer down. "Digital projectors?!"

"Ah ... yes, to project on smoke the image of Santa acceding to the roof," George mumbled, not feeling good about any of this.

"You never used digital projectors for us," Jamie wailed. His daughter was now crying profusely.

Jeremy shook his head and looked at his father.

"You told me when I was nine that Santa would spontaneously combust from the g-load. Do you remember that, Dad, when I asked you if Santa was real?"

"Yes, and I regret it, son."

"You never even told me about Santa," Jamie wailed, wiping black mascara on her napkins.

"But for your new daughter you're going to recreate Santa Claus." Jeremy leaned into the table. "Do you see, Dad, why we might be a little pissed about that?"

George nodded slowly. "Yes ... but I never meant to favor one child over another."

"Well, you are, Dad, you are."

"You are giving her a Real Santa, and you won't even give me a car," Jamie screamed, standing outside the booth suddenly. "I hate you! I hate you! *You're a ... dickhead, Dad!"*

George realized then the entire restaurant had paused to watch his daughter call him a *dickhead dad.* He spoke out of the side of his mouth. "Jamie, sit down!"

The Goth woman with mascara flowing would not stop.

"YOU WONT EVEN GIVE ME A CAR! YOU'RE A DICKHEAD!"

Then she stormed out the door, passing patrons—a heavyset, ink-stained Goth woman, pierced and tattooed in seventeen-year-old angst. The restaurant stared collectively at the man who wouldn't even give his daughter a car. *Scrooge. Dickhead!*

"Well that didn't go well," he muttered.

Jeremy shrugged. "You can't blame Jamie, Dad. She was only eight when you left. Mom told her in Florida there was no Santa while she was with that Guido guy on the beach. It really sucked."

"That's just terrible."

"Yeah, I already knew ... but it pretty much blew."

George sat back down and stared at his son.

"I wish there was something I could do for you guys."

"I can't help you there, Dad. You blowing all this money on your new family kind of speaks for itself." Jeremy frowned. "I heard you lost your job."

"Yes, I did."

"That's got to kind of suck, but it doesn't seem like it's slowing you down."

The waitress appeared.

"Are you ready to order?"

"Give us a few minutes."

She left, and George stared at the laminated tabletop. He paused. "You're right. I was a bad father in some respects."

"Oh, yeah," Jeremy said into his beer.

"But ... I always wanted you and Jamie to have the best too."

"Really? That why you worked all the time?"

"Partly. Partly because I was building a career."

"Well, good luck with that."

"Look," George leaned in. "Why don't you come out on Christmas Eve and help me?"

Jeremy frowned. "I don't get it."

"Come out and help me be Santa. You can be my helper. You and Jamie. It's not the same as being Santa for you, but you could be in the sled with me as Santa's helpers."

Jeremy finished his beer.

"I don't think so, Dad. You know we go to Florida that morning."

"I know, I know. Just think about it. It's something we could all do together one last time. Maybe I can give you back some of the magic that we lost."

Jeremy put his empty bottle on the table and stood up. He zipped up his army coat and looked down at his father.

"I know Santa's not real, Dad. Some asshole told me he sponta-neously combusted from the g-load on reentry."

20

Macy's Santa

IN *MIRACLE ON 34th Street* Mr. Gailey took Susan to see Santa in the hope Santa Claus would seem more real to her. George felt like Mr. Gailey waiting to see the Macy's Santa with Megan and the other children and parents who had lined up five days before Christmas. But of course Megan had seen Santa in their town already. Mary thought the traditional Macy's Santa visit wasn't necessary. But their house had become a street corner in New York, with twin jackhammers shaking the walls and floors daily. The wheel barrels of fallen cement and bricks had grown into a pile in their backyard. Men pounded away in the attic, putting rebar under the roof to support the load limit his father had specified, and added their hammers to the madness of the home. Dust covered all.

George suggested they go downtown to see the Macy's Santa, but Mary had a cold and stayed behind. So George had taken Megan down on the train and had to admit to a double motive in going to see the Macy's Santa. He wanted Megan to see Santa, but he also wanted to ask the big man if there were any special things he should know. He had spent the night before in chat rooms of Santas who sparred over who manufactured a better suit and how to really produce a gusty *HO HO HO*. Some of the Santas became vitriolic.

Take your fake beard and padded stomach and go find some Walgreens to fleece kids with your bullshit, one poster known as *Santaman* wrote.

Eat reindeer shit and die, Yo Santa responded.

George was looking for a pearl of Santa wisdom. He liked that Santa had started out as this benevolent soul in Italy who tossed bags of gold down chimneys to luckless girls without dowries. St. Nick had evolved then as a saint who brought gifts to the poor. Of course the American version was a marketer's dream, but George wanted to return to the benevolence of that original Santa Claus. The Santa wannabees on the Internet were not inspiring.

... Just eat the cookies and drink the milk ... throw some horse manure around the yard and tell your kid it is reindeer turds ...

... Just tell every kid they will get exactly what they want ... that will hold the little shits and you can get through your shift without some kid going wacko ...

... Secret to Santa? You tell me. I have been freezing my balls off in these shopping malls for minimum wage for years. The only secret to being Santa Claus is that if you can get another job, then take it!

So he had decided to go see Macy's Santa in Chicago. The line snaking back through the store had been moving along for the last hour. Megan stood like Natalie Wood with her muff, patiently staring ahead as they entered Santa's village with giant ornaments and candy canes and twentysomething elves telling everyone to get their credit card ready.

"I know this isn't the real Santa," Megan whispered, in her fluffy white coat, blue eyes drawn together.

"How do you know that?"

"Because, the *real Santa* is in the North Pole getting ready to come to my house, and this is just one of his surrogates."

George nodded slowly. "Ah ... a surrogate. I didn't think of that before."

Megan stared ahead.

"Oh, yes. Santa has lots of surrogates to go to all these stores, and they report back what kids want."

"I see ..."

George felt his phone vibrate.

"Hello, mate!"

"Dean."

He stepped away from Megan.

"Everything going as planned?"

"Nothing to worry about, mate. We have the digital projectors ready and the necessary smoke machines and snow machines ready to go. I've had to secure some special lighting and that has cost a pretty penny, but all is under control. My carpenters are working on your ramps, and we will all be ready to film on the twenty-fourth."

"Great!"

"But I need to film you with your reindeer and in your Santy suit in the sled so I can project that onto the scrim and make your little one believe Santa is flying. And we only have four days, mate, so we better get it done ASAP!"

"Alright, let's try for tomorrow out at the reindeer farm. He said he had a sled I could use, so this could be a good dry run."

"STUPENDOUS! Now, you have your Santy suit ready?"

"EBay ... just delivered today in fact."

"Stupendous, mate! Shoot me a text with the address, and I'll bring me crew out and we'll shoot you on the sled and we'll be ready for the big day where you become Santa Claus and I get my movie!"

"Great."

"Oh, listen, mate. Going to need some more greenbacks. I have to pay these carpenters, and I've had to hire some gaffers and grips to handle the construction at the set, so maybe you better bring your checkbook along."

George saw they were coming to Santa's house.

"How much are we talking?"

"Better make it ten, mate. Those union carpenters are a bit pricey, you know."

George reeled back. Another ten thousand dollars! He would have to break into his 401(k). There was no other way. The credit line was toast.

"Dean," he whispered fiercely, "do we need all these people you are hiring?"

"Mate, I am a director, and we need people who can run these projectors and we need the proper lighting or we won't see a flipping thing up there on the roof. Trust me, mate, if you want this thing to come together for the little one, you need the proper people and equipment."

"We're almost there, Daddy," Megan sang out, jumping up and down.

George stared at her, keeping the phone pressed to his ear.

"Daddy. We are almost there, Daddy!"

"You still there, mate?"

"I'll bring the money with me," he said.

"STUPENDOUS! Alright, mate, shoot me that address, and I'll see you out at the farm!"

George put his phone away as they entered Santa's home. He had mentioned in the *Santa.com* chat room that he was going to see the Macy's Santa, and several Santas had told him that Macy's was the *premiere* Santa gig.

George examined Santa and admired his bright red suit, shiny black boots, and his red velvet throne. His beard shone brightly and his *HO HO HO* was deep and baritone. His cheeks glowed red and his spectacles were prisms of Christmas ice. Here was the Elvis of Santa Clauses. He held the children lightly on his knee and laughed and rumbled and shook before he smiled for the camera. Megan squealed.

"It's our turn, Daddy!"

He let Megan go as she climbed into the big man's lap. George stood back and watched while his daughter whispered into Santa's ear and he exploded with a *HO HO HO* that shook the windowpanes. George gave his credit card to a blonde elf who swiped it as the camera blinked three fast shots, and then Megan jumped off his lap.

"He was a great Santa, Daddy," Megan gushed.

"That's fantastic, honey."

"Sir, you can wait for your pictures in that room," an Asian elf told him with a hint of a lisp.

George hesitated. "Ah ... I'd like to speak to Santa for a moment," he whispered.

The Asian elf with heavy makeup frowned.

"Sir, that is not possible," he said, planting a hand on his hip.

George flipped out a twenty.

"Just give me a moment, alright, bud?" The elf took the money. "You have one minute."

George walked into the high-intensity lights.

"Do you mind if I ask you a question?" he said, leaning close to the Macy's Santa.

The eyes behind the glasses lost their gleam, and the voice lowered.

"Little old for Santa, don't you think?"

George laughed lightly.

"Ah, no, no ... I just have a question for you about being Santa."

"What can I do for you, sir?"

"Well ... I'm going to be Santa for my little girl on Christmas Eve," George began. "I'm going to land the sled on the roof and do the whole chimney thing."

Santa's brow furrowed as he looked sideways.

"What are you, crazy? You'll kill yourself."

George smiled, seeing his daughter watching him.

"I have it all set up with the reindeer and everything, but my question is, do you have any special insider tips to being Santa? Anything I should know about?"

"Get your life insurance policy paid up before you go up on that roof."

"Sir, your time is up," the Asian elf sang behind him. "Other people want to see Santa too."

George turned back to the Santa leaning back in his chair.

"You're really going to go up on the roof with a sled and go down the chimney?"

"Yes. They are jack hammering my chimney so I can fit, and I have ramps for the reindeer being built to go on and off the roof."

The Macy's Santa shook his head and leaned back on his throne.

"Why are you doing this?"

"My daughter is doubting Santa, and I still want her to believe."

"Alright, your funeral," he said, shrugging. "I don't have any advice for you, but Google a guy named Kris Kringgle—with two *g*'s. He might be the one you want to talk to."

George nodded slowly. "Who is he?"

The Macy's Santa shrugged and motioned to the next child.

"Just another wacko who believes he's Santa."

21

Dry Run

"STUPENDOUS!"

George, Kronenfeldt Sr., Bill McGruff, and Dean stared at the sled, with its large red velvet cushioned seat, plenty of room for payload, winking lights on the front, and curled runners slicked with wax and wood gleaming the color of a ship's cabin. The nine reindeer harnessed to the sled turned their heads and stared at the humans in the clearing.

"Aye, got her on eBay, and she shines up right nice. Haven't used it in a couple of years, but I think she'll do yer just fine," McGruff said, nodding.

"STUPENDOUS! This will look fantastic in the movie!" Dean exclaimed.

McGruff looked at George in his Santa suit.

"Where'd yer get the suit?"

"EBay."

"Bit tight."

George looked down. The boots pinched his feet, the pants looked like he was waiting for a flood, the sleeves didn't reach his wrists, the vinyl belt was cracked, and the suit had faded to a light pink. It took a lot of *Spray 'n Wash* to overcome the vinegary cat piss from the last owner's cat. His father had gotten in the car, sniffed once, and said, "Did a cat piss in your car?" George had stood in the bathroom mirror and thought he looked like a homeless man.

Now he was staring at nine reindeer standing in McGruff's fenced in pasture with snow falling on their backs. While he was watching, two of the reindeer pumped out large brown turds. Another one shot a brown stream into the field that sizzled and made his eyes water. Dean was already filming with his handheld camera.

"Just getting some B roll here, mates," he announced, squatting down.

McGruff nodded his beard peppered with snow. "Had to scramble a bit to get all nine together, but I did it."

"These goddamn animals stink," George's father declared, waving his hand.

"Aye, one of them has the squirts."

As if on cue, two other reindeer let fly.

"I didn't think about manure," George murmured as another reindeer farted.

"They eat all the time and shit quite a bit. I would have a man with a shovel and a garbage pail on site," McGruff told him.

Dean stood up with his camera.

"No problem, mate. I'll handle that and edit out their shitting. Now I need you to get in the sled and take the reins, and if you can, get the sled to move a bit, mate. This will be the footage projected onto the scrim. We'll edit out the background, and we'll have our flying Santa!"

McGruff eyed Dean. "Yer going to do all that with that little camera?"

He held up the camera with the large lens.

"Digital, mate. Super high def. State of the art!"

"Son, I don't know if I would get in that sled behind those reindeer," his father grumbled.

George turned to his father in his floppy hat and parka.

"Dad, they're reindeer," he scoffed. "They hardly look dangerous."

"What if they bolt?"

McGruff shook his head. "Aye, they don't bolt, Mr. Kronenfeldt. They can gallop a good clip, but reindeer aren't like horses. They usually start slow then get up to speed."

George's father shrugged. "Like I said at the beginning: your funeral."

"Thanks for the vote of confidence, Dad."

"You're welcome, son."

Dean positioned himself in front of the sled.

"Alright, George. I just need you to get in the sled. The first shot will be of you just sitting there holding the reins, mate. Then I'll want you to get them moving, and we can get a nice lot of B roll of the reindeer pulling you in the sled. Then I'll shoot from behind for the exit projector. Shouldn't take us long at all."

George looked at McGruff.

"Anything I should know about getting them to move?"

McGruff shrugged. "Aye, just slap the reins on their back, and they'll start moving. Nothing real sudden, just call out to them and let them know."

"I have sound," Dean yelled. "Maybe we can get a few *HO HO HOs*, mate, and call out the name of the reindeer to set the scene."

"Jesus," George's father muttered.

George stared at the reindeer standing as if they were on Valium. They just stared straight ahead and didn't seem to care about the humans. This gave him confidence. The most that would happen is the sled would move across the snow-covered field and Dean would have what he needed. George pulled on his big red mittens he had been keeping in his back pocket. The one nice thing about the Santa suit was it did have a pocket.

"Alright then ... here I go," he murmured.

George stepped into the sled and sat down. He gingerly picked up the leather reins. McGruff nodded.

"Aye, now wrap them around yer mittens there."

"Alright."

George carefully wrapped the reins and stared at the furry, snow-crusted animals. Dean walked around slowly with the camera.

"Mate, could yer take off your glasses?"

"Right, sorry."

George handed his glasses to his father, and suddenly the world beyond thirty feet was a snowy white haze.

"STUPENDOUS! Okay ... *action, mate!* Do a few *HO HOs* for me!"

George cleared his throat. "HO HO HO."

Dean held down the camera.

"Mate, you sound like yer dying! I need some real *HO HO HOs*."

George nodded. "Sorry, I'll try again."

"Okay ... action!"

He inhaled deeply and shouted, "HO HO HO!"

Two of the reindeer looked back at him sleepily.

"Alright, perfect, mate!" Dean held the camera down. "Now, do yer think we could get them to move a bit?"

George looked at the reindeer. "I'll give it a try," he muttered.

"Just give the reindeer a gentle snap with the reins," McGruff nodded.

"Alright, Prancer, Vixen, Comet, Cupid, and Blixen ... let's go!"

George flicked the reins. The reindeer just stood with their heads low. One reindeer farted. Another one let go with some fresh diarrhea.

"God, these animals stink," his father muttered.

Dean held the camera low.

"We need them to move, mate."

"I know," George grumbled, flicking the reins. "Giddyap!"

Another animal defecated.

"I think you are telling them to crap, son."

He looked at his father. "Thanks, Dad."

Dean frowned. "We really need them to go, mate. I need the footage for our projectors."

"Just snap it a little harder on their backs there," McGruff called out.

George snapped the reins three more times, but the reindeer didn't move.

"What kind of shitty reindeer are these?" his father wanted to know.

"'Tis not the reindeer, Mr. Kronenfeldt, 'tis the driver. They have to know who is boss, or they won't go," McGruff replied.

"Let's go. *C'mon, giddyap*! Let's go!"

His father shook his head. "Son, if these reindeer don't move, you will never get them on your roof."

Dean held his camera down again.

"Mate, we need these buckaroos to do something, or we won't be able to pull this off you know."

The snow was coming down harder and it was getting cold.

McGruff shook his head. "Like I said, they have to know who is boss."

George breathed heavy, feeling the frustration of his torn-up home, his diminishing finances, his kids' hatred for him, and on top of all that, that it was Christmas Eve in three days. And he was sitting in a forest in a sled with nine reindeer he had paid five grand for so they could shit all over the place.

"Son, I told you this thing was nuts," his father called out.

George stared at the fur-covered backs, breathing the heavy ammoniac scent of fresh manure. He raised the reins high and brought them down as hard as he could, shouting at the top of his lungs.

"C'MON, YOU BASTARDS!"

George fell back with a jerk and lost the reins as the reindeer bolted. The world started whizzing by with the reins trailing outside the sled. George grabbed the sides like a man bracing for a horrible accident. The snow filled his mouth and blinded him. He couldn't even wipe his eyes for the fear of being pitched out.

"HELP! HELP ME!"

The thunder of the nine reindeer pounding through the snow filled his ears. George stared at the cleaving muscles of their backs rolling up and down as they followed the fence. He saw his father then McGruff then Dean whiz by.

"STOP ... THESE ... BASTARDS!"

George then saw his funeral. There were Mary and Megan with their heads bowed and people sniffing as they lowered him into the ground. The minister spoke of his tragic death behind a herd of reindeer, and his father called out over the gathering, *"I told him it was a stupid idea! I told him he would kill himself!"* George felt the sled turn then bang off the fence as he fishtailed back toward the center of the corral. Snow sprayed back into his face. The reindeer galloped head down as his beard flipped up.

"Mate! Mate! Slow down!"

Dean's voice ran up then went away. George shouted, gripping the sides while the nine animals galloped full-out. He saw his father shaking his head and McGruff motioning to him.

"Grab the reins. Grab the reins!"

"I CAN'T!"

Dean had now gone to the center of the field and was turning with him.

"STUPENDOUS, MATE!"

George wondered if the reindeer would tire. They showed no signs of fatigue but seemed to have increased to a frenzied gallop. The sled began fishtailing crazily back and forth through the snow, whizzing around the white fence again. George saw his father then McGruff then Dean then his father then McGruff then Dean then his father then McGruff. He was whizzing in circles and now he saw McGruff had come out into the field, waving a stick at the reindeer that veered suddenly and shot the sled around like someone water-skiing. The g-force pulled George's grip loose as he was launched like a man shot out of a cannon.

"SHIIIIIIIIIITTTT!"

Like Charlie Brown he went straight up and came down flat on his back. The reindeer bolted to the far side but the sled had flipped over. The reindeer came to a slow galloping stop and turned back into the phlegmatic shitting, farting animals of before. George raised his head as Dean crunched over through the snow with his arms straight up.

"STUPENDOUS, MATE! JUST BLOODY STUPENDOUS!"

22

Real Santa Down

GEORGE FLOATED IN the suds with the jets puckering bubbles toward his lower sacroiliac and sciatic nerve. The hot tub in the bathroom was the only modern upgrade the owner had done to the early twentieth century home. He apparently had a bad back and gutted the bathroom, replacing the tub with a whirlpool. George rarely used the tub, but now he was thankful for the whooshing bubbles swirling around him, moving his beard like seaweed.

Mary called in. "George?"

"Yes."

"I have your ibuprofen."

He sat up and moved bubbles over him. Not that he minded being naked around Mary, but she was strangely prudish about such things. She often averted her eyes when he would walk through the house naked in search of a towel. George didn't see the big deal about being naked and suggested to Mary they go to Hawaii and try a couple of nude beaches. She told him he could go if he wanted to.

She walked in and set his ibuprofen and water on the hot tub.

"How's your back?"

"Feels better in here."

Mary sat on the tub and looked at the black boots and the pink heap on the floor. Santa had had a hard day. The day would have been comical if George's back didn't hurt so much. He had risen from the snow like a quarterback knocked cold that everyone is amazed can still play. But when he took his first step he had screamed out in pain. His father and McGruff helped him to the car, and he rode home like a man in a straitjacket. Dean had been in movie heaven.

"STUPENDOUS, MATE! I think I will use some of this for the promo trailer! You were HILARIOUS!"

George nodded with his eyes closed.

"Glad you got what you needed."

"You just get better, mate. Three days and it's showtime! Don't worry about anything. I'll take care of everything ... Oh, mate, do you have that check?"

He had managed to hand him the check, and then he walked into the house. His only hope was that heat and massive amounts of ibuprofen would allow him to be Santa.

"George?"

He opened his eyes, realizing he had been dozing in the tub. Mary was looking at him, and he moved more suds over his middle.

"We received a notice from the bank. They reduced your credit line to forty thousand."

He knew this already. He knew it when he received the TEXT ALERT that said he had reached his limit. The voice on the phone was apologetic, but the value of his house had fallen, and they had to freeze the line.

"Yeah, I know. They sent me a text."

Mary paused and adjusted her glasses.

"George, your accountant called too. He just was asking if everything was alright, because he heard you had cashed out your Roth IRA."

George positioned his back into the churning jets of water.

"Yeah, I needed to pay Dean and the carpenters, and the reindeer guy wanted more for the sled."

Mary rubbed her hands, fingering her wedding ring.

"George ... I never have questioned what you do. I believe when people marry later in life they have to give each other a lot of space."

"Me too," he murmured, turning on the hot water with his toe.

"But my house is covered in dust. I have people on my roof and in my chimney, and my husband has spent forty thousand dollars in less than a week, and now he just cashed out a fifty thousand dollar IRA."

George nodded slowly. "I think that about covers it."

Mary tipped up her glasses.

"I guess, my question is," she continued, "what the hell are you doing?"

"I think you know very well what I am doing. I am trying to extend our daughter's childhood by allowing her to believe in Santa."

"That is all well and good, George, but you can't take us to the poorhouse to assuage parental guilt."

He silenced the hot tub. George looked like a dripping wet dog with the suds sliding down his chest and clinging to his beard.

"What is that supposed to mean?"

Mary stared at her wet and steaming husband.

"I think you know."

"No, I don't think I do know, Mary."

"Your relationship with Jeremy and Jamie isn't good, and from what you said, there were a lot of problems in the home and—"

"Spare me the drugstore psychology. My relationship with my kids is fine! And I am not doing this out of guilt. I am doing this because in this crappy world we live in, a kid can't even believe in Santa Claus anymore without some *idiot teacher* trying to pierce her beliefs. Well, I'm not going to let that happen this time!"

George saw his wife's cheeks turn red. She pulled off her glasses and wiped her eyes then looked at him. Her undereye circles shocked him.

"I can't sit by while you put us in the poorhouse. You don't have a job, and I have worked hard to get where I am—"

"I'm not using any of your money," he snapped.

"It is *our money* now, George."

"Could have fooled me," he muttered.

Mary paused. "What are you going to do when you go through this money, Clean out your 401(k)?"

"If I have to."

Mary looked down and put back on her glasses.

"Then you are going to do what you want to do, regardless of my wishes?"

George looked up at her and wished he had some clothes on. It was hard to fight in a hot tub covered with suds.

"I'm going to be the Real Santa ... like I promised to Megan."

"You didn't promise to be Santa for Megan, George. You promised it for *you*."

"That's ridiculous."

"Is it? Why do I think if you hadn't lost your job none of this would be happening? Megan would either believe or not believe in Santa just like every other child."

"Losing my job has nothing to do with this."

She raised her eyebrows. "No? Some men go have an affair when they turn fifty, others buy a fast car, you, George, you decided to become Santa Claus!"

"This is not a midlife crisis. I had one of those after my divorce, for your information."

"Oh? And what did you do?"

"I screwed a lot of women."

Mary stared at him dully.

"Is that why you joined every online dating site?"

"Maybe."

"Really? I didn't know I married a stud muffin."

George looked up and raised his eyebrows. "There are a lot of things about me you don't know."

"Apparently," she murmured.

His wife stared down at her ring again, turning it slowly.

"I think we should rethink our situation after Christmas."

"Fine with me," he shrugged, feeling his back stiffen again.

George felt he was back in those days after his divorce, with lawyers and therapists and ultimatums. One thing people didn't understand about him is that if pushed, he would dig in like a mule.

His wife's eyes welled up. "I knew you were stubborn, but I always trusted you would do the right thing in the end."

"And I thought you would support me, so I guess we were both wrong," he replied, shrugging.

Mary stood up stiffly and looked down. George didn't bother to cover himself up.

"Your bulge is showing," she said, walking out of the bathroom.

George looked down and felt himself go soft.

"My bulge," he grumbled, sliding back into the warm water.

George pushed the jets on, angling himself toward the pulsing warmth. He stared darkly at the water, muttering above the bubbles, "I didn't join *every* online dating site."

23

GI Santa

GEORGE COULDN'T SLEEP and watched the Christmas movie *Holiday Inn* with the sound on low. The Christmas tree winked silently beside the television as Bing Crosby and Fred Astaire laughed, danced, and sang while they fought over girls. These movies were supposed to get him in the mood for Christmas, but he was facing divorce while going into the poorhouse.

George ate several bowls of Cap'n Crunch and walked into his living room. He stared at a Panzer taking aim at him. Shanti's house of inflatables beamed like it was Jack Frost's palace. George could hear the pumps of Santa and the reindeer sled that glowed weirdly in pneumatic glory. Shanti's Christmas tank flashed a red MERRY CHRISTMAS. Then the Panzer continued its rotation, looking for other sport to flash away its fiery message.

George held his bowl down and muttered, "enough is enough." He went back into his kitchen and slipped out a carving knife. Then he slipped on his blue parka and stepped into his snow boots. His back felt pretty good after three ibuprofen and the hot tub. George slipped out of the side door into the bracing northern air. He listened, clutching the kitchen knife. There was nothing but an airy hint of snow and woodsmoke. The pump for Shanti's pneumatic menagerie hummed like a small factory.

George moved stealthily to the snow, running across his yard to the clump of pines directly across from the Shanti palace. He could hear the plastic on plastic sliding of the turret. He pushed the pine needles aside and stared at the rotating Panzer. The turret was taking aim at his house again. George stared at the dark windows of the Shanti fortress.

George took a breath. It was like his plan to be Santa Claus. A man had to say *enough is enough. I will not have a Christmas tank taking aim at my house anymore!* He examined the darkened windows one more time then broke from the pines like the GIs in the Battle of the Bulge he had watched on The History Channel. George ran low and approached the Christmas tank as it turned toward him.

He raised up with the knife and charged the tank, not unlike those maniacal soldiers who charged up the beaches of Omaha. He plunged the blade into the turret. The hardened rubber plastic gave way but the knife slid off. George couldn't believe the knife hadn't penetrated the tank. He raised the knife again and plunged it into the turret. Again the rubberized cover gave way and the knife slid off. He hacked and hacked, but to no avail. The turret rotated and nearly knocked him over. George glanced up at the windows and then like a GI fighting in hand-to-hand combat, he brought the knife in low, thrusting as hard as he could into the base.

The explosion of air was a pop as the tank began to wilt in front of him. The turret sank like that famous scene in *The Wizard of Oz*, melting away from the lack of pressure with the pump working furiously to reinflate the moribund Panzer. George felt an orgasmic glory as the tank sank in front of him. He had just taken revenge on his boss for firing him, his wife for doubting him, and the world for forcing his daughter to grow up too fast. He raised his knife over the dead tank and shouted in the winter night.

24

Homecoming

THE WHITE, MOTTLED stucco bungalows with city yards and a porch were built in the twenties. The porches were for people to sit and nod to neighbors. It takes a village. That's what Hillary Clinton was saying when George bought the three-bedroom bungalow for one hundred and seventy thousand. He would live in a village, and his kids would ride their bikes, and he would sit on the porch and inhale the last scent of the American dream in the American century.

But of course his kids didn't ride their bikes. And George never really sat on the porch in the evening and nodded to neighbors. There were no neighbors, and the people didn't seem too interested in a man on a porch swing. Even the nights where he did sit out on his porch, he felt weird. Most people came home from work and went inside. A man sitting on his porch in the dark was a little suspect if not crazy.

Park Ridge was a village with parking problems, high taxes, and stressed middle-class people with homes hammered in the crash. And then his marriage went south, and his equity swirled down the drain along with his 401(k), and George was stuck with his home. That was why the stucco was falling off it and the garage leaned at a forty-five degree angle. His ex-wife was under the illusion their equity would reflate and there would be money left over. George knew they would be lucky if they didn't owe the bank after they sold the house.

He rang the doorbell and hoped Julie wasn't home. He had really come to see Jeremy and Jamie under the guise of dropping off his support check. He had sat in the tub a long time and thought about what Mary had said. There was an ache in his heart over the way things had turned out with his kids.

"Mom's not here," Jeremy said, opening the door.

George smiled. "I don't want to see your mother."

His son stared at him like he just woke up.

"I came to see you and your sister. Can I come in?"

Jeremy shrugged. George followed his son into the kitchen, where a mountain bike was flipped upside down with one tire off.

"Jamie's been working on her bike," he said as his father examined it.

"I can see that," George murmured. "Mom doesn't care that she works on it in the middle of the kitchen?"

Jeremy shrugged again. "She's never here. She doesn't give a shit what we do."

"I see," George said, glancing into the living room, where an artificial tree stood with no ornaments. "Does she even decorate the tree?"

Jeremy shook his head. "Not unless we do it. Sometimes she and Dirk will drink a bottle of wine and decorate some of it Christmas Eve before they pass out or go upstairs to screw."

George winced, looking at his son.

"That's just terrible."

"Yeah … I'm going to have a cigarette, Dad, on the deck."

"You mind if I join you?"

"Suit yourself."

They walked outside onto the deck George had built fifteen years before. He had designed the deck, had the wood delivered, then worked on it every weekend. But the Wolmanized lumber didn't fare very well. It had turned a dirty grey, and then individual boards started to give. George thought he had worked out the load factors, but building a deck was different from building a bridge. Soon they were all walking across the deck like pogo men.

Jeremy leaned on the railing and lit up a Marlboro. George walked carefully to the banister, taking in the leaning garage and the old grill covered in snow. He listened to the leaking gutters and the slow plop of snow falling between the cracks in the deck.

"I'm amazed that garage is still standing."

Jeremy puffed on his cigarette. "Dirk says he's going to knock it down and build a new one in the spring. Nobody is holding their breath."

With a Facebook suggestion they go to Vegas, Dirk had taken Julie there to see if their high school romance was still real. A lot of screwing apparently transcended the years, and his wife moved into Dirk's apartment, and then Dirk moved into George's house. The word he got from the kids was Dirk watched a lot of NASCAR and adult Netflix until he blew through his case of beer.

"It's not a small job," George said, staring at the garage. "She do anything about the sewer?"

Jeremy frowned. "Are you kidding? You can't take a crap without it backing up."

George had given her the money for the main sewer line. Where the five grand went he could guess with the trips to Vegas. He was sure Dirk had lost it at blackjack and craps. George turned around and looked at his son in his army coat and jeans.

"Jeremy, I want you to consider coming to my house for Christmas. I'd like you and your sister to come out and spend the holidays with me."

He threw the cigarette over the railing.

"That's why you came out here, Dad?"

"Well ... yes, that and to give your mother a check."

"Not a chance Jamie's going to miss Florida. I think she likes having Christmas on a beach."

George nodded slowly. "How about you?"

"I don't know, Dad. It seems a little late for all that now. You didn't seem to give a shit until now if I came out or not. You have your new family." He frowned. "I guess I just don't give a shit either."

George nodded slowly. "You're right, Jeremy. I want to apologize for that. I wanted to get away from ... from the pain. And in the process I lost you and your sister."

"Dad, it started before that. Even when you were here, you seemed like you wanted to be somewhere else."

"That's not true. I wanted to be here."

Jeremy leaned forward on the banister, flipping ash into the snow.

"Maybe, but you know the last time I remember you doing something with me, Dad? Do you remember sleeping in the Field Museum with the Cub Scouts with all the dinosaurs?"

George nodded slowly. "Yes, we slept on the floor in our sleeping bags."

"And remember how we got up at one AM, and the McDonald's was still open, and we bought burgers and ate it and walked around the museum?"

"I do."

Jeremy turned around and held his cigarette low.

"That's my last memory, Dad. After that, I don't remember you and I doing anything together."

George felt his heart grown heavy again.

"I'm sorry, son. I really am. I screwed up, and … and I'm sorry."

"That's alright," he said, shrugging. "It's over."

George jammed his hands down in his parka and stared at the falling garage.

"Would you at least consider coming out for Christmas? I could really use your help with this Santa thing, and I just want to spend time with you."

"I don't know, Dad."

George turned to his son. "Do you think you could give your old man another chance?"

Jeremy looked down. "I'll think about it."

"Okay."

"You better give me the check, Dad, and split. Mom was really steamed when she heard about you being Santa and all. She said she was going to take you back to court."

He raised his eyebrows. "How surprising."

"Yeah."

They grinned, and George felt himself grow a little lighter. He handed his son the check and walked to the edge of the deck.

"Think about it … okay?"

Jeremy flicked his cigarette into the snow. "Okay."

"Take it easy, son."

"Thanks for stopping by … Dad."

George tried to speak but could only hold up his hand.

25

Real Santa

THE APARTMENT BELL had been built in the last century sometime after the Wright Brothers flew. The bell buzzed up through the tenement like an angry bee with a faint echo. George waited in the musty alcove of chipped tile, breathing old smoke, hearing the crotchety voice again.

"Oh ... another wannabe Santa?"

He leaned close to the brass speaker and pressed the button.

"Not exactly."

"Then what the hell are you?"

George paused. The man he had found under KRIS KRINGGLE did not sound friendly. In fact, he sounded downright hostile. George pressed the button again.

"The Macy's Santa told me I should contact you if I have questions about being Santa."

"Jerry doesn't know his ass from a hole in the ground as far as being Santa goes," the old voice grumbled. "Just goes to show you how hard up Macy's is."

"Well, I'd appreciate if you could just give me a few minutes. I'm not really a Santa by trade. I'm doing it for my daughter who is nine and doubting the existence of Santa Claus."

The voice on the speaker grunted. "It's that Internet and the Xboxes and DSis and cell phones and the rest of the shit kids waste their time on. Of course she doesn't believe in Santa with all the crap that's out there now!"

George stared at the rolled newspapers piled up by the heavy lacquered door. He pressed the button again. "That's true. That's why I wanted to be Santa for her and try and bring back some of the magic."

"Well good luck with that," the speaker blared back.

George paused then pressed the bell again.

"Jerry at Macy's said you were one of the best Santa's he knew!"

"What an asshole. *I am* Santa!"

George chuckled and pressed the button again.

"Aren't we all."

"No ... I ... AM ... SANTA, YOU MORON!"

George swallowed and considered that going into the dark tenement wasn't such a good idea after all. He pressed the bell again.

"You're kidding."

"Why should I kid about something like that?"

George rolled his shoulders and pressed once more.

"I just didn't think Santa cursed as much as you do."

"You try getting all these goddamn gifts together and getting behind a bunch of smelly reindeer who shit all over you and fly through the air with the shit freezing so fast it feels like a cannonball when it hits you, and you'll be cursing too."

George nodded slowly and held the button.

"You have a point there. Reindeer do seem to defecate quite a bit."

"Defecate! They *shit* is what they do!"

George paused and breathed deeply, leaning close to the scorched speaker. "So do you mind if I come up and have a few words with you?"

"Your nickel."

The electric latch buzzed angrily as George pulled back the heavy door. He slipped up the musty stairs that smelled slightly like piss and continued down a long, dimly lit hallway that led to the door with a single piece of garland stapled to the center. *Kris Kringgle* was posted on a four-by-six notecard. George paused then knocked.

"It's open!"

He pushed on the door and thought of his grandmother's house up in Wisconsin. The smell of butter combined with cigarettes and a faint scent of dust and musty clothes. The long bowling alley hallway was dark, with a light bleeding from a room at the far end.

"Hello?"

"I'm back here," a voice called down the narrow passage.

George walked along the hallway that became an organ of creaking floorboards following him into a living room where a man with a white beard and long hair sat wearing a blue sweatsuit in La-Z-Boy with thick woolen socks and *White Christmas* playing on a black and white television. Newspapers were stacked level to his arm along with pizza boxes. He didn't bother slapping the paper closed nor did he remove the spectacles on the tip of his nose.

"The Bears need a damn quarterback. That man cannot have a game without an interception!"

George stared at the newspaper.

"What can I do for you?" he asked, keeping the paper high.

George sat down on a couch that poofed up dust. The man in the chair snapped the paper to another page. George stared at the man behind the paper.

"Well... you certainly look like Santa Claus."

He snapped the paper shut and looked at George.

"What are you, some kind of L.L. Bean moron? I don't *look* like Santa Claus. I *am* Santa Claus, you idiot! Jesus!"

He opened the paper again. George looked at his coat. He had never heard his parka summed up quite that way.

"Well ... I'm sorry."

"You have some questions for me. I have a lot of work ahead of me as I'm sure you can imagine," he murmured, looking over his glasses.

"Busy, huh?"

He snorted. "You think?"

"Well ... I assume so."

"I'm due to leave for the Pole tonight, as if it is any of your business."

"Ah ..." George paused. "Well, I guess I was wondering if there is any ... ah ... secret to being Santa."

The paper snapped again.

"Say *HO HO HO,* and give out a lot of gifts, and don't get stuck in the chimney, and wear goggles so you don't get reindeer shit in your eyes." He looked over the paper. " How's that?" He slapped the paper to another page.

"That comes from experience, I suppose."

"Yes."

"I'm sorry ... I don't really know your name."

The paper crackled again. "Kris Kringgle! Can't you even read?"

"I saw the name on the Internet. How did you get yours changed?"

The man dropped the paper onto the stack and looked over his glasses, leaning slightly forward.

"Let me ask you a question."

"Sure."

"Are you retarded? Did you escape from some institution?"

George smiled slowly. "Me? No, I'm an engineer. I build bridges mostly, or I design them. Well, I used to before I got laid off."

Kris Kringgle leaned back and stared at him.

"Can you give me a list of bridges you designed so I never go over them."

George laughed lightly.

"They are safe, I can assure you."

"Uh huh. Well, what else do you want to know?"

"Just if there is any secret I should know. You know, tricks of the trade to being Santa."

"I told you—wear goggles."

George pursed his mouth up and nodded.

"Well, I guess if there's no real secret to being a good Santa Claus, then I appreciate your time."

Kringgle put his paper on the stack and flipped out a lighter and lit a Marlboro. He clapped the lighter shut and studied George with the cigarette by his cheek.

"Why are you doing this?" He motioned the cigarette. "I mean this thing with your daughter?"

George rolled his shoulders.

"I want my daughter to believe in Santa. She's only nine. She wants to videotape Santa and prove to the world there is one. So I'm going to be the Real Santa for her."

Kringgle waved his hand.

"They all try and do that, and I catch them every time. Never get me on YouTube."

"Well, I want her to video me. It's the only way I can give her the magic back."

Kringgle flicked ash from his cigarette.

"Yeah, giving the magic back. That's where most parents screw up. They are so intent on their careers and their iPhones and their iPads and iPods, they forget about their kids. They forget the magic they had when they were kids."

George nodded. "That's right. That's what I want to give her. I lost my job, and I don't know, I think I've missed a lot. I screwed up my other family, and I don't want to do it again."

Kringgle picked up his remote and switched the television to *It's a Wonderful Life.*

"You going down the chimney?"

"Yes … I had it all hollowed out so I could fit."

Kringgle shook his head. "Don't fall down the bastard. That first step is a doozy."

"I hope not to."

"Relativity cloud is a lot easier you know. Just zoom, and you are there. No creosote or getting stuck halfway down. "

George chuckled. "Well, I don't have one of those."

Kringgle tipped his cigarette toward him.

"What about getting the sled to fly?"

"Digital projectors and smoke machines," he replied. "I will have the reindeer on the roof with ramps at both ends."

Kringgle watched George Bailey with the cigarette fuming in his mouth. "Lot of trouble. Relativity clouds are a snap, like I say. You just move faster than the speed of light and pop down the chimney."

"That's pretty good."

Kringgle looked over his glasses. "Just get done with your bullshit before I get there. I don't like people screwing up my landing zone."

"No problem."

Kringgle put down his remote and looked over his glasses. The cigarette whisked by his cheek.

"Anything else?"

George shrugged. "I guess not …" He paused. "But … well … you really believe you are Santa?"

Kringgle rolled his eyes, puffing perfect smoke rings.

"I *am* Santa, you moron!"

"But ... well, how did you know?"

"What do you mean, *how did I know*?"

"Santa Claus. How did you know you were Santa Claus?

Kringgle opened a box and took out a piece of pizza.

"I just knew. Same way you knew you were an engineer."

George stared at him.

"I never told you that. How did you know?"

"Santa knows everything, you moron." He bit the pizza.

"Huh!"

"Anything else?"

George looked around. "How did you end up in this apartment? Isn't Santa supposed to be at the North Pole?"

Kringgle shrugged. "Mrs. Kringgle and I separated about a year ago, and I let her stay at the Pole. She said she was tired of being alone every Christmas Eve and that all I do on the off-season is watch football, smoke, and eat pizza and read the paper. I told her everybody deserves their downtime. Anyway, she found some old boyfriend on Facebook." Kringgle raised his fingers in quotes. "Said he had a normal nine to five."

"That happened to me too," George cried out.

"Yeah ... she married me for excitement, and now she wants this boring guy. So I got the bachelor pad, and she kept the Pole. Did the divorcee bars for a while, but they're brutal. And I'm not going to cut my beard just to look younger."

"I never would have thought Santa had marital problems," George murmured.

"Hey, I am who I am." Kringgle stubbed his cigarette. "She knew she was marrying a fat guy who smoked and has to work the graveyard shift."

George nodded. "Yeah, my wife isn't too crazy about the money I've spent so far on being Real Santa."

Kringgle waved his hand. "Don't get me started ... she shops until she drops, and I give her anything she wants. But I drink a little beer and watch a little football, and it's a problem."

"I guess everyone has the same problems"

"Maybe." Kringgle lifted the paper. "Well, if you don't mind."

"Oh, yes." George stood up.

"Get the door on the way out will you?"

"No problem." He turned and walked toward the hallway.

"George!"

"How did you know my name?"

Kringgle's mouth flattened.

"Please! I knew you when you thought I had been incinerated in the ionosphere. Your dad ... now there is a *real moron*. He should read up on relativity clouds." Kringgle paused. "So, you really going to do this? This Real Santa thing?"

"Yes."

"This is going to cost you a lot of money."

"I have already spent forty thousand."

"And it's dangerous being on a roof, and your wife thinks you have lost your mind."

"We might split up over it."

Kringgle looked up. "So ... why are you doing it?"

"I told you—I want my daughter to believe in Santa."

Kringgle waved his answer away. "I know that. *But why?*"

George hesitated.

"Look ... you want to know the secret to being Santa?"

"I do.

Kringgle gestured with the newspaper. "Then tell me why you are doing it."

George paused and looked down, then back up. "Because I love my daughter."

Kringgle snapped the paper open.

"Shut the door on your way out will you, and give my best to Megan. Tell her I'm working on the guitar."

"Sure ..." George paused. "Wait a minute. I didn't tell you my daughter wanted a guitar."

Kringgle snapped the newspaper to another page and shook his head.

"Morons ... I'm surrounded by morons."

26

A Class Party

MRS. WORTHINGTON'S MOUTH turned down like the sun going into total eclipse when she saw George, and she would have banished him, but Megan held firmly to his hand.

"My dad has come to help with the party," she declared.

"I think we have enough helpers today, Megan," Mrs. Worthington said like a ventriloquist, sending hate while commanding her mouth to speak. The effect was like two people speaking out of both sides of their mouth. One side said *your father is an asshole* while the other side said *I think we have enough helpers today.* That was when Megan teared up, and that was when George knew he had Mrs. Worthington.

"Alright, your father can read *'Twas the Night Before Christmas,* Megan, but I hope he reads it *properly.*"

Daggers. Icepicks. Fileting weapons. That's what her eyes said as she moved off to command the other two mothers.

"I'm so happy you are going to help, Daddy," Megan whispered, then she ran off with her classmates to make reindeer.

George made himself useful helping the kids cut out their hands on brown paper for antlers. He found it interesting the way girls zipped through cutting out their hands and pasting on the antlers while the boys sat around unable to cut out their hands and some of them ate their glue sticks. His phone began ringing in the middle of the reindeer project and carried over to musical chairs. They had three days, and like all projects, the problems were coming to the surface. McGruff was not used to anything more complicated than having the kids touch his reindeer.

"One of the reindeer has started shitting blood. My question is, do yer need all nine reindeer?"

This was said while George helped a boy who couldn't trace his hand.

"We need all nine. Can you get a replacement?"

"Aye, I can try. But three days before Christmas, it's going to be tough. We might just have to bring him along and hope he doesn't shit all over the place or croak."

"Do what you can," George murmured, feeling the flamethrowing eyes of Worthington as she marched across the classroom.

"We don't allow *cell phones* in the classroom, Mr. Kronenfeldt!"

George put it back in his pocket, but he couldn't turn it off. His father was having trouble with the union carpenters, who said they built the two ramps to spec but his father said they had screwed it up. And since Dean hired them, there was an issue of who had the authority to fire them.

"It's useable though ... right, Dad?"

"That's not the point, son! They did not follow the specs, and I can't vouch for the job."

George hunched over, trying to hide his phone, whispering, "This isn't the railroad, Dad. We don't have time to rebuild the ramps. If they work, then we have to go with them."

"I can't vouch for the work."

Mrs. Worthington glared across the room.

"Dad, I don't care if you vouch for it or not. Are the ramps usable?"

His father grumbled the words *assholes, morons, unions,* then grumbled he would call back. Mrs. Worthington swept across the classroom again.

"What did I tell you about using your cell phone in class?"

"I'm sorry," George muttered. "Business call."

Mrs. Worthington raised her eyebrows.

"What is so important that you could not answer it later?"

"It was a Santa call," he muttered.

"Either give me the phone *or leave.*"

George stared at her outstretched hand, the imperious shelf of bust, the brooch, the hard grey eyes, the silver bowl of hair. *What a bitch* almost came out of his mouth.

"I won't use it again. Sorry."

Mrs. Worthington stepped closer, her outstretched hand in his face.

"I want your phone ... *now!*"

The Black Sabbath ringtone started again.

I AM THE GOD OF HELLFIRE AND I BRING YOU ... FIRE!

It was Dean. George had to pick up the call.

"Hey, mate, Dean here. Listen, everything is going according to plan. Had to hire a few more blokes to help with the snow machines and smoke machines, and we're going to need some trucks to transport so yer better get in a little more in the kitty there so we can finish the job."

Mrs. Worthington breathed like a bull, eyes burning, nostrils flaring, veins pulsing at her temples.

George nodded slowly. "Okay, fine. Let me call you back with a credit card number," he murmured.

"STUPENDOUS, MATE. This is going to be a stupendous shoot!"

George pushed the call off and looked at the seething, blood-filled face of Mrs. Worthington.

"Sorry. Business call," he mumbled.

"Give me that phone ... NOW!"

All the kids were watching. Somebody was going against Mrs. Worthington. George stared at this teacher, this master bull of every matriarch the Midwest had ever produced. He shook his head. "No, I'm not going to give you my phone."

That's when Barbara Worthington made her move. Tired of the years and years of taking shit from men and boys, she lunged for George's BlackBerry. He held firm, and they started to dance. Mrs. Worthington had half of his phone in her hand, and they looked like a couple tangoing across the room. The class watched in rapt awe as the phone went back toward George and then toward Mrs. Worthington.

"Give me your phone," Mrs. Worthington demanded.

"Let go of my phone!" George shouted, feeling the outrage of the boy who always felt wronged by detentions after school, trips to the principal, and always for the same thing: asking inappropriate questions. And yes, one of them had been, *How could Santa survive in the North Pole in Arctic conditions?* Here was the woman who would have sent him down to the principal for that one. Worthington was gritting her teeth, pumping coffee breath into George's face as her color deepened to a raging purple. Like the old bull she was, Mrs. Worthington yanked the phone free with all her might, but broken free from his grasp, the old teacher of seventy-years-plus, due to retire in the spring, fell back with the force of her effort, tumbling over Charlie Blunkenfeldt's desk in a back flip of support hose and a Playtex girdle that hadn't seen the light of day since 1965, and, like a mighty tree falling in a forest, flipped backward with her floral print dress rolling up over her shoulders and crashing among chairs, crayons, rulers, calculators, and all the odds and ends Charlie Blunkenfeldt had stashed in his desk.

Mrs. Worthington rolled on the floor with George's BlackBerry still clutched in her hand like a baton ready for the final dash to victory. A mighty tree had fallen and the fourth grade class stared in shocked silence as their teacher lay on the floor with her dress up, girdle up, support hose over girdle, and George's phone by her head, like someone bent on making a final desperate call.

Then the Black Sabbath ringtone screamed out for all the fourth grade to hear.

I AM THE GOD OF HELLFIRE! AND I BRING YOU ... FIRE!

27

Incarcerated Santa

MARY POSTED GEORGE'S bond. Mrs. Worthington had said he assaulted her. "What a crock of crap," he said to the cops, who said they had to book him. Mrs. Worthington said he had deliberately pushed her over the desk. Only Megan saved his bacon by saying that Mrs. Worthington had tried to take his phone. Still, his mugshot was taken, he was fingerprinted, underwent a cavity search, and was then given a nice clean cell. George's one phone call brought his wife, who posted the five hundred dollars bond with a court date the next month and a banishment of five hundred feet from school property. Mary said nothing to him on the ride home then nothing to him that evening, but at the kitchen table the silence ended.

"I'm leaving, George, after Christmas and taking Megan with me."

Just like that. She tossed the grenade into his lap with the pin out and good luck getting it back in. The grenade of loneliness, unemployment, and divorce would detonate on December 26th. Until then, George could juggle the grenade, play with it, do what he wanted, but the resolution in his wife's voice let him know there was no way to get the pin back in.

"But why?"

Mary ticked off his transgressions like a judge.

"You have put us into bankruptcy after losing your job. You have made Megan a pariah at her school, assaulted her teacher, and you have destroyed out home."

George frowned, sitting in his BVDs and T-shirt. A man really should have pants on when his wife says she is leaving. But he didn't want to get up from the table. For one thing, incredibly, he had a hard-on. For another thing, he felt if he left he would lose all leverage and Mary would go through with her plan. So he sat with his hands between his legs, hunched against the setback temperature on the thermostat of sixty-five. "The house isn't destroyed," he said, looking into the living room covered in dust from the chimney.

Mary stared straight ahead, not really looking at him but through him. That's what scared him most. She had already left.

"I asked you to stop this nonsense, but you have persisted. I am afraid to see what is going to happen tomorrow night. I will ask you one more time to stop this. Do not continue down this road of ruin."

Even to George it sounded melodramatic, but Mary did that often. She spoke in the humorless voice of the prairie schoolmarm—she had taught first grade for ten years. A bar had to be set for errant children, and he was now in that category.

"All the work has been done. Tomorrow night will be the easy part," he pointed out weakly.

Mary blinked, taking off her glasses like a man drawing a gun.

"Then you will not stop this crazy plan even though it has resulted in you going to jail and breaking our family financially and destroying our home."

"This had nothing to do with what happened with Mrs. Worthington! That crazy bitch tried to take my phone!"

Mary sniffed, putting her glasses back on.

"I have to believe the stress of everything, George, is the reason for your assault on Megan's teacher."

"I didn't assault her. She *assaulted me!*"

But Mary had a point. The barrage of phone calls, the problems, the money—it had all played a part, and when Mrs. Worthington demanded he give up his phone, well, he just went off the rails.

"Whatever happened, Megan has been scarred," Mary continued.

George waved away his wife's words. "Oh, she's fine."

"Then you are going through with your plan?"

George felt his spine stiffen. It was the same with Mrs. Worthington, his boss, and now his wife. People wanted him to conform to their way of thinking, to their world.

"Absolutely."

"Then I will leave with Megan."

"No you won't," George said, standing up in his BVDs. "Megan stays, but you can feel free to go anytime you want."

Mary stood up and faced him.

"Don't friggin' mess with me, George."

And that was how they left it.

28

'Twas The Night Before

GEORGE STARED UP at the grey sky floating wisps of snow like the ashes he had seen coming out of the school incinerator on the day before Christmas when he was twelve and had climbed to the top of a train trestle and contemplated falling off. George saw that same world below him now—chimneys belching smoke, families huddled in for the holiday, the dabbing of a white Christmas sprinkled onto the pines—and for a moment, he felt that same excitement as that boy on the trestle. Then his phone rang.

He carefully pulled up his phone, making sure he had one hand on the chimney.

"Ya this is Yergen the climber. You want me at your house what time?"

"Ah, why don't you come around ten."

"This will cost you extra you know."

George nodded his head tiredly. "I know. Just bring everything we will need."

"And you want to go down what—a chimney?"

"Yes."

Yergen the German climber of *mountainexpeditions.com* was silent. Then he said, "That sounds crazy you know. Are you Santa? Ha Ha."

"Yeah, I'm Santa. I'll see you tonight."

"*Ya vol.*"

George put the phone in his pocket and looked at Joe.

"I think you have enough room now to go down her."

George leaned over, breathing creosote and the dry scent of busted bricks and cement. The enlarged opening did look large enough, and far down the dark hole he could see the light of his living room. It made him want to crap. The thought he could fall to his death down the chimney never occurred to him. But now, looking down into the black chasm, he saw himself clearly falling to his death.

"You really going to do this thing?"

George looked up Joe's rodent eyes.

"Is it hard going down a chimney?"

Joe spat off to the side, relieving his swollen lip.

"No, you just have to make damn sure you don't lose your grip or look down."

George looked back down the hole. Mary was right—he had lost his mind.

"Yeah, well, I put some footholds in there for you. I put a half-brick about every ten feet. Figured you could use that to balance yourself going down."

"Thanks ."

Joe leaned over and spat down the chimney. The glob of tobacco sounded like a rifle crack when it hit the hearth. They both stared down the long black tunnel he would descend into in less than twenty-four hours.

"Long way down," Joe muttered.

29

Christmas Eve Dinner

THE FONDUE SMOKED in the middle of the table, and George felt like a boy waiting for Santa except he was waiting for a semi loaded with two three-hundred-foot ramps, lighting equipment, snow machines, digital projectors, a sled, smoke machines, tracks, grips, handlers, cameras, closed circuit television, a boom, a film crane, walkie-talkies, union carpenters in case there were any last minute changes, pyrotechnics, a director, a director's latest girlfriend and first assistant, two German mountain climbers with rappelling gear, and finally nine reindeer and Bill McGruff.

Dean had arranged to have everyone follow the semi and assured George he would handle the setup and breakdown. "The director, mate, is the general. I'm in charge, and these blokes will have to do as I say and we should have a STUPENDOUS film!"

George understood there had to be a project manager or otherwise the bridge would not get built. Dean had taken on the role of project manager and interceded between his father and the union carpenters, navigated problems with McGruff, who couldn't get a trailer big enough to haul the nine reindeer, and arranged for the semi with a sectioned off part for the reindeer. All McGruff had to do was get them to a parking lot, and Dean would transport them the rest of the way.

George heard the roar of a diesel engine and the hiss of pneumatic breaks. He looked up from the table as his father nudged him. They both looked out the window at a tractor trailer rolling to a stop in front of the house followed by three dark SUVs, McGruff's truck, three older cars, and a concession truck.

"You have to feed the crew, mate," Dean told him later.

George stared out the window and saw the hundred thousand dollars he had spent. So his kid wouldn't go to college. So he had no retirement savings left. *Megan would believe in Santa Claus.*

"Shit!" his father muttered.

"Don't say a word, Dad."

"I just lost another shrimp, Daddy," Megan announced.

"I'll get if for you," George said, watching his wife stare out the window at the lights on the sixteen-wheeler and the people congregating in front of the house.

"Why don't you pull the drapes together. It will keep the house warmer," Mary suggested, staring at him icily, raising her eyebrows.

"Yes, it is cold in here," George replied.

"You can say that again," his father muttered.

But it was too late. Megan was already staring at the semi and the cars and the people standing around the lit concession truck.

"What is that truck doing in front of our house, Daddy?"

George whisked the drapes together, facing his wife and father and his daughter, who was already out of her chair. Kronenfeldt Sr. crossed his arms and looked at the ceiling.

"Now let's get back into our seat, Megan. It is just the Shantis getting some furniture delivered."

"Lots of furniture," his father mused.

"Why would they have furniture delivered on Christmas Eve, Daddy?" Megan asked as he continued pulling curtains and shades in the living room, dining room, and kitchen.

"Oh ... that's normal. A lot of people do that. They are giving it as a gift. People give pool tables and couches and dining room sets as gifts, and that's what the Shantis are doing."

"Oh." She shrugged. "Seems weird to me."

"You have no idea," Kronenfeldt Sr. said, looking at his son.

George made sure Megan was safely in front of the television watching *Elf* for the tenth time with Mary and his father. He then slipped out the door and ran across his lawn to where Dean was standing with a group of men with LOCAL TEAMSTERS U35 pinned to their hats and several young women with clipboards and walk-ie-talkies.

"'Ello, mate! Are we all ready for the shoot?"

"It's not a shoot, Dean, and what are all these people doing here?" George hissed.

Dean shrugged. "Gaffers, grips, electricians, digital technicians, Teamsters, assistants first and second, cinematographers, crane op-erators, handlers, pyro technicians—all necessary, mate, to give your little daughter the STUPENDOUS show she deserves!"

"We don't need all these people, Dean," he whispered fiercely. "This is not about your movie!"

Dean sipped his latte and took George by the shoulder. He carried his riding crop under one arm and cocked his beret forward.

"Look, mate, you hired me to do a job. What you basically asked me to do is create *a world*, create a character, an *illusion*, mate." He stopped and stomped his riding boot. "That's what I'm doing !" Dean tapped his chest. "I'm an artist, mate, and I am a perfectionist, which is a good thing for you. What if I didn't bring the necessary equipment and blokes who know how to operate snow machines and smoke machines and digital projectors? And yer ass is on yer sled, and your little daughter there sees that it is daddy and not Santy Claus coming down the chimney? Then you would say, *Listen, Dean, I hired you to do a job and you didn't do it,* and you would have every right to fire me, mate."

George rubbed his forehead, seeing two bearded men with rap-pelling equipment walking toward him in the darkness.

"Alright, but did you need all the film equipment too?"

Dean held up the leather-riding crop.

"Remember our deal, mate. I'll create the visual of Santa Claus for your little mite there, but you'll allow me to film for my STUPEN-DOUS upcoming feature-length movie!"

The two men with rappelling ropes over their shoulders and spiked boots clicking on the street walked up.

"Ya. You are George, ya?"

"Yes, I am."

"Vee are Yergen and Sven. Vee are your climbing coaches," Yergen said, shaking his hand.

George nodded, glancing toward his home. "Nice to meet you."

"We came early to get you down the chimney, ya?"

"Uh … yeah. Yes. We are going down the chimney and back up."

"Hello, mates! I'm Dean, and I'm the director of this shoot," Dean announced, shaking their hands. "Why don't you speak with my first assistant Leslie there, and she will get you all set up."

"Ya …Ya …"

Dean adjusted his beret and looked at George.

"You see. All under control, mate."

George watched people getting coffee and donuts from the concession truck. Already, several neighbors were looking out their windows. He realized then his father and his wife were correct—he had lost his grip on reality and had created a monster.

"Just give me a jingle on the cell phone and let me know when we should start getting set up. Then when you are ready to suit up, mate, I'll give you your cues and spots, and she should all go like clockwork," Dean assured him.

George stared at the short, swarthy man who had taken sixty grand of his money. He wondered if he had just built another bicycle bridge people would laugh at again. He looked over the people milling about with the low thrum of the diesel engine coming back from the houses across the street. He didn't have many neighbors, but the Shantis were nosy enough to blow the whole thing with a bunch of questions.

"Alright, I'll give you a call within the hour," George said, turning to Dean. "I have all the shades down around the house, so you can start setting up. Then I need you to get these trucks and cars away from the house. Spread them out or whatever, but I can't have it looking like a movie set around my house!"

Dean clapped him on the shoulder.

"Don't worry about a thing, mate!"

A blonde with a clipboard and a walkie-talkie set up a folding chair with DIRECTOR on the back. The assistant turned around with a logo on her jacket: REAL SANTA.

George walked back to his house as his father met him at the door.

"What's going on?"

"You don't want to know."

George shut the door and looked around his shoulder.

"Megan still watching *Elf*?"

"Yeah. What's going on out there? Is everything here?"

George pulled off his parka and shrugged.

"It looks like the whole world is out there, including a concession truck."

His father stared at him. *"A concession truck?!"*

"Shhh, keep it down. I have to keep Megan away from the windows. She already is talking about a white Christmas and wants to look out the windows."

His father frowned. "How are you going to keep her away from the windows?"

"How the hell do I know? But I have to get Dean and his guys going, because it doesn't look right having a tractor trailer in front of the house."

His father frowned. "The ramps are in the truck?"

"Yes. So are the reindeer."

Kronenfeldt Sr. whistled. "I'll bet that truck is full of shit!" He shook his head. "Are you sure it's worth all of this, son?"

He stared at his father.

"Do you really think I need to hear that, Dad, when I've spent close to a hundred grand and it's Christmas Eve?"

"No."

He reached past George for his coat on the hall tree.

"Where are you going?"

"I'm going out there to check on those ramps and see if these knuckleheads screwed up my specifications."

"Where do I say you went if Megan asks?"

"Tell her I went to get some milk."

Kronenfeldt Sr. went out the door, and George realized then he might not have milk for Santa. The details were mind numbing. Santa gifts had to be hidden in a special place then loaded into the "payload bag," and they all had to be a certain diameter to fit down the chimney. Even though Joe had given him room, there was no way he could go down carrying the gifts. The gifts would go down ahead of him or behind him.

George rubbed his head. A million things could go wrong. He might get stuck in the chimney. He might fall to his death. The reindeer might bolt. The reindeer might not move. The digital projector and smoke machine wouldn't give the proper illusion. He could fall off the roof. The reindeer could fall off the roof. He might not be able to get back up the chimney. The sled and reindeer could tumble down the ramp. Megan might not buy any of it.

"George ?"

He jumped and turned in the hallway to his wife.

"What's going on?" Mary asked.

"Nothing. Just half the world is in front of our house."

Mary opened the door a crack, and she saw cars, lights, an idling truck, and people milling around. She shut the door and turned, her face white.

"Oh, my Lord!"

"I know. It won't be as bad once they are set up in the backyard. But I think I really screwed up."

George's cell phone rang. "Yeah."

"Hey, mate, listen. We have to let these reindeer out of the truck. They have to go you know, nature's call and all that."

"Alright. Start setting up in the backyard. I'll keep Megan away from the windows." He paused. "We probably should start."

"*Right-o, mate!*"

George held down his phone and looked at his wife. "It's begun."

"Oh, shit," she murmured.

30

A Clatter

"WHAT WAS THAT, Daddy?"

George looked up from the book toward the window.

"What?"

"I just heard a clatter," Megan said, her blue eyes growing larger. "I think I just heard a clatter! I think it's Santa! Where's my video camera?"

George felt a ticking down in his groin. He heard footsteps on the roof and something bumped the house. He had managed to keep Megan away from the windows through dinner. Now he was in the final countdown. *'Twas The Night Before Christmas* was usually read to Megan by them both, but Mary had nodded grimly, telling him to go ahead.

"Sweet dreams, precious," she said, going back to her wrapping in the bedroom.

George couldn't help thinking this was a presentiment of things to come. Then he had started reading, and the world seemed distant. He had set the video camera up for Megan and put it by her bed. He had gone over how to operate the camera and made her press the buttons to get the camera in RECORD mode. He explained how the bell would ring by her bedside when Santa came.

"I want to wake up every hour to make sure I catch him," she whispered, peeking out of the curly blond hair edging her eyes.

"I am certain you will catch him," George assured her, glancing at his watch. "But with the bell, you don't have to worry. When he comes it will ring."

And then he had started to read and now there was this "clatter" on the roof. Megan already had the camera in her hand, pulling back the covers.

"I'm going to look!"

"No!"

George stood up. "Let … let me look first."

Megan stood by her bed with the camera in her hand.

"Okay, but let me know if you see Santa."

George walked to the window and lifted the blinds to a scene of utter chaos. Lights shined crazily all over the lawn. Reindeer were standing in the middle of his yard with a man trying to herd them toward the ramp that looked like a runway to the stars. People were all over the roof with glowing screens—men with computers and smoke machines and snow machines. The reindeer were shitting in the grass. Dean appeared like the Wizard of Oz on a camera boom, rising above the roof behind a large camera.

"What do you see, Daddy? Is it him?"

He dropped the blinds down quickly and shook his head.

"Nothing. Nothing at all."

Megan frowned. "Is it snowing?"

"Snowing—not yet, but soon I'll bet."

Megan started to get out of the bed.

"I want to look outside."

"No—"

There was another thump, and Megan's eyes grew large.

"Is that Santa?"

George's phone rang, and he saw that it was Dean.

"Hold on … stay in the bed," he commanded, walking into her large closet of stuffed animals, dolls, a rocking horse, and clothes. "Can you guys keep it down?" he whispered.

"Sorry, mate. The little mite asleep?"

George stared out the door and saw Megan starting to get out of the bed.

"Megan, I told you to wait in the bed!"

She crossed her arms and pouted.

"Still up then?"

"Yeah, and she heard you guys and wants to look out the window."

"Oh, don't let her do that, mate. These reindeer are shitting all over the place and do they stink! The buggers keep breaking loose. I don't think that McGruff knows what he's doing. I'm right outside the window now on the boom, mate. You in the first window there with the light?"

"Yes," George whispered. "But she wants to look out the window and wants to see if it's snowing! Can you hide everything?"

"Ah, no way, mate. We are constructing the set you know. But listen, mate, I have an idea. Give me ten minutes, and I'll give her a snowy Christmas, and then the little bugger will go to sleep with sugar plums in her head."

"Alright ... ten minutes. But you can't have all those people!"

"Leave it to me, mate! Just leave it to me!"

George pushed his phone dead and walked out. "Now where were we?"

"*We* were going to look out the window," Megan declared in her red Santa pajamas, arms crossed. "But you won't let me!"

George sat down on the bed.

"Well, how about this—how about we finish the book and *then* look outside and see if it is snowing?"

"We're going to miss Santa Claus," she grumbled, slipping down in her covers. "And I want to see if it is snowing."

"Megan, I *promise* you won't miss Santa Claus, and we will check and see if there is any snow."

"Okay," she grumbled, still pouting.

George opened the book again and began reading. And as he read he remembered his own father reading to him. It was one of the few things his father did that showed he recognized Christmas as a reason to stop working and leave the basement or garage and participate in a communal holiday. He read the entire book to George, sitting on the edge of the bed, his heavy bass voice reciting the words while the snow fell outside his window. Then he tucked him in and gave him a kiss good night.

" '... and to all a good night.' "

George closed the book and stared at the window.

"Can we look outside now? Can we, Daddy?"

George looked at his watch again and stared at the curtains. He breathed heavy. "Well, I guess we can," he murmured. "Maybe we should read another book—"

"No way!"

Megan jumped out of the bed and ran to the window, throwing back the curtains. George felt his heart leap.

"Daddy! Daddy!"

She jumped up and down. "Look! Look!"

"Okay," he murmured, sure now they were done.

He got up slowly, walking toward the window. Megan turned to him, her eyes shining.

"It's snowing, Daddy!"

George frowned and looked out the window. Thick white snow was falling down in front of it and piling on the roof. It was an amazing amount of snow.

"It's so dark out, I can't see anything except the snow," Megan said, jumping up and down.

"It is dark out," he murmured, feeling his phone vibrate. He held the phone to his ear, and Dean laughed

"What do you think, mate—enough white Christmas for you?"

"Yeah. How are you doing it?" he whispered.

"Movie magic, mate. Got the snow machine pumping away, and there are some people holding a scrim just beyond the snow, but your little mite just sees a snowy night."

"Amazing."

"Well, lots of work to go, mate, and you are due in makeup once the little one falls asleep."

George put his phone in his pocket and stood with Megan watching the manufactured tufts of snow piling up. His daughter turned and looked at him.

"We are going to have a White Christmas, Daddy, for Santa!"

"Yes we are, so you better get in the bed so you can catch him."

Megan jumped back in her bed and yawned.

"I have to get to sleep so I can wake up and catch Santa," she declared, looking at her clock and the video camera by her bed.

George turned out the light and only a single Christmas candle lit the room from the far window. This too reminded George of when he was a boy and sat in the yellow glow of the candle and waited excitedly for Santa. He remembered the crust of snow on his window and how the world seemed to pause. George leaned down and felt his daughter's arms go around his neck. She hugged him tight.

"I love you, Daddy," she murmured sleepily.

"Merry Christmas, Megan," George whispered.

He stood up and walked to the door then turned. Megan was staring at the movie snow just outside her window.

31

Training Camp

WHEN GEORGE WAS a boy he imagined Santa in a sled with his reindeer in order, the reins firmly grasped, the wind in his hair, toys snug in his sack, flying over the rooftops with a great *HO HO HO*, landing on a dime, then scampering down the chimney with the grace of a ballerina and climbing back out after a snack of milk and cookies, throwing his sack of gifts into the back of his sled with a hearty, *Away Dasher, away Dancer, away Cupid, Comet, and Blitzen!* Then he would fly off to the next house after leaving a note for George telling him what a good boy he had been and somehow knowing what he had wanted because there it sat under the tree.

What he didn't think about was what it took for Santa to gear up for just *one* house. As a boy he assumed other kids got their gifts, but he really didn't care how Santa did it. George now stood outside in the cold darkness and saw chaos. Reindeer were galloping back and forth. People were running after the reindeer. The smell of a farm hit him like a blast of city sewer gas. Nine animals had produced an amazing amount of reindeer manure. Men were moving the giant wooden ramps that looked like something for Noah's Ark. Other men were swearing as they bumped the roofline, and George knew what the *clatter* had been.

In the middle of all this was Dean on a camera boom in his beret, riding crop, and breeches. George crossed the yard as Bill McGruff whistled and amazingly the reindeer trotted to him. He snapped them into a long harness like something you would see in an old Western. George was amazed at the docility of the animals under the grizzled veteran's commands.

"These assholes couldn't build a ramp to specs if their life depended on it!"

George turned to his father. "Hi, Dad."

Kronenfeldt Sr. shook his head, standing in his parka like a fat snowman. A woolen BEARS hat sat just above his eyes.

"The ramps are off, so the reindeer are going to fall on the roof and off," he grumbled.

"What can we do?"

"I'm having the numbskulls build a small gap bridge for the difference. Hopefully it will hold, or you're going off the roof."

"Hopefully," George murmured.

"I better go see what these assholes are doing," Kronenfeldt Sr. muttered, stomping off.

"Mate!"

George turned to Dean, who had descended from the camera boom walking with his two twentysomething assistants in matching REAL SANTA coats.

"Everything is going exactly to plan, mate! We are getting the roof all set up."

George turned and saw lights all over the roof and an image dancing on the far shingles. Men walked around the chimney and the windows, stringing wires through gutters and down off the side of the house like long black snakes. A generator hummed by the street with thick black cables going into a large operations tent, where men sat with laptops and walkie-talkies. The general hum of the hive was impressive. Dean rolled his hand across the vista of the roof.

"We ran the smoke machine and the digital projectors, mate, and it looks STUPENDOUS! All we have to do is make sure you are suited up, and we get the reindeer on the roof and then jingle the Santa bell I rigged by the window for the mite." Dean framed the house with his hands. "She wakes up, and then I will speak to you on an earpiece and tell you to go. You go through the clouds and smoke and stop in front of her window. You get out of the sled, let go a few *HO HO HOs*, then up the chimney and down with the mountain blokes, deliver your gifts and then up again and out, then you give the reindeer a little tug through the smoke and snow, and we shoot Santa in the sky again and you, mate, have your Real Santa, and I have my movie!"

Dean held his hands out. "What could go wrong?"

George stared at Megan's window covered by a spotlight with a snow machine spraying confetti.

"I'll keep the snow up if she wakes again, mate, then we drop that for the real thing, and bingo!"

"You think it will all work?"

He held his hands to the sky.

"Mate, I think this could be my greatest work yet! This could be by my *Lawrence of Arabia. It* is simply going to be stupendous!"

"I'm putting my trust in you, Dean."

"Don't worry about a thing, mate." Dean pushed him along lightly. "Now go get suited up, and I want to get you in makeup."

"Makeup?"

"Mate, you can't look like her daddy. I'll have you looking more like St. Nick than St. Nick himself!"

32

The Suit

GEORGE PUT ON long underwear first and wondered if Santa made this precaution against the elements. Did Kris Kringgle wear long underwear under his suit? He lifted up the pullover shirt with white ribbing that still smelled like cat piss. The shirt had some room for extra padding. George shoved in two small pillows, moving them around to both sides of his own stomach. He then slipped on the pants and realized he had forgotten about the suspenders. He had to start over.

"Dammit," he muttered, yanking the shirt over his head then slipping on the trousers, looping the suspenders, slipping back on the shirt, and stuffing in the pillows.

He looped the fat belt and pulled it tight, snugging it around the pillows. George looked in the bathroom mirror, punching up the pillow on the right side. He then pulled on thick woolen socks and stepped into the knee-high shiny boots that pinched his toes. He sat down on a stool and had to yank hard to get them over his thick socks.

The right boot stuck then broke free and slipped on. George stood, clunking around on the tile, trying to get feeling back in his pinched toes. He approached the mirror and picked up a can of hair color. George lifted his chin, spraying white paint all over his beard and the fringes of his grey hair. He coughed the hazy paint away and stared at himself. He looked like a man who had just sprayed white paint on his beard and hair. He put down the can of paint and picked up his hat, positioning it carefully on his head. He took off his glasses then paused.

"Yeah," he muttered.

The man staring back at him did not look like Santa. He looked like a fat, middle-aged engineer in a tight-fitting faded-to-pink Santa suit with two pillows pushing out like prenatal twins from a bad movie, with road paint on his beard and hair. George took off his glasses and couldn't see a thing. He stepped back from the mirror and came into clearer focus. He put his hands on his hips and tried to look jolly. "HO! HO! HO!" The man staring back at him looked even more ridiculous. "Shit," he muttered, walking into the living room.

Mary looked up from the couch and stared at him.

"What do you think?"

His wife had her legs folded up under her, with presents already arranged under the tree. George would place several strategic presents for Megan to watch, but the majority were already there. He and his wife had not spoken much beyond logistics for the last twenty-four hours. George kept looking for a thaw, but her pressed lips let him know the deep freeze would continue until she walked out the door.

Mary tilted her head and nodded slowly.

"You look like Santa Claus."

George nodded, moving the pillows again.

"I had to add some padding, but I don't think she will notice."

"No, I don't think she will."

He walked over to the couch and saw himself in the mirror—a Santa with marital problems. *Kris Kringgle had marital problems too.* The guy was gone for twenty-four hours probably every Christmas. He probably was MIA for the whole month of December getting ready. Maybe even from November on he was doing the late at the office thing, barely seeing his kids, supervising the elves. George was sure Kringgle's apartment was waiting for him too now.

"I know things haven't been good between us," he began, brushing some paint from his fingers.

Mary raised her eyebrows. "You think?"

"But I want you to know my heart has always been in the right place."

Mary frowned.

"I don't worry about your heart, George. It's your brain that concerns me. We have people running all over the yard, a semi parked on our street, cables, lights, machines, cameras, reindeer, ramps, and a concession truck in the back of our yard." She looked up at him. "Don't you find that a bit odd for Christmas Eve?"

"I told Dean to get rid of the concession truck."

Mary picked up her magazine.

"Well, you better go. They are all waiting for you."

George lingered, hoping he could straighten out his marriage on the way out the door. Mary stood up.

"I'm going to bed. I guess I will see you in the morning then."

"You won't hear a thing ... but by morning you'll have a daughter who believes in Santa Claus again!"

His wife stared at him.

"Is that what this is all about?"

"Of course it is."

"Maybe you should ask yourself who you are really being Santa for."

"I don't understand."

Mary turned at the bottom of the stairs.

"It's not Megan."

"Who then, if I may ask?"

She smiled faintly. "It's for a little boy who found out too early there really was no Santa Claus."

"And?"

"And he turned fifty, and he's still trying to believe."

33

Papa Elf

GEORGE STARED AT the electric candle in his window. It had been burning all night in his bedroom, and he checked every thirty minutes to see if the yellow glow had dimmed by horizon light. But it was just three AM. His parents had tucked him into bed seven hours before and then gone down the stairs. He had lain awake, willing himself to fall asleep, but he just couldn't. So he stared at the candle and imagined it as a beacon for Santa and his sleigh. Several times he went to the window to look at the sky, examining the clouds for a big man with a beard and reindeer.

Then he heard something. He wasn't sure if he had imagined the hard steel runner of a sleigh touching down on the roof. George jumped up and went to his window, a boy lit by a solitary candle on a snowy city street. He tried to crane his neck and see where Santa must have landed, because that was where the chimney was. He threw up the window, inhaling an Arctic blast of Chicago night air. George stuck his head out and looked up on the roof. The dormer eaves of his window kept him from being able to see the chimney.

He pulled his head in and ran to his desk, pulling out the Kodak Instamatic he had squirreled away for this moment. George went back to the window and held the camera up over the eave, shooting a cube flash into the night. Then he pushed the window down, feeling the biting cold still on his face and hands. Several crystals of ice were on the hardwood of his bedroom. He crept to the door and walked out into the hallway. He listened.

There was someone down in the living room. Even up on the third floor he could hear the sound of someone walking. His father had told him a month ago that Santa would implode on reentry when he had asked if there really was a Santa. He had stared at George and frowned with the slide ruler in his top pocket, taking off his glasses. "Think about it, George. You know those astronauts with a heat shield in their capsule? Imagine them without that heat shield. They would be French fries. Besides, the g-force would make Santa combust like an overboiled egg."

It had taken him a good two weeks to reason his father had not said there *wasn't* a Santa Claus. He had just said the physics behind Santa Claus didn't add up. He had done some reading himself and reasoned his father could be wrong. Santa might not go up in the atmosphere and might fly at lower altitudes. His father was just being cranky, he concluded. Besides, he now had a picture that would prove his father and all the other doubters wrong. And now he would get another one.

George crept down the stairs to the first floor, passing outside his parents' darkened doorway. He paused and heard the rhythmic low snoring of his mother. His parents were asleep, and Santa was down in their den where the fireplace was. He felt the excitement in the pit of his stomach. No one he knew of had ever taken a picture of Santa Claus. He would publish it worldwide and start by sending it to the *Chicago Tribune*. Surely they would put his picture on the front page.

George made the last turn, holding on to the banister like a man holding on to a dock. After this, he was going into history. He checked his camera and saw the glowing orange light. His flash was charged, and he had advanced the film. He placed one bare foot ahead of the other on the cold oak boards. His father kept the furnace low at night, and George shivered but he thought it was from nerves as much as a fifty-nine degree setback. He carefully placed his toes on the floor, trying to minimize the creaks and gasps of the hundred-year-old joists.

George heard Santa's breathing. He sounded like a man laboring up a hill. Well, of course he was tired! He had probably been up and down hundreds maybe thousands of chimneys. George didn't know how old Santa was, but he had to be over fifty. He probably wasn't in the greatest of shape with that big belly. George saw the light spilling from the den into the hallway. The breathing was louder and he heard the tinkling of metal striking metal.

George raised up his camera and positioned his finger on the top. He had to be ready because Santa might just shoot up the chimney. The breathing was loud, and he thought he heard a muffled *shit* followed by another muffled *dammit. Santa curses!* He wish he had a tape recorder, but the pictures would be enough. He would soon be famous as the boy who proved the existence of Santa Claus!

George turned into the den and heard an even clearer, "Jesus Christ. Do they have to make these bolts so damn tiny?"

He paused in the doorway with his heart pounding in his ears, then peered into the den and saw a formless shape by the fireplace. There was only the one light on. George saw the Christmas tree and piles of presents around the base. *He's already left the presents!* That meant all he had to do was go back up the chimney. George hunched over behind the couch, and again he heard the low cussing: "Piece of Japanese shit ... Japs really screwed us with these ..." So even Santa's toys were made in Japan! He had to get the picture now before it was too late. George gave himself a count. One ... two ... *three!*

He jumped into the den, swung up his camera, and pressed the button.

"Santa!"

His father jumped straight up like someone had shot him.

"What the ... ?!"

POP!

Santa was blinded, and George had his picture for all time—a disgruntled parent in the middle of the night trying to tighten the last bolt on a Schwinn bicycle. His father recovered, holding the crescent wrench out like a scepter.

"What the hell are you doing up?" he roared.

George stared at his old man. "Dad!"

"Who the hell else do you think is down here in the middle of the night?"

George shrugged, feeling his face warm.

"I, I, I thought you were Santa."

His father frowned. "Whadaya, nuts? I told you there ain't no goddamn Santa! Now get the hell to bed so I can get to bed," he shouted.

George turned and walked up the stairs silently. He cried himself to sleep and got up late the next morning, causing his mother to feel his forehead.

"He always was up at the crack of dawn before," she murmured worriedly.

His father never said a word about their nocturnal meeting and neither did he. But George developed the picture and kept it in his dresser drawer for years. It was now the faded photo of a tired fortysomething man with a crescent wrench. George tied the end of his childhood to that picture. And maybe Mary was right. Maybe he was trying to put the genie back in the bottle for that ten-year-old boy. Maybe that's why he went into his bedroom and slipped the picture into the pocket of his Santa suit.

34

Defecating Reindeer

GEORGE HELD THE reins and watched the nine reindeer relieve themselves in unison. It was as if they were playing musical crap with the *plop, plop, plop* hitting the frozen ground while the man with the green fifty-five-gallon tote swore at the beasts who calmly chewed the hay McGruff had thrown down. George looked up the ramp leading to his roof like a runway and felt his stomach churn. It had begun to snow, and the plywood looked slick.

Lights illuminated the runway like something out of a science fiction movie. His whole yard had been turned into something out of Hollywood. Lights and men with laptops were all over the place. George looked up to the yellow window of Megan's room. He could actually see her sleeping. Dean had a monitor installed in the sled, and George stared at his daughter clutching a stuffed panda bear, her hands folded under her cheek. The snow still flowed outside her window under a solitary light with a scrim strung up behind. This was just in case she woke and wanted to check on the weather. George breathed deeply and stared at his daughter.

"Alright, Megan," he murmured.

"Mr. Kronenfeldt?"

George turned to a man in a long overcoat, fedora, and glasses.

"Yes?"

"Quite a setup you have here ... Phil Stanton, *Chicago Tribune*. Do you mind if I ask you a few questions?"

"What type of questions?"

"Well, I understand you are doing all this to prove to your daughter there is a Santa Claus."

George looked at the man with the pad in his hand. He had already noticed a crowd of people along the street behind a barricade Dean had set up.

"People always want to watch a movie being made, mate. It's good publicity."

George had pointed out he didn't want any publicity.

"I understand, mate, but this won't affect the little tyke. Believe me, she will never see any of this. There's a bloke from the newspaper who wants to ask you a few questions. Just be nice to him. It will help the buzz on my movie, mate."

"Yes ... I am doing this for my daughter," he replied.

The reporter looked at the reindeer and the lights and the men tromping all over the roof.

"It looks like you are filming a Hollywood movie."

"Yes, " George acknowledged tiredly.

"It must have cost you a pretty penny."

"Yes, it did."

The man took off his fedora and smoothed back his hair, laughing lightly. "Excuse me for asking, but couldn't you have done something simpler to prove there is a Santa Claus to your daughter ... or just told her the truth?"

"And what is the truth, Mr. Stanton?"

The man stared at him through his round accountant glasses.

"Well, that there really is no Santa Claus."

"Are you a Christian?"

"Well, yes ..."

"And you believe in God?"

"Sure."

"But you have never seen him and yet you believe in something a lot of people say is nuts. Why is that?"

The reporter opened his mouth. "Well, I have faith."

"Exactly. It is no different than your belief in God. You believe, and therefore it must be true. Well, children have faith too, and they believe there must be a Santa Claus, and for them there is one. Their belief makes him true the way your belief in God makes Him true."

The reporter scribbled something on his pad, murmuring, "Interesting." He looked up and nodded to the roof. "Could you walk me through how this is all going to come together?"

George looked up the runway. "The reindeer and I will go up this runway and make a turn on the roof there. You can see the pitch of the roof has been corrected with plywood. My daughter will wake up," he explained, motioning to the monitor, "and she will come to the window. I will be behind a black scrim with snow coming down in front of it, and she will see a digital projection of Santa Claus in the air beamed against smoke, which will fold into the scrim, and then I will advance the sled and stop in front of the window."

"So she will see Santa ... *fly?*"

George nodded. "That's right. And then I will go up to the chimney and descend with gifts," he continued, motioning to the bright red bag behind him. "My daughter will then go down to watch me emerge from the chimney—"

"Hold on, hold on." The reporter looked up from his pad. "*You* are going down the chimney?"

"Yes." George nodded solemnly. "I have two mountain climbers who will lower me down, and when I get to the bottom I'll eat the cookies, drink the milk, put some gifts around, then ascend in the chimney with the mountain climbers assisting."

The reporter shook his head, writing furiously. "This is going to be awesome," he muttered.

"Then I will come back down and get in the sled and go down the ramp on the far side of the roof, but my daughter will see a digital projection in the sky again showing Santa flying away."

The reporter looked up. "What if something goes wrong?"

"We have some backup plans."

"I see." He put his pad away and stared at the ramp and the roof lit dramatically from several different angles. Smoke and snow were spouting out from the corners, and the digital projector shot George flying through the darkness behind his sled.

"Amazing," the reporter murmured, shaking his head. "This is just amazing."

"You do what you have to do for your kids."

"I have a daughter, but I don't know if I would do all this."

George looked at the man a good fifteen years younger than himself. "Wait until you only have a few chances left to make things right."

The reporter stared at George then put out his hand.

"Good luck, Mr. Kronenfeldt."

"Thank you," George replied, shaking his hand, watching him tramp off through the light snow on the ground. George looked up the long ramp and watched a man fall on the slick roof, catching himself just before he fell to the ground. "I'm going to need it," George murmured.

George's father slogged up through the snow and ice. Already the back lawn was turning into a muddy, snowy trough. Too many people and machines and reindeer had pummeled the dead grass into wet earth. A slushing sound began to fill in the hubbub of people trying to orchestrate a movie. Dean floated over on the camera boom, rising above the roof and then coming back to earth.

Kronenfeldt Sr. watched him levitate past and shook his head.

"That guy should be in a movie."

George leaned back in the sled. It was eleven thirty, and he was to start up toward the roof at midnight when the bell outside Megan's window started ringing. His father turned with his floppy fedora pulled low over his face and his puffy down coat pushing his arms out.

"So, you ready for this?"

George shrugged. "Ready as I'll ever be."

His father stared at the crowd gathered on the far side of the lawn.

"How do you think all those people got there?"

"Like Dean said, everyone wants to be in the movies."

"So you think it's all worth this, son?"

George felt the picture in his pocket and fished it out.

"You remember this, Dad?"

He squinted at the faded picture.

"What the hell is that?"

"That's you, Dad."

"I can see that! But where the hell did you get that?"

"Don't you remember the night I snuck down on Christmas Eve and snapped this picture?"

"Oh, yeah. You scared the shit out of me that night."

"That's right. And then you yelled at me to go back to my room.

You didn't even try and cover up that I had just discovered you were Santa Claus."

"I thought you knew already."

"Because you said he would spontaneously combust in the atmosphere?"

"Well ... yeah."

George shook his head. "I didn't believe you, Dad, because I didn't want to accept that Santa Claus could be explained away with science." He paused. "But when I saw you there, putting that bike together, I knew then—there was no Santa. And you were the guy who put all the presents under the tree."

"How the hell should I have known you'd come down? You were supposed to stay the hell in bed until I finished!"

"I know. It wasn't your fault. I did the same thing to Jeremy and just about in the same way. So I guess the apple doesn't fall far from the tree." George looked at his father. "But maybe I can get it right this time."

Kronenfeldt Sr. stared at the men on the roof.

"In my time it was easier," he said. "You weren't expected to be such a great parent. Now you got to be Mother Theresa for God's sake."

George crossed his arms over a large black belt.

"That's probably true."

"I wouldn't have done all this for you."

"I wouldn't have expected you to do it, Dad."

George saw Dean floating toward him.

"Well, I guess it's getting close to showtime," he murmured, sitting up.

His father turned. "It's a crappy world, son, but I am proud that you would do this for your daughter, if that makes any damn sense."

George picked up the reins and smiled.

"It does to me."

35

Sugar Plums and Candy Canes

MEGAN STARED AT the clock. The hour hand would not move, and the minute hand was taking its time. By her estimation it would be seven hours until she would run downstairs and see the presents under the tree Santa Claus had left behind. Every year she watched the clock and suffered through the night. She wanted to sleep but she just couldn't fake her body into it. She had counted sheep. She had counted backward from one hundred. She had recited the Gettysburg Address that she had memorized for her class project. Nothing worked.

But of course she only wanted to sleep an hour. Her father had rigged an ingenious device with a string tripwire connected to a bell by her bed. He had stretched the string across the roof and explained that any person, reindeer, or sled would trip the string. Megan stared at the brass bell on a pivot wheel. She had tested the string several times going out the tiny crack in the window. When she pulled on the string, the bell rang out. She had shut her eyes and done it to see if she would wake up. She did.

Like a fisherman, she kept one eye on the bell and the string. She had heard some funny noises outside. It sounded like people were walking on the roof, but every time she went to look all she saw was fat, juicy snowflakes. And the funny thing is the snow didn't even look real. The flakes looked like soggy cotton balls and fell in large clumps on her sill. Beyond the snow she could see nothing. So she was left with the bell and the string, and so far the string had not budged and the bell had not rung. She turned over several times with her stuffed animals, hugging her Tweety Bird close. Her room was lit by the electric candle on the sill, and she considered turning it off to get more sleep. But the candles gave her comfort and told her it really was Christmas and it really was the 24th of December—*finally*, Christmas Eve.

Megan reached over and picked up the video camera. Her father had plugged it in and made sure it was charged up. He had explained that all she had to do when she heard Santa was press the red button and point it out the window. He had even put a piece of masking tape by the button. Megan had practiced several times jumping out of bed and running to the window with the camera and pressing the red button. She really didn't press it, but she wanted to make sure everything would go smoothly when the big man arrived.

Megan had great fantasies about the fame that would find her when she proved to the world there was a Santa Claus. She saw herself as a guest on popular TV shows, giving interviews and describing how she caught Santa Claus on video. She and her father had also gone over the procedure for posting the video to YouTube, though she already knew how to do this after posting a video of Whiskers, her cat, hanging off the side of the maple tree in front of the house then falling ten feet to the ground below.

Megan heard another thump on the roof and turned over. The string was not moving, and the bell didn't move. The glowing diode in the video camera announced all was ready. She wondered what would happen if Santa saw her string and stepped over it or flew over it with his sled. Megan imagined girls and boys had probably tried to catch him before and had failed. He was probably very clever about avoiding detection. She stared at the string and followed it to the crack in the window. She turned back over.

Megan had asked her father what time he thought Santa would come. He had stroked his beard a moment then replied without hesitation, "Everyone knows Santa comes at midnight." So she had a half-hour to go. Megan snuggled back in under her covers and yawned. That was a first. She had not yawned or felt her eyes become heavy. None of her usual sleep rituals had kicked in, but now she felt her eyes actually drooping. She fought against it, feeling that with one hour this was no time to sleep. But she felt it coming now.

Megan promised herself a ten-minute nap and promptly fell fast asleep.

36

Francis Pharcellus Church

SNOW WAS FALLING hard now and blanketed the countryside like the white wool of a Christmas tree skirt. George stared at the chimney of white frost. Sven and Yergen waved to him with their rappelling ropes, hanging off both sides of the chimney like they were standing on the ground. That he was going to go down a chimney seemed unbelievable to George, and he blamed it squarely on Francis Pharcellus Church.

Church was the correspondent who had written back to Virginia O'Hanlon in 1897 and said there really was a Santa Claus. The editorial he wrote was on Megan's wall, and they read it together every year. George had read it alone this year and wondered what made a man write such a letter. He had researched Francis Pharcellus Church and found out he was a Civil War correspondent who had seen humans at their absolute worse. He had taken that damaged faith in man and given another view of the world. He had pointed out that the joy of the world is mostly unseen. His was an extremely religious age which would soon give away to the modernism of the twentieth century. But this war-weary man gave a spiritual platform to the Dutch legend of Sinterklaas brought over in the seventeenth century and Americanized by Clement Moore's poem *'Twas the Night Before Christmas*, where reindeer were added and the method of entry became the chimney.

George could feel Church's pain as he wrote, "Yes, Virginia, there is a Santa Claus. He exists as certainly as love and devotion exist, and you know that they abound and give to your life its highest beauty and joy." He could see the man in his study by gaslight, with his fountain pen, giving meaning to a world gone mad. "Virginia, your little friends are wrong. They have been affected by the skepticism of a skeptical age. They do not believe except they see. They think that nothing can be which is not comprehensible by their little minds. All minds, Virginia, whether they be men or children, are little."

And there was the rub. This is what gave George courage to go the distance and put his marriage and his financial health on the line. This man who had seen the absolute worst of human beings had been able to summon up a belief there was something better in the universe. And George knew his pain. He had felt the pain when he lost his son and daughter to the carnage of his first marriage.

And as he sat facing a ramp to a roof behind nine reindeer being slowly covered with snow, he thought about what Church had wrote: "There would be not childlike faith then, no poetry, no romance to make tolerable this existence." That is what he failed to give Jeremy and Jamie—the childlike faith and poetry every parent should give their children. He had snatched away their childhood under the guise of making a buck, and he would not commit this carnage twice. Megan would have a childhood, and if he fell off the chimney or the roof, then it was worth the risk.

What had Church said in the end of his editorial, a man who had seen the hell of our bloodiest war. "You may tear apart the baby's rattle and see what makes the noise inside, but there is a veil covering the unseen world which not the strongest man that ever lived could tear apart. Only faith, fancy, poetry, love, romance, can push aside that veil and view and picture that supernal beauty and glory beyond ..."

George looked at the monitor showing his sleeping daughter. It was fifteen minutes to midnight, and he was about to push that veil aside for her. He only wished Jeremy and Jamie were here. He would love to push that veil aside for them too.

37

A Christmas Story

DEAN WALKED TOWARD George sitting in the sled. He was intercepted by Jeff, who was running the snow machines and said the one snow machine had already crapped out. "Well, get another one, mate. We are fifteen minutes away from showtime." Jeff pointed out there was no other snow machines and that's where Dean had his moment. "You're wrong, mate. I picked up one just in case—a backup." Jeff looked at him admiringly and ran off to the truck.

Dean looked at the set he had created and felt pride swell up in him. The four novels and five screenplays and ten shorts and one feature did not slow him down. His other films might have gotten off the ground if the distributors had gotten their head out of their ass and seen the market for it. The indie business was a lot like the big studios—uncontrollable, nobody quite sure who is pulling the strings. Dean lived for the one-shot deal, and he knew immediately that this Real Santa movie was the answer of providence.

Financing was always the sticking point. Everyone had an idea for a movie, but nobody had any money. But Mary's husband was a Christmas gift with a red bow. He not only *gave him* the plot of his movie, but it came with built-in financing. He had already blown through almost sixty grand, and George didn't seem to miss a beat. Now after this shoot he would have the golden demo reel to show investors to finish the job. There were dentists and doctors and lawyers out there *dying* to give their money to touch a little Hollywood gold. Let them come on the set and they would become lambs to the slaughter.

So that's why everything was riding on this shoot tonight. This was a one-take deal because after tonight, Christmas would be over and his benefactor would withdraw. Dean knew his position of power was only good until midnight. Then like in *Cinderella,* the carriage would turn into a pumpkin and he would be back in his dark Chicago apartment wondering how to pay the rent for another month. And there was something else riding on this film. He had four kids who might be back within his reach once they saw Dad's new movie about Santa Claus.

True, he had left them back in Australia with his wife, and they wouldn't even speak to him, but with this film he could point to the reason behind his departure and say: *This kids, this is why I had to leave!* In Dean's scenario, all would be forgiven. Seeing what George was doing for his daughter elevated the film to an almost holy status. He had been living and breathing this shoot for the last ten days, and he wanted everything to go perfect. Planning was key to every film.

Dean had broken it out in storyboards in his apartment. He had gone over the sequence with his cinematographer, his gaffers, assistants, the union guys laying the tracks for the camera, the steady cam operators. There must be no screw-ups. George had to take those reindeer up to the roof on his signal and stop behind the scrim while the projector threw his image up against the smoke and snow, and then on his signal he would slide to a halt in front of the little tyke's window. Then he would go up the chimney and down where Dean had cameras positioned in the living room in secret places, filming Santa coming out of the cinders and parceling out the gifts. Then he would film George going back up the chimney by the mounted camera and then out the top and onto his sled and through the fog and snow and down the ramp while he shot the final scene of Santa flying away in the sky.

One take. It would be like the opening of *The Player* with Altman's long extended shot that kept rolling and rolling. This would rival even that and make his name in the film world. He would out-Altman Altman. And all would be forgiven—the lack of child support, the hand-to-mouth existence, his wife suing him for divorce. All these problems would be remedied with fifteen minutes of film. He had put it all on the line, and he was ten minutes away from destiny.

The only thing that was bothering him was the bloke in the sled with George. Who the hell was he, and why was he holding the reins to the reindeer?

38

Second Chance Santa

JEREMY HAD SEEN Santa Claus and stopped. His suit was a reddish pink, his belt black and shiny, his beard a cotton-candy white. He was sitting in a sled behind nine reindeer getting covered in snow with lights crisscrossing their backs, breathing smoke, chewing, defecating. People were walking around with laptops and on the roof where green diodes lit the darkness and snow funneled in front of a window. A camera crane floated overhead with a man wearing riding boots and a beret. His father was filming a movie in his backyard, and that really blew Jeremy away.

He still remembered the days when his dad was the coach for his baseball team. He knew nothing about baseball, and the other coaches treated him like a college freshman. Jeremy noticed his dad had to always collect the balls and couldn't throw straight and dropped the ball when playing catch and couldn't even hit the ball in the fielding drills. But he kept showing up with his thick glasses and pens in his shirt.

The other boys' fathers all had played little league and most of them had played high school baseball. Even then Jeremy knew his father was making an ass of himself for his benefit. When the coaches couldn't make it to one game, his dad had ended up coaching. His father sent kids into disaster with steals from third and gave kids the take sign when the pitcher was nailing the strike zone. When the coaches returned, they apologized to the boys for *Coach George's* lack of knowledge. But his father kept coming to practices and that was how Jeremy saw his father now—a man who would keep coming even if it meant disaster.

After seeing his mother and sister off to the airport his cell rang.

"Jeremy, pick me up."

It was his sister and she was crying.

"I just dropped you off. Is something wrong?"

"That bastard Dirk ... he's drunk, the filthy pig. Just pick me up!"

Jeremy spun the car around and headed back to the airport.

He found out later Dirk had drunk margaritas while waiting for the flight, declaring it the drink of Florida. When Jamie's mother went to the ladies room, he had leaned over, his old man breath mixed with the foul airport swill, and whispered, "Next time, sugar pie, it will be you and me on the beach as long as you bring your bikini. You know I love your mom, but you know a man gets urges. In high school we did it all the time but you slow down, but I wouldn't slow down with you ..."

When her mother returned, Jamie had run down the terminal hallway. Jeremy picked her up by baggage claim. They drove toward their father's home, and Jeremy reasoned that he didn't really blame his father for starting a new family. This whole Santa Claus thing had echoes of disaster written all over it, but he wanted some closure with his dad. There had been the property in Michigan that would supposedly be worth a fortune that turned out to be inaccessible. There had been the legendary sailing boat disaster, where his father tore a gash in the side of the boat. There had been the famed bicycle bridge turned into a railroad trestle. And now there was this scheme to become Santa, complete with chimney descent.

"I just want to make sure Dad doesn't kill himself," he explained to his sister as they drove out.

They parked on George's street lined with cars.

"I'll wait in the car," Jamie said.

Jeremy frowned. "Come on, sis."

"No, it's freezin' out, and I don't have a coat. I'll watch from here."

So he had left his sister, and now Jeremy was walking up to his father, and the churning emotions gripped him by the throat and he was having a hard time with that one central question: *Why didn't he do this for me?*

"Hey, Dad," he called out.

His father turned with his horn-rimmed glasses under the bushy white brows.

"Jeremy!"

He jammed his hands down in his pocket and nodded.

"You look pretty good, Dad. You should lose the glasses though."

George nodded sheepishly. "Yes, I just wanted to keep them around if I get in a tight spot. But when I head up the ramp, I will take them off."

"Cool," Jeremy murmured. "So, this is all pretty wild. When is the big moment?"

George glanced at his watch.

"Ah ... just about in fifteen minutes."

"Wow, just like a movie."

George sighed. "Yes. It's gotten a little out of control."

"You could say that."

His father lowered his voice. "I think Mary is going to dump me after it's all over."

Jeremy looked at his father. This didn't surprise him. Women could only take so much of the Kronenfeldt antics, and then they headed for the hills, though his mother had hung in there right through the cat toilet that allowed a cat to shit and then flush. The misses really stunk up the house, and the cat had more than once fallen into the whirling blue water. The Facebook flame from high school was more of a symptom than a reason.

Jeremy looked at the people all over the yard.

"So, is it all worth it, Dad?"

"I think so," he replied. "Megan can believe in Santa Claus a little longer." He looked at his son. "But you know how it is—once I get rolling on a project, it's hard for me get off the train."

"Yeah ... I know."

George leaned back. "So ... you didn't go to Florida."

Jeremy shrugged. "Yeah, I wanted to see some snow I guess. Dirk is a pretty strange dude, and I think we would have killed each other by the end of the week. We almost did last year. Jamie's in the car."

George stared at his son. "She is? What is she doing there?"

"She didn't have a coat, but I think she is unsure of all of this."

"Well, you are going to spend Christmas with us, and that's an order!"

"Sure. Guess that's why I'm here."

George held up the reins. "Want to command nine reindeer?"

"I don't think so, Dad."

"C'mon. How many times do you have the opportunity to sit in Santa's sleigh?" George held out the reins. "Take them."

Jeremy shrugged and climbed in the other side of the sled and sat next to his father. George handed him the reins, and he looked over the snowy backs of the smoking animals.

"Pretty cool, Dad," he whispered.

"You know what? Why don't you accompany me on my sled tonight?"

"But, Dad ... there can only be one Santa Claus."

"Nonsense. You are Santa's helper! We can get you dressed up like an elf. We have a wardrobe person that has three Santa outfits."

"I don't know ... this is between you and Megan."

"Bullshit! This is for all of us. You are coming with me."

Jeremy looked at his father. "You really want me to, Dad?"

"Damn right I do. You are going with me tonight. Besides, I'll need all the help I can get climbing up that chimney."

Jeremy held the reins in his lap. "Okay then."

"Alright, mate! We are all set, and it is time for all nonessential people to clear the sled!"

Dean was out of breath and staring at George's son. George nodded to Jeremy.

"We better get a costume for my son here. He is going to assist me."

Dean shook his head. "Sorry, mate. The script only calls for one Santa Claus."

"I don't need to go, Dad," Jeremy murmured, starting to get out.

George grabbed his son's arm. "You are going with your father." He turned to Dean. "The script now calls for Santa and his helper. My son goes or Santa doesn't fly."

Dean turned red, sputtering, whipping up his walkie-talkie.

"Wardrobe, get the hell over to the sled!"

Jeremy looked at his father, and George leaned over and whispered, "You gotta be tough with these Hollywood types."

39

It's a Wonderful Life

MRS. WORTHINGTON SETTLED in by the fireplace with the flowers in the hearth. She had hung two stockings over the mantel, but they were Walgreens stockings bought for decoration. In fact they were sewn together so Santa couldn't put candy and goodies or even coal in there if he wanted to. Her husband, Walter, had pointed this out and asked her why she bothered.

"Decorations, dear," she had replied the same way she explained the candles she bought that were never burned.

Their Christmas Eve ritual was not much different from any other night. The television was on low, and Walter was reading in his chair. *It's a Wonderful Life* played, and Mrs. Worthington looked up from her romance novel to see if George had realized he did have a wonderful life. George deserved whatever he got. The man had a perfectly good family and was going through hard times but to contemplate suicide was ridiculous! Every year Mrs. Worthington pointed this out to Walter, and every year Walter said all men have different breaking points.

But this year her novel was not holding her. It was supposed to be very randy, but she found it boring and not very well written. Getting a turkey ready for her daughter and her grandchildren had not held her either. She was bothered. Maybe it was the knowledge that this was her last Christmas as a teacher. Maybe it was the stillness in the house. The kids' Christmas party was the usual carnage of sugar and pop and games and, of course, the incident with Megan's father.

Mrs. Worthington look at the television again. George was looking for Mary at the library. *She is better off without him. Imagine
running through town like that! Men.* Mrs. Worthington turned back
to her novel and heard her husband chortle. She looked up.

"What are you reading, dear?"

Walter, a big man in his slippers, held up the green and red book.
"'*Twas the Night Before Christmas.*"

Mr. Worthington looked over her glasses.

"Why on earth are you reading that?"

"I read it every year on Christmas Eve."

The teacher dropped her book and stared at her husband.

"You do not!"

"I do. But if you don't want to believe me, that's fine."

"I don't see why you would read a children's poem even once,"
she grumbled.

"I enjoy it."

"It is for *children,* Walter!"

He looked at his wife.

"On Christmas Eve we are all children, Barbara."

"Oh, don't be ridiculous."

Walter shrugged again. "Suit yourself. Some of us still believe."

That one cut her. Mrs. Worthington carefully marked the page
of her novel and saw that George was now in his old house looking
for his wife and children. She could have told him that it was all in
vain. The man had thrown away a perfectly good life with both hands.

Ms. Worthington gripped her armchair.

"What do you mean by that, Walter?"

He looked over his glasses.

"I mean, I still believe in the magic of Christmas."

"I suppose next you will tell me you still believe in Santa Claus."

"I might."

Mrs. Worthington jumped up.

"I have had it with all this foolishness. You are as crazy as that
Kronenfeldt man who is going to prove there is a Santa Claus by
flying a sled onto his roof!"

Walter put down his book and frowned. "I heard about him. I
heard he had hired a whole movie crew to pull it off, and he was going

to do it tonight. I wonder if he really is going to fly a sled onto his roof."

"How should I know? He has been warned by the principal and many parents not to try anything that would disappoint the children."

Walter looked at his wife.

"I don't see why it's the principal's business what he does for his daughter."

"Of course it is the principal's business and mine! If he disappoints hundreds of children after promising Santa Claus will come and his daughter promised to put it on the Internet, then it most certainly is my business!"

"Bah humbug, huh, Barbara?"

Mrs. Worthington put her hand on the mantel and saw that George had stumbled back to the bridge.

"What do you mean by that?"

Her husband looked up at her.

"I mean that for forty years you have been knocking the stuffing out of Santa Claus because that strict old German bastard knocked the magic out of his daughter."

"My father was a very logical man who didn't believe in fairytales. I appreciate that he told me early on how the world was."

Walter sighed. "He told you his view of the world, Barbara, not the way the world is. He didn't know what it was like. All he knew was how to work from sunup to sundown in his fields and sell eggs off his back porch."

"I resent that Walter—"

Her husband sat up, his eyes flashing uncharacteristically.

"And I resent that you have imposed your beliefs on hundreds of children who do believe in Santa Claus. What the hell is the harm in believing there is something better than this life?"

Mrs. Worthington was sure the world had gone crazy. Her husband never talked to her like this. He never crossed her; he usually acquiesced to her demands with the same placid demeanor he had when they married.

She raised her eyebrows.

"You are angry, Walter."

He paused then nodded. "Yeah, I guess I am. You try and stop a father from giving his daughter the gift of childhood. I guess that does piss me off."

Piss him off. Mrs. Worthington felt like he had sworn at her.

"I will not tolerate this kind of talk!"

"What ... are you going to give me a time-out? I'm not one of your students, Barbara."

"You deserve a time-out with that kind of talk," she declared

Walter shrugged and stood up, walking into the front hall. He took out his coat and slipped into his boots.

"Where are you going?"

Walter popped on the hat with the large earflaps she hated because it made him look like a farmer.

"I think I'd like to see Santa Claus. I think I'm going to go see if that guy can give his daughter something to believe in."

"Don't be ridiculous! You stay right here! Going out in the cold on Christmas Eve. You are as crazy as this man George," she declared, gesturing to the television.

Walter opened the door and turned back to his wife.

"I'm eighty-five years old, Barbara. Maybe I need to believe in something again." He looked at the television where George was running through Bedford Falls. "Go, George, go!"

And with that he walked out the door. Mrs. Worthington stared at the door then turned to the television where George had been reunited with his family. Zuzu was telling her father that every time a bell rings an angel gets his wings. Mrs. Worthington collapsed in her chair, staring at the happy family in disbelief.

40

Santa Cop

THE ROOKIE SIGNED up to catch crooks and crouch behind cars like the cops on television. He saw himself like on *NYPD Blue* or any of the other cop shows where he could run behind a car and draw out his nine-millimeter and blow away a few bad guys. But here he sat in the parking lot of Caputo's with the radio telling him to go investigate the appearance of Santa. He should be at home with his wife and his baby, not driving to arrest some nut in his backyard dressed up like Santa.

But that was how the call came in. *"Man dressed as Santa Claus in a sled with reindeer."* He had asked dispatch to repeat the report. "MAN-DRESSED-AS-SANTA-WITH-REINDEER IN BACKYARD. PLEASE INVESTIGATE. POSSIBLE MOVIE SET." That was Ruth, and he could just see her rolling her eyes. *A movie set?* He wondered if there had been any permits given to production companies in the area. Usually they notified the police.

As the rookie drove through the snow, he wondered if he might make a contact. He had written a screenplay that he had sent around and received no response. If it wasn't a movie, then he would have to figure out if a man in a Santa suit with reindeer was disturbing the peace. He would think a homeowner would be allowed to sit in his backyard in a sled. The reindeer might be a problem. It might be some dad trying to convince his kids that there really was a Santa Claus.

He turned his squad car and could see lights shining down the street. Cars and trucks were parked on the sides of the street, and he saw people walking toward a lit-up house. Definitely a movie shoot. The rookie felt excitement down in his stomach as he flipped on the squad's cherries and drove toward the lights.

George watched the cop crunch across the snow talking into his shoulder. The radio hissed back as he stared straight ahead like someone pulled over for drunk driving.

"Mr. Kronenfeldt?"

He turned to a cop with smooth skin and perfect hair.

"Mr. Kronenfeldt?"

"Yes," he said, with Jeremy next to him dressed like an elf.

"Sir, is this your sled and ..." He paused, looking at the chewing reindeer. "And your reindeer, sir?"

"Yes, officer, they are." George nodded. "What can I do for you?"

Dean crossed the snow in a frenzy and held out his hand.

"Dean Sanders, officer. I'm the director of this production, officer," he announced, shaking the rookie's hand.

The cop stared at the camera crane and nodded slowly. "So ... this is a movie?"

"Oh yes, sir, officer," Dean answered, nodding. "*Real Santa* is the name. We were just about to shoot our scene when you pulled up."

The rookie smoothed back his hair.

"Okay, now did you get a permit to shoot this film, because we have had some complaints from the neighbors."

Dean frowned. "You know we filed for our permit, but we never heard back, and you know it's just one scene, and then we are all finished."

The cop's eyes darkened.

"I'm afraid that without a permit, I'm going to have to shut you down. There are some traffic issues, and you have a lot of lights that are bothering people—"

Dean held up his hand like a man requesting divine intervention.

"Look, officer, we have invested thousands of dollars for this one shoot—if you could look the other way, I could make it worth your while," he said in a low voice.

"Are you trying to bribe me, sir?"

Dean held out his hands.

"Oh, not a bribe, officer—*a favor.*"

George could see this was going off the rails very quickly.

"Officer ..." He handed the reins to his son and turned in the sled. "I know this looks ridiculous, but I think I can explain." He gestured to his house and the room with the movie light shining into the snow. "You see that yellow window with the snow? My daughter is up in that bedroom. She is nine years old and has started to doubt the existence of Santa Claus."

The rookie crossed his arms. "Go on."

"And so I thought that I could give her faith back to her if I became the Real Santa Claus—if she was able to see a real Santa fly onto the roof and deliver her gifts and then fly away in a sled."

The cop looked at the sled and frowned. "You're going to fly in this thing?"

"If I may interject, officer," Dean said, gesturing to the roof. "He will not actually fly, but we will create the *illusion* of him flying. See those smoke machines up there and those digital projectors?"

"Yes."

Dean took him by the arm and pointed to the far side of the roof. "We will project the image of Santa flying against the smoke, and then George here will run the reindeer up on the roof and come to a stop in front of his daughter's window, creating the illusion of flying. Then when it's time for him to leave, he will do the same thing and go down the ramp on the other side."

The cop shook his head. "That's pretty neat. What about the chimney? How are you going to do that?"

George motioned to the two mountaineers hanging off the chimney like acrobats.

"I'm going to rappel down the chimney with the gifts, then I'm going to be hoisted back up."

"Holy shit," the rookie muttered, staring at the chimney lit by three movie lights. "And you hired all these people here—this isn't really a movie shoot?"

George shook his head. "Dean is a film director who I hired to help me and has decided he wants to film it, which I'm fine with, but no, this is really all about keeping a little girl's belief in Santa."

The cop stared at Jeremy.

"Who is the elf?"

"My oldest son."

Jeremy held up a hand. "Hello."

George turned around and saw his father behind him.

"And this is my dad."

"Glad to know you, officer," Kronenfeldt Sr. said, shaking his hand. "My son is crazy, but it's a good kind of crazy, officer," he added.

The rookie rubbed his jaw and puckered his mouth.

"So you see, mate, all we really need is about thirty minutes, and then we are all done here, and we can restore the faith of a little girl!"

The rookie stared at the ramp and the reindeer and the people on the roof and the lights set up in the corners of the yard. He shook his head slowly and looked at George.

"You did all this to convince your daughter that there is a Santa Claus?"

He nodded solemnly. "Yes."

"I got a baby at home, but I don't know if I would do all this if she didn't believe in Santa Claus."

"Wait. You'll do whatever it takes to keep her happy."

"What did this cost you?"

"About eighty grand."

The cop looked at him then at the reindeer and the ramp.

"Alright, I'll give you a half-hour. But if the neighbors call in again, I'm going to have shut you down."

Dean motioned the crane operator and his assistants.

"Alright, folks," he announced. "IT'S SHOWTIME!"

41

Santa's Comin' to Town

GEORGE STARED AT the snow-covered ramp and felt the same as before he gashed a hole in the two hundred and fifty thousand dollar boat. The circumstances were not so different. A large amount of money had been invested in the gleaming white sailboat George was to bring down from Waukegan to Chicago. It had become a ritual and Matt Demler had always called on him with the promise that if he would bring down his boat, then he could have access to it all season long.

George was a self-taught sailor and approached it like engineering. He was proficient and methodical, but he was not a natural sailor. He did not have the instinct some men possessed that allowed them to find the edge of the wind. George was an expert sailor, but like the expert he had to stick to the rule book. The day that he was to take *The Sally Jane* down to Monroe Harbor was windy. He jumped on the boat with the two men who had come to help and took his place behind the wheel. The owner knelt down on the dock. Matt owned several boats but *The Sally Jane* was his pride and joy.

"George, when you back up the wind is going to try and take you. Just goose the shit out of the motor, and you'll clear the dock."

George had saluted in his yellow foul-weather gear with his fur hat and glasses. He ordered his assistants to guard against the dock wheels, which were small tires to keep the boat moving along the wooden rim. George cast off and felt as he did holding the reins in his Santa suit. It was a feeling of freedom combined with the suspicion he had no idea what he was doing.

The Sally Jane was immediately taken by the wind, and they start-ed going straight out toward another moored sailboat. Matt cupped his hands, and George became confused. Did he say goose it or did he say go for it? He wasn't sure, and while trying to hear exactly what Matt said, he froze. The Sally Jane was about to crash into The Norma Jean, and that's when Matt Demler screamed again.

"Give it the gas, George!"

And like a man woken from a dream, he pushed the throttle all the way up and The Sally Jane churned through the water toward the dock. George jerked the wheel hard to starboard but the big boat scraped the dock with all her tonnage against the bumper wheels, crushing the wheel and exposing the bracket that tore a foot long gash in her fiberglass hull. Matt cried out in agony, and George turned a bright-sunset red.

"You stupid bastard!"

That's what Matt Demler called him. Then he banished him from sailing any of his boats, and George never did sail again. He eventually let his membership in the Columbia Yacht Club lapse as well. George knew he had failed some critical test, and he wondered as he waited for Dean to signal him, with McGruff standing by with an electric cattle prod, if he was about to do it again.

The clock touched five to midnight, and Dean was up on his camera crane. "Alright, mate. You are going to go up onto the roof and through the snow and the smoke machine, and then you have to stop those bastards and dismount. You ready? I'm going to ring the bell now for the little tyke."

"Roger. Ready to roll." George looked at Jeremy. "Ready, son? I really wish your sister were here to see this."

Jeremy shrugged. "She'll probably come along eventually, Dad."

"Alright, quiet on the set," Dean announced through a bullhorn.

George saw him on his camera boom.

"Alright, then—hit your snow and smoke!"

A long roll of vaporous fog enveloped the roof, then the air filled with thick white snow like detergent blown out of a pipe. It was amazing. The light snow that had been falling was replaced by this raging fogged-in blizzard.

"Hit your projectors!"

George looked down at the monitor as the bell began to ring.

"Alright, mate, she's up!"

Megan was sitting up in bed and staring at the window.

"Alright ... she's got her camera, and she's moving toward the window. Looks like she's filming now ... keep those projectors rolling," Dean continued into everyone's ear on the set.

McGruff appeared by George. "Snap them reins!"

George snapped the reins, and the reindeer remained where they were. McGruff's men began pulling on the reindeer.

"C'mon, George, get those shitting bastards moving up the ramp!" Dean screamed.

George snapped the reins again. The reindeer continued breathing smoke and farting like popcorn. McGruff's men had taken to punching the reindeer. Jeremy leaned over.

"Dad, I think you have to yell at them you know—Away, Donner, Prancer, Vixen—"

George shouted, "Away, Donner! Away, Prancer! Away, Vixen, Cupid, and Blitzen!"

"George she's at the bloody window," Dean said into his ear. "You got to get up on that bloody roof! I can only cover with the snow so long!"

"The bastards won't move," George yelled into the wireless mike." He stared at McGruff and felt *The Sally Jane* starting to drift into another boat. "Do something, McGruff!"

"Hang on to yer ass," McGruff shouted.

He then leaned over and goosed the three lead reindeer with his cattle prod. The reindeer bolted like they just heard the starting bell. George and his son were thrown back against the sled as the animals charged the long wooden ramp. George grappled the reins watching the backs of the nine reindeer rolling up and down as they hit the angled ramp. It sounded like a hundred horses clopping across a bridge as the wood groaned and snapped under the weight load. George felt the sled swing back and forth as they gained momentum and bumped onto the ramp.

"ALRIGHT!" Jeremy screamed.

George watched the world fall away with the snow and the wind

and the reindeer pounding up the wooden ramp. Then he realized
he was behind the nine seven-hundred-pound animals, who had
dumped him before. The reindeer had decided that going anywhere
was better than getting shocked. They bolted for the roof in the deafening thunder of hooves. The question was then: Would they turn
and would they stop?

"Fantastic, mate!" Dean blared in his ear.

George hung on tightly to the reins and heard Dean's shout again
as he doubled up the reins and entered a void of oily smoke and
chemical snow. Dim train lights strafed the smoky, snowy gloom as
the digital projectors shot an image into the sky. But now George
saw nothing. He was lost in the smoke and the snow with the digital
projector blinding him like the light of a train. His son was holding on
to the sled like someone on a rollercoaster, and George pulled back
on the reins as he felt the sled turning. McGruff had men on the roof
who were to assist in guiding the reindeer on the turn.

"YOU ARE ON THE ROOF, MATE!"

"I can't see a damn thing with all this smoke and snow," George
shouted into the microphone.

"She is still at the window, and you are not in front of her. You
got to stop them, mate, when I tell you, or you're going to go right
back down the other ramp!"

George could hear the hissing and the hum of the smoke and
snow machines and tasted the oily chemical snow. He wondered what
his daughter was seeing right now. Like a man in a fogged-in ship,
he looked for any kind of landmarks. He was a jet on final approach,
waiting for a signal from the tower and praying he could stop.

"Alright, assistants, get the hell back before you get seen. The sled
is lined up, and those reindeer have got to stop! Get ready, George!
Okay, you are in front of the window! STOP!"

George felt the sled slow, but the reindeer were still trotting forward. He jerked back with all of his might and still they didn't stop.

"Mate, you got to stop those bloody reindeer so the assistants
can grab them!"

And just then, George saw *The Sally Jane*. She was heading for
the dock again, and he was about to tear a foot-long gash in the side.
George stood up in the sled and pulled on the reins as hard as he

could, screaming out: "STOP! STOP, YOU BASTARDS!"

The reindeer stopped. George looked at Jeremy in his elf hat, coated in the same white paste that had painted him like a cream-colored minstrel. They looked like two men who had just flown in from the North Pole. His son shook his head, eyes beaming like a twelve-year-old.

"That was awesome, Dad!"

42

'Tis the Gift Given

THE BICYCLE WAS by the tree when she came down. The blue Schwinn stood out like a diamond. The red ribbon on the handlebars beckoned her, and Mary and her father went outside. It had been snowing all week, and the streets still had a thick layer of slushy white. Her father walked with her on the new bike, holding it up, letting her glide through the quiet snow.

Santa had brought her what she asked for in the letter her mother mailed. *Dear Santa, I want a blue Schwinn Stringray Banana bike with five gears.* Her parents told her Santa might not be able to deliver such a bike. But there it was when she came down the slippery wooden stairs. Sylvia and Shirley and Daffney were wrong. They had walked home one day, and she had been the lone holdout: Santa was real.

Riding out in the bracing air, she was a happy ten-year-old as her father huffed by her. And then it happened. The handlebars shifted, and when she turned straight the handlebars pointed to the left. Her father frowned and looked at the bike, pulling out an adjustable wrench from his coat. "I thought I had tightened that bolt down enough," he murmured. Mary stared at him as he tightened the steering wheel, turning the wheel between his legs. *Had he really said he had tightened the handlebars?*

"I thought Santa put the bike together, Daddy."

And years later she realized how tired her father had been. He had come home from his sales job, and then stayed up half the night assembling toys. His eyes were red rimmed with heavy bags under them. He was bent over the bike with a stubble, cranking the bolt in the center of the handlebars. He wasn't thinking, and that's why he said what he said.

"You're looking at Santa," he muttered.

And Mary had stared at him. He kept torquing the bolt with his bare hands chapped and slightly red from the cold. He finished and handed her the bike. "There you go." Mary held the bike and put one leg over and then paused. She looked at her father, whose eyes had started watering from the cold, his long overcoat tailing out in the wind.

"You're Santa Claus, Dad?"

"Yeah, but don't tell your brothers. They still believe."

And Mary felt her breath leave. She felt the cheery white world go away. She brushed away the tears and pushed off, but the bike slid in the snow, and she felt the rutted ice on her cheek. Her father picked her up.

"Hey, kiddo, maybe we should try this when it's not so cold."

And she had nodded, keeping her head down, brushing away the tears she blamed on the wind. Her father never knew he had delivered the hammer blow to her belief in Santa Claus. Even then she knew that would crush her mother, who went to elaborate means to keep her belief alive. But she had lost it, and there was simply no turning back.

And that day is what she thought about when she heard the reindeer trampling overhead like thunder. It's what got her staring out the window at Dean floating in space in the green beret with the snow and fog enveloping the roof. And as she stood at the window, she felt like that little girl again who had cried on that cold, snowy Christmas day. And she realized then what George had said was true. She would have paid a million dollars to have her belief in Santa back.

"I am practical, dammit," she muttered, hearing nine reindeer scuff about on her roof.

But there was something about a man who would lead a sled of reindeer onto a roof for his daughter. And now that man was about to go down a chimney. Mary considered for the first time that her husband just might kill himself.

43

Christmas Bell

THE BELL STARTED ringing, and Megan opened her eyes.

"He's here! He's here!" she exclaimed, jumping up.

Megan threw off the covers and stepped into her slippers. She grabbed the video camera and ran over to the window. She moved the curtain aside and pressed the *on* button. She saw fog and thick white snow in the viewing screen. There was a whirring sound.

"Oh, my gosh," she gushed.

The world had become quite still. There was only a thick fog and a light like a distant train coming toward her. Then she saw Santa and his reindeer in the sky.

"It's Santa," she whispered excitedly.

Megan kept the camera on as Santa and his sleigh floated down through the sky. Then the house shook and the crystal horse on her dresser crashed as pictures fell off the wall and the bedside lamp fell to the floor. The house groaned and shook, and Megan thought it might just come apart. Then she heard a man scream out a swear word. Megan kept the camera glued to the image floating against the fog and snow.

"I can't believe it, I can't believe it," she whispered, feeling her legs shaking and a strange warmth all over her body. "Santa is real ... *he is real*!"

The pounding hooves became louder and louder as the china figurines fell and her picture of summer camp flew off the wall. Then the whole house shook again, and she felt something under her feet. Megan knew then Santa had landed because she heard the creak of the roof and the heavy drumbeat of hooves. Reindeer hooves! Her softball trophies and bowling trophies and her bulletin board fell from the wall. The windowpanes shook. The lights flickered. Megan kept her eye to the camera, feeling her hand shaking. This was the moment! Now was when Santa would pull up outside her window. The snow was thick and the fog was like a grey veil. The house sounded like it was splitting apart as Megan saw reindeer crash through the white, filmy snow and smoke like phantoms.

The reindeer seemed to be trying to stop and the windowpanes were shaking again, and she heard snorting and a man's voice. It sounded oddly like her father, but of course all men sounded like her father.

"I can't believe reindeer are on my roof!" Megan screamed, squealing, talking to the camera. And then the nine reindeer streamed past her, shaking snow, snorting, smoking, slushing, lunging, eyes wild, fur wet, and antlers high. Then a sled broke into view with a large man in a brilliant white beard, standing up and pulling back on the reins with all his might, screaming: "STOP! STOP! STOP, YOU DUMB BASTARDS!"

And the reindeer locked their legs, and the terrific shaking stopped. Megan couldn't speak. She just couldn't speak. She had Santa's voice on tape as the sled slid to a halt with the reindeer snorting and shaking their heads. They stood in front of Megan with their fur slicked and steaming, puffing smoke from their nostrils like locomotives.

"The reindeer are pooping," Megan whispered, moving her camera down the length of the nine large reindeer stepping on the poop, then centering on Santa and what looked like one of his elves. "Santa has an elf with him," Megan whispered, staring at Santa as he wiped his brow, shaking his head, looking like an astronaut getting out of the command module, taking a step onto the roof with a loud thump.

"Shit!"

Megan exclaimed to the world in tearful joy, "Santa Claus has just landed on my roof!"

Just then Santa Claus paused, and she wondered if she had been too loud. He looked directly at her window, and she stepped to the side. "He might have just seen me," she whispered, feeling like the TV character iCarly, explaining to her viewers what was happening. She peered around and saw Santa moving again with his elf. "His elf has a beard and is smaller," Megan continued in a low voice. "Santa is just like you think he would be ... maybe a little fatter ... a little older, kind of dumpy looking."

"HO HO ..." He coughed and began spitting.

"Santa has a cough," Megan whispered.

"Uhhh," Santa groaned.

Megan followed him as he picked up an enormous sack of toys form the sled.

"He has the presents!" she whispered feverishly.

Santa approached the chimney with the elf and stopped at the base and looked up. Megan thought Santa shook his head and the elf said something. Santa shook his head again, and the elf held out his hands for his boot. Santa pushed up then grabbed on to the sides of the chimney like a man hugging a tree. Megan zoomed in and couldn't be sure, but Santa did not look happy on the side of the chimney.

"He's starting to climb the chimney," Megan whispered, keeping the camera pointed out her window.

Santa slowly started to climb the chimney with the presents over his shoulder, almost like there were steps. Megan followed Santa to the top of the chimney, where he paused and wiped his brow. He seemed to be waiting for something.

"I better get down to the living room. He's going to be coming down the chimney, and I want to see him come out," she whispered, turning off the camera. Megan then left the window to run down stairs and wait for Santa Claus.

44

The Santa has Landed

GEORGE FELT A great relief not unlike the spacemen who had landed on the moon. And like the spacemen he found himself in an alien land. It was windy and cold with light snow biting into his cheeks. He saw the distant rooftops of other homes and the twinkling lights of houses farther away. The temperature had plummeted to eleven degrees, and the wind swirling over the rooftop made it feel twenty degrees colder.

George felt a strange presence overhead and looked up.

Dean hovered above him like a high-tech avenging angel. He sat behind the cameraman waving to George before levitating higher. In the void of the snow and oily smoke, men watched him like an elaborate tech support staff. George saw McGruff's handlers up by the sled keeping the reindeer from bolting off the roof.

"Alright, mate, yer on the roof, and the little tyke is watching you," Dean crackled into his earpiece. "Now it's time to get on … yer ready Santy to get up that chimney?"

"Hell no," George muttered.

"Now she is by the window, mate, so don't go looking over there," Dean directed while he looked around.

"Can you guys cool it with the snow and smoke," George murmured, getting ready to step out of the sled.

"No can do. I need to keep my techs and equipment hidden. It makes for great effects!"

"It tastes like motor oil."

George stared at the dark chimney before him like an ominous monolith.

"What now, Dad?"

He turned back to the sled and looked at his son.

"Alright, let's get the presents out of the sled," he said to Jeremy. "And act like an elf. Megan is watching from the window."

"No problem."

And then George had a glimpse of Megan by the window. Her video light peered out like a star through the glass. George wondered if she would get anything through the window with the reflection.

"Alright, Santa. How about a *HO HO HO*, mate?"

"You gotta be kidding," George groused, trying to keep his footing on the slippery roof.

"This is yer director speaking. Give us a big Santa *HO HO HO* and hold on to yer sides!"

"*HO HO ...*," George bellowed, feeling his throat constrict. He had inhaled some of the chemical snow, and he thought he might barf.

"Yuck," he muttered, still gagging.

"Alright, mate, forget about the *HO HO HO*. Let's concentrate on getting up that chimney, shall we?"

George looked up and saw the nose of the camera peering down at him. A man on the roof with a handheld camera followed his every move. Jeremy had the red bag of presents over his shoulder.

"Ready, Santa?"

George glanced at his son up on the slushy roof in the middle of the night with nine reindeer and men floating around with cameras. He was smiling.

"I better take those for effect," he said, taking the bag of presents. "Alright, let's move toward the chimney. And remember, Megan is watching us," he cautioned under his breath.

"Got ya, Dad."

George moved toward the chimney like a man underwater, stepping carefully through the sticky slush and oily residue from the smoke machines. The chimney had rungs that Joe installed for him like metal horseshoes going up water towers. But the first one was very high, and George could not bring his boot up high enough.

"Alright, mate, ready to climb?" Dean sparked in his ear.

"The step is too damn high."

"Careful there, Santa, we don't want a foul-mouth Santy. She can hear you know, mate."

George looked up and saw Sven and Yergen crouched down against the sides of the chimney with their rappelling ropes. They motioned him up, and George tried to bring his boot up again. The coat and pants wouldn't allow him to get his foot up high enough.

"It's no use. I can't do it."

"Dad, let me give you a boost," Jeremy said, taking the bag of presents that George had hooked onto a harness over his shoulders. He had brought up the fact he couldn't carry the presents and climb the chimney with one hand. The harness had a hook, and the presents would dangle free, allowing him to use both hands. His son was bent down, with his fingers locked.

"Alright, ready?"

"Ready," Jeremy replied, nodding.

George put his boot in his hands and pushed up against the chimney. He hugged the bricks, leaning against the brick tower like a small bridge.

"Get yer foot on the first rung, mate," Dean directed from above.

George saw the first rung, but it required him to free his death grip. "I'm going to fall," he muttered.

"George ... yer got to go up that chimney, mate! The little tyke is watching!"

George saw Sven and Yergen motioning to him to get his hands over to the steel horseshoes. George looked down and saw people staring up at him. Dean had trained several lights on the chimney. He just had to get his hands over to the first rung, and he would be fine.

"Alright, here goes," he muttered, lunging for the rung.

For a moment Santa swung free, his feet dangling in space, an acrobat doing a high-wire chimney stunt, hanging on with his hands for life. George kicked around, finding the bottom rung with his fat boot and steadying himself, pushing up, his heart beating like a fast drummer. He hugged the chimney like his mother.

"Jesus Christ," he cried out, kissing the frozen brick.

45

Dear Virginia …

MRS. WORTHINGTON'S LIFE had gone along like a train on a track that had few bends. But why was she crying over a silly movie? Why did she care if George Bailey was happy? Was she crying because her husband had left and gone over to watch that maniac Kronenfeldt play Santa Claus? Why would anyone want to watch a grown man endanger himself and others by landing a sled with reindeer on his roof?

Mrs. Worthington stared at the fake Christmas tree. Walter always liked a fresh tree, but the mess and the needles were simply too much. Ten years ago she had bought the Christmas tree that could be set up in ten minutes. No lugging the tree in the house. Just take the tree out of the box and set it up. Mrs. Worthington felt that she had scored one against Christmas. She resented the silliness the holiday generated in her classroom and in her home. The only real way to deflate the myth of Christmas was to deflate the biggest myth and that was Santa Claus!

Mrs. Worthington stared at her father on the mantel with his fierce dark German eyes. He had taken Santa away from her early, and she resented the other children who believed in the ridiculous fat man with a beard. She had told them it was their parents. She had told them Christmas was ridiculous and a waste of a good working man's day. That was what her father had said. And she found herself an outsider among her friends. The teacher admonished her to keep her beliefs about Santa Claus to herself. She was a spritely thing who had them sing Christmas carols all month long while she played the piano.

Mrs. Worthington picked up the picture and stared at the man on the front steps of their home. She was there between his legs, a young girl of ten. Her father taught her how to milk a cow and stack hay bales and even to slaughter a chicken. He treated her like a son, and she took his revelation about Christmas as evidence that he viewed her as an equal. But she envied the excitement of the other children when talking about the arrival of Santa Claus. Who wouldn't be excited about a man who comes down your chimney and leaves gifts around your Christmas tree and then vanishes? Why, he was a bit like God when you thought about it.

God promised human salvation. He promised the greatest gift of all—the gift of life. So the advertisers who had created Santa Claus had tapped into a very powerful emotion—the human yearning for someone to come in and save us all. And for children, Jesus and Santa Claus were all mixed up together. Mrs. Worthington had read a recent poll that Santa Claus was what children associated with Christmas, not the baby Jesus. That alone was justification for her war against Santa.

And her war consisted of one simple human emotion—doubt. She put doubt into the children's head over the existence of Santa Claus. Some might think it was an evil thing to do, but they didn't have to deal with twenty-five screaming children for the twenty days before Christmas. The holiday party was her concession to the children and their parents. But she would not lie to the children. She would not perpetuate this myth of gifts for nothing. Children should understand the relationship between work and getting things they wanted. Santa Claus told them that if they were good children, then they were rewarded. That was ridiculous. Children should be good and not expect a reward.

Mrs. Worthington set the picture of her father down and paused. And now this moron was going to potentially undo all her work. He would give his daughter an opportunity to prove to the children that there was a Santa Claus. She did not want a celebrity in her classroom for the remaining six months of school. She did not want her class to be home to the girl famous for proving the existence of Santa Claus. And now Kronenfeldt had lured her husband away on Christmas Eve. That made Mrs. Worthington so mad she picked up the phone and dialed. She would make Kronenfeldt pay.

"Yes, I would like to report a man with reindeer on his roof ... Yes ... he is creating quite a disturbance, and I cannot get any sleep," she said to the policeman, meeting her father's disapproving glare.

46

Stockings Hung by the Chimney with Care

MEGAN STARED AT the fireplace. Bits of black creosote fell down onto the hearth like black snow. Megan kept her video camera on the fireplace, barely breathing, scarcely able to believe she was going to see Santa Claus emerge from the chimney with his gifts. This moment contained the biggest question for her: How did Santa mange to fit down the chimney with all his gifts? How did he actually climb back up the chimney? Was he able to simply recreate the chimney the way they did in *The Santa Clause* movie?

More pieces of creosote rained down into the fireplace and littered the hearth. Then larger black pieces fell with heavy thuds. Some exploded like small black bombs. This had never happened in any movie Megan could remember. Now she became aware of other sounds. Santa Claus was breathing heavy, grunting, thudding. Megan lowered her camera and walked closer to the fireplace. The creosote was falling like sand, as if someone was kicking the sides of the chimney. A cloud of coal dust rolled into the living room, and somewhere far above her she heard Santa again. His voice was deep and hollow, but that might be because he was in a chimney. Megan stepped back into the shadows and positioned herself. The sounds were getting louder, and the size and amount of creosote had increased to a black avalanche.

Megan felt her heart and raised the camera again. Santa was breathing very heavy and seemed to be grunting. A large black rock of creosote hit the hearth and exploded like a small meteorite. The sound stopped and Megan kept her eye on the camera, waiting for Santa Claus to emerge in her living room. She bit her lip to make sure she wasn't dreaming. Here was the undisputable proof that not only did Santa *exist,* but he had come down her chimney after landing on her roof, and this proof would stream out into the world! She just had to keep her camera aimed at the opening of their fireplace

A minute went by. Then another. Then another. Megan hit the stop button and looked over her camera. She tiptoed up the fireplace and bent her head, listening closely. There was no sound, then she heard a single grunt, an expulsion of breath, then some dull cursing followed by Santa's voice echoing far up the chimney.

"I'm stuck!"

47

The Santa Sweep

"YA ...YOU READY?"

Sven had a beard and sparkling eyes and looked like he wanted to go down the chimney. He gestured into the gaping mouth. "This will be cake piece."

His German accent broke apart the epigram. Yergen, who was darker, had black eyes, and also had a beard, waited with the harness to keep George from flying down the chimney. George didn't want to break his grip on the chimney and raise himself over the top. It felt like he would fall straight down to the roof below if he did. It was Dean's voice that got him moving again.

"C'mon, mate! The little tyke is waiting for you down in your living room with her camera!"

George gave himself a count. He had taken off his mittens, and his fingers were numb and bloodied from the rough brick. He had one black vinyl boot on the rung and one positioned on the crevice between the mortar and the brick. He was a man clinging to a brick edifice that had been used only to transport smoke to the heavens. Now he would go down into the mouth that smelled like the old coal chutes he used to play in as a kid, a mixture between burnt wood and oil stoves from cabins up in Minnesota. Far down below he saw a glimmer of yellow light. Warm air rose up, and he thought he could smell the pine Christmas tree.

"Alright," he muttered, hoisting himself up over the chimney while Yergen slipped on the harness.

"Ya ... you be fine," he said, tightening straps and buckles, making George think of those men who had jumped into darkness over France in World War II. He knew now they were wondering how they came to be jumping out of an airplane. George wondered how he was about to hover over a fireplace sixty feet below.

"Okay. All set, ya?"

Sven nodded to him and helped him lower his legs into the chimney. George was now sitting on the edge of a high dock. His legs swung in space, and the warm house air fanned him like a blast furnace. The air was literally rushing out of the house.

"Ya, you be fine." Yergen nodded, holding on to the rope with Sven on the other side.

"Don't you guys let go," George muttered to the men who would bear his weight once he plunged into the open darkness. Yergen said nothing, his black eyes registering neither fear or judgment on the man in the white beard and Santa hat. George slid his butt to the edge and supported himself with his hands on the side of the chimney.

"Alright, here goes."

His heart pounded beneath his suit. He was sweating. He felt weak, and then he slipped his butt into space, and the weight of his body pushed down on his arms. For a moment he was Iron Man, the Santa gymnast suspending himself over space, kicking for a toehold as his arms gave way and he dropped into darkness. He shouted like a woman, like a girl, like a child, and disappeared into a woody, burned creosote darkness, bashing his forehead against the blackened brick, seeing stars, smashing his back against the other side, feeling his shoulders pull like someone yanking him toward the heavens. He stopped, kissing the creosote that coated the chimney like a flaking black paint.

"YA ... WE HAVE YOU, SANTA CLAUS," Sven called down in a long echo from the top.

George turned around like a puppet, kicking the fire-blackened bricks.

"JESUS CHRIST! DID YOU GUYS DROP ME?"

"Ya, you much fatter than we thought."

"Thanks a lot," George croaked, spitting out creosote.

He looked up and saw four eyes peering down and stars far above. He had gone a third of the way down the chimney in seconds before the ropes pulled tight and the two mountain men arrested his fall. George was black with soot, and creosote sprinkled down below every time he kicked for support. He held on to the harness as Sven's head loomed over the pinwheel stars.

"Ya, you are a big boy. We didn't think you would jump like that. We stopped you though," he called down.

"Great," George grumbled, triangulating himself across the chimney in the rising warm air, looking down to the light that was closer now.

"We lower you down slowly, ya. You ready?"

"Yes," he called, feeling the rope slacken as he started a slow kicking descent.

"How you doing in there, mate?" Dean crackled in his ear.

"I feel like I'm in a furnace."

"I'll bet ... the little tyke is waiting with her camera."

George turned around like a rotating top, kicking from the close wall, going down a few feet at a time. Creosote broke off in large chunks that tasted like a burnt stick. He pushed off from the bricks looking up at the stars getting farther away. George thought only Santa Claus would understand the claustrophobia of being in a wood blackened space that made breathing hard and battered your back with sharp-angled bricks. The chimney closed in, and George realized then chimneys were not uniform. They moved sideways. They had irregular bricks and suddenly became small.

George kicked back from the wall, straddling the space of the two chimneys that forced him to move sideways, slipping down like a man in a slot. And now the slot had become so narrow he felt his belt buckle hook on something, and for the second time he hovered in space.

"*I'm stuck,*" Santa announced to the world.

"What do you mean you're stuck, mate?"

"I mean I can't move," George muttered, trying to lift his buckle off the brick. "My belt buckle is hooked on something."

Dean made these breathy noises in his ear. George struggled to move himself over the brick, trying to lift his body weight, but he was hanging by a five-inch-wide leather and vinyl belt.

"It's no use," he grunted, leaning his head back. "I'm stuck."

"Listen, mate ... Sven is lowering you down a knife to cut yourself free."

"Alright."

George looked up and saw a black glittering object float down toward him. Bits of creosote fell in his eyes. When he cleared his eyes the knife was just above his hat. He reached up and grabbed the knife.

"Got it."

"See if yer can cut yourself free, mate."

George opened the knife and slipped it under the vinyl belt. He began to saw. He felt the material start to give, and he continued sawing. The sharp knife jaggedly ripped through the thin leather and vinyl belt. He stopped and felt something tear, and he moved slightly lower.

"I don't know if this is such a good idea—"

The vinyl leather belt tore in two and for the second time Santa went into free-fall down the chimney. George felt the rushing warm air, the rain of creosote, the smell of cold fear, the bricks hitting his back arms, legs, boots, the bumping sound of a full-grown man falling down his own chimney. He saw the bright yellow light getting closer where a cinder block hearth awaited him.

George didn't remember swearing, but he did remember saying a prayer just as he felt his shoulders pull and he was winched upward and then he collapsed into a sooty black pile of creosote blackened detritus. A fine black cloud of coal dust spread out into the living room, where his daughter captured the arrival of Santa for the world.

48

Santa Routine

"SANTA IS STUCK, Mom!"

Megan lowered her camera and looked at her mother. Mary saw a dark cloud of creosote rising from the fireplace. She could hear George swearing, gasping, and wondered again if he might kill himself.

Megan's face was flushed and anxious.

"Do you think he can make it down, Mom?"

Santa was not supposed to get stuck in chimneys. Mary had never had a husband who had become lodged in her chimney on Christmas Eve with her daughter waiting to videotape to show to the world there really was a Santa Claus. She felt like she was watching *Miracle on 34th Street* and the lawyer for Santa Claus had just approached the bench and said: *"Oh, but there is a Santa Claus your honor … I intend to prove that my client is the one and only Santa Claus!"* The derision that greeted that lawyer might greet her own daughter as well.

"I'm sure he will be down in just a moment," Mary murmured as the doorbell rang. *What now?* she wondered, walking toward the front door.

She pulled the door open to find a policeman with his hat kicked back.

"Mrs. Kronenfeldt?"

"Yes?"

"Mrs. Kronenfeldt, we are going to have to shut this thing down. Your husband is creating a nuisance in the neighborhood with all these people and trucks and lights. You gotta have a permit for this kind of thing, and I was willing to go along with it, but we just had a complaint from some lady in another suburb who said she could see the lights from her house."

Mary looked behind her and saw Megan by the fireplace. She turned back around and looked at the policeman. Here was chaos. Here was what she had been careful to avoid her whole life. But this was for something else ... wasn't it? Mary pulled the door closed and looked at the rookie cop.

"Tell me, officer, did you ever believe in Santa Claus?"

"Yeah, sure I did."

Mary crossed her arms.

"Well my husband is stuck in our chimney right now, trying to prove to his daughter that there is still a Santa Claus." Mary felt her eyes well up. "And I cannot have him fail now. It was a stupid idea that will probably send us to the poorhouse, but it is for the innocence of a little girl and her belief in something magical. I think that will be worth whatever fine or incarceration this event produces, don't you?"

The rookie blinked twice, staring at the woman with tears in her eyes and the sweater pulled around her shoulders. She wasn't budging, and he wasn't going to arrest her.

"Alright." He nodded slowly. "I'll try and keep a lid on things until your husband is done with his Santa Claus routine."

Mary wiped her cheeks under her glasses.

"Thank you, officer."

"Yeah, well ..." He didn't know what to say. He stepped back into the yard and looked up at the chimney. He shook his head and looked at Mary.

"I have a daughter, but I don't think I'd have the balls to do something like this."

49

Black Santa

SO FAR MEGAN'S video showed Santa Claus floating down through smoke and snow then crashing onto the snowy roof. The dark figure then jumped down from the sled with his elf helper and trudged toward the chimney. The video followed Santa as he slowly ascended the chimney, climbing like a man hugging his mother. Santa clutched the chimney for a long time then climbed to the very top, barely visible in the smoke and snow. Then the video went to black and picked up on the fireplace and Christmas tree in Megan's living room.

There was a sound like laundry falling down a long chute and then a muffled voice. Megan whispered that Santa was stuck and the video rolled on, bits of creosote falling down into the hearth. The video stopped then and picked up again on the fireplace with Megan whispering, "I think he's coming now." The Christmas tree winked next to the fireplace as the video zoomed in on the hearth speckled with black paint. The video pulled back, and then Santa's voice was forever immortalized on magnetic tape.

"SHIIIIIIIIIT!"

Megan felt this moment alone was enough to prove Santa was a real man.

The Santa that emerged in Megan's viewfinder from the fireplace was African-American or maybe Bing Crosby in the old minstrel number in *Holiday Inn* with white eyes and a mouth outlined in caricature. Even his beard had turned a dirty shade of grey with black eyebrows that pirated his expression. His eyes blinked like two white Oreos. Megan stared at Santa, whose red suit was now carbon with black streaks running down his pants. He resembled those coal miners who emerged from underground and blinked into the light like men from Hades. Every inch of Santa's suit, face, and hands had been painted creosote black.

And this was after Santa had crashed down into the hearth and rolled out like a man who had just landed from another planet. The creosote cloud mushroomed into the room, followed by a sprinkling of burned soot and wood particles. The room smelled like the inside of a chimney or those old lodges her parents had taken her to in Minnesota with the giant stone fireplaces. It sounded like half the chimney had come down with Santa Claus, and Megan kept rolling her video camera thinking that she was solving the greatest question of all: How did Santa come down the chimney? Not very well obviously, but now she knew—he came down as a chimney sweep and made a big mess.

Santa Claus grunted to his feet and seemed disoriented in the video. He wiped his eyes and swore then brushed clouds of blackened particles off his suit. He approached the chimney wearily and bent down. He seemed to be waiting for something. A large dirty sack then plopped down into the fireplace with a gentle thud. Santa disconnected a rope and dragged the heavy sack to the Christmas tree. He began to reach down and pull presents out, tossing them under the tree.

The video camera whirred on, following Santa as he moved around like a dirty burglar, sampling the cookies and milk, distributing the gifts, staring at the Christmas tree like a man appraising his own work. He burped, and Megan wasn't sure but he might have farted as well. Santa looked at the fireplace then walked over and shoved the empty sack into his belt.

It was at this point Megan turned off the camera and stepped forward.

"Santa?"

Santa Claus froze with his back to her.

"Santa?" she said again.

50

Santa on High

GEORGE THOUGHT ABOUT the fact he was a fifty-year-old unemployed man stuck in his own chimney on Christmas Eve while he hung suspended like one of those wooden dolls jumping up and down but never moving on their own volition. Even when he was waiting for Sven and Yergen to get him free by lowering down a knife, he wondered if he had finally found the perfect metaphor for his life. He was always doing things that made his life a mess, and he considered that maybe his hands weren't so clean.

Maybe he knew becoming Santa Claus would send his kids over the edge, rupture his marriage, put him into the poorhouse, and basically screw up his life. Saving Megan's vision of Christmas might have been a convenient foil. The way his wife's old boyfriend popping up on Facebook had been a foil for a marriage he had screwed up long ago. He had not been a great husband or father, and he found irony that he should have this epiphany while stuck in his chimney with the warm air of his own home blowing up between his legs. Below him was his daughter and his wife and the conjugal mess he had created.

Even as he sawed away on his belt with the knife, he wondered if he had been sawing his own branch all his life. Why did he create such havoc all the time? But this time he was trying to reset the clock. It was amazing how fast children grew up. In fact it was frightening because while they were growing their parents were simply becoming older. And like a candle they finally melted down to a puddle of wax and that was simply it. He had seen this puddle of wax lately. He felt his candle was nearer the dish now, and he wanted his children, Megan, Jamie, and Jeremy, to be left with dreams that would sustain them through life.

And one of these dreams was a belief in Santa Claus. It was optimistic to believe there was a benevolent man going down chimneys and dropping off gifts. It was a glass half-full view of life to believe that one man was capable of bringing joy to children all over the world, and what was amazing was that people *did believe* in Santa Claus. Millions of children believed in a man with a white beard and a red suit and a hat who could land a sleigh of reindeer on a roof and go down a chimney and drop off gifts and then take off from the roof for another home. And in that minute, sawing on his own belt, George understood his true mission: *It was to prove that Santa Claus was real.*

He then flew down the chimney like a cork unleashed. After Sven and Yergen arrested his fall, he ended up rolling into his living room. George caught sight of a black man in the mirror on the wall. He was a soot-covered chimney sweep. His beard was brown, and his suit had become a drab brown. His lips and eyes resembled a coal miner. The creosote had painted him black. George unhooked his harness, hearing Dean cracking in his ear. "You alright, mate?"

"Yeah," he muttered.

"The gifts are coming down now. The little tyke is behind you videotaping. Be a good Santa."

George went to the fireplace as the sack of gifts floated down. The plan was simply to put the gifts around the tree and then hook back up to the harness and have Yergen and Sven hoist him up. George pulled the heavy sack to the tree and began to unload the presents. And then a second glow came into the room. Maybe it was the lights, maybe it was the spirit of Christmas, but he suddenly *felt like* he was the man bringing gifts to children the world over. It started as a warm feeling in the middle of his stomach and then radiated out like a bath. He was moving in the glow of the Christmas he had known as a boy, when he ran down the stairs and saw what Santa had left him.

And it was Santa that left him gifts. It was never his parents. Even when he knew intellectually there was no Santa Claus, he still believed these gifts came from above, from some place that rested in the heart of a nine-year-old boy. And he felt that same excitement of a heavy box or a bicycle or his first stereo. These memories were not invalidated by adult knowledge. They remained strangely inviolate.

And he was giving this to his daughter—he was giving her a belief that would last a lifetime, a warmness of the heart that she could rely on when the world seemed dark. He was giving her the moment in *A Christmas Story* where Ralph clutched his BB gun in Christmas bliss, certain he had received that Red Ryder BB gun from the big man. And in this spirit George ate the cookies and drank the milk and walked around the living room like Santa, a man who had many homes to get to, and he approached the fireplace, letting Dean know he was ready to go back up the chimney, when he heard a voice.

"Santa?"

And all George could think of was little Cindy Lou Who, who asked Santa why he was stealing their Christmas tree. And like the Grinch, George froze, seeing the dangling harness rope he was about to clip on and make his escape up the chimney. Dean was crackling in his ear to get moving and Yergen and Sven were waiting for the signal to start hauling him up the chimney. If he spoke he was dead meat. So he didn't move, facing the hearth.

"Santa ..."

She was not going to stop. This he was certain of. Megan had a plan. She always did, and so George dropped his voice down as low as he could, peering over his shoulder at his daughter in her Mickey Mouse pajamas and said, "Shouldn't you be in bed?"

"Yes, but I wanted to see you. I wanted to prove you were real!"

George didn't move. He had to get up that chimney. He couldn't even tell Dean, who was freaking out in his ear, to hold off. *"I'm going to have them start hauling you up, George. These bloody reindeer are starting to go crazy."* And George stood, staring at the mantel on his fireplace.

"Santa, I wanted to ask for one thing not on my list. My daddy lost his job ... and I'm worried about him."

George felt his skin warming, his vision blurring.

"And I was wondering if you could get him a new job for Christmas. You can keep all my presents, if you just bring him a job, Santa."

George breathed heavy, trying to get hold of himself. He had to respond, but he thought he might lose it. That his daughter was worried about him came as a shock. He had not talked about losing his job, but of course kids knew everything. She was willing to give up all her presents so her father could have a job. George felt a single hot tear go down into his beard. He breathed heavy and dropped his voice as low as he could.

"That's not necessary, Megan. He will find a job. I promise. Now why don't you get some sleep?"

He heard his daughter breathe.

"Thank you! I love you, Santa."

George felt the second rush of warmth and breathed again, steadying himself with one blackened hand on the fireplace.

"I love you too, Megan."

And then he heard her footsteps go back into the hallway.

"Let's go," he muttered into his beard.

George groaned and huffed as he crawled into the hearth, clicking on the harness. He stood up in the chimney and felt his shoulders bunch and his muscles tighten. He kicked against the sides of the chimney and left the ground and started going back up toward the stars. George bumped back and forth between the blackened bricks, trying to keep himself centered as he rose up into the still night. He could hear Sven and Yergen grunting and breathing heavy as he rose steadily. Halfway up, the warmth of the rising air mixed with the snap of descending cold air, and he felt like he had plunged into a pool.

George continued to rise steadily, staring up at the blue pinwheels above him and muttered, "This is pretty friggin' cool," as he emerged from the chimney, reaching up and pulling himself into the bitter air and the lights, the noise of reindeer, computers, cameras, and smoke machines. Yergen smiled at him, wet with perspiration, gripping his hand.

"Ya, welcome back, Santa Claus!"

51

Away Dasher, Prancer, and Vixen, Comet, Cupid and Blitzen!

DEAN WATCHED GEORGE emerge and realized he had a movie. He had something that trumped all the screenplays he had sent to New York and Hollywood. He had something that trumped the agents and producers and directors that ignored every demo reel, every tape he sent them, every pitch, every e-mail blast, every phone call, every name change, epiphany, mood, trend, every moment he pigeonholed as his moment. He was doing what he meant to do all his life: *directing a movie!* Up here in the darkness above the lights and cameras and action unfolding, he felt like God.

You had to dance with the big boys, and the big boys were Hollywood. *Christmas movies!* The plot was simple—a man who wants to keep the myth of Santa alive for his girl, and so he becomes *the* Real Santa. *Real Santa!* Dean could see it up on the marquee. He could see himself giving interviews, talking about his low-budget film that became a cult classic and then a classic. *Real Santa* would take its place next to *It's a Wonderful life, White Christmas, Holiday Inn, Home Alone,* and *Elf.*

And as he watched George climb down the chimney, he realized he didn't have an ending. Something supernatural would be good. Something that would allow the audience to keep the magic going. People wanted to believe in the big man. *Elf* ended with Santa flying away over New York and of course *The Santa Clause* redeemed Tim Allen when he became Santa. These movies told us that there is such a thing as Santa. Why else would movies like *Miracle on 34th Street* stand the test of time? You have to have a pitch, *proving* Santa is real. Much like the famous scene where Natalie Wood picks out the house she asked Santa for and Maureen O'Hara sees Santa's cane by the fireplace and Fred Gailey stares at the cane and leaves the audience with the question, *Is Santa real? Was the old man really Santa after all?*

And watching George hit the roof, trudging through the snow like Santa himself, Dean murmured, "Santa *is* bloody real, alright." Now would be his greatest cinematic moment. He would film Santa leaving the roof and flying off into the heavens. He had real reindeer on his roof, and he would show real reindeer taking off into the sky. He just hoped they didn't bolt off the roof and kill George in the process. Of course, William Holden's death in *The Twilight Zone* hadn't hurt the movie or the director. There was no such thing as bad publicity and looking at the reindeer, bucking up and down, snorting, looking more like pent-up bulls, Dean saw a disaster in the making.

They had to trot across the roof and down the ramp on the other side through a blizzard of manufactured smoke while digital projectors shot their image into the sky. Anything could happen. They might bolt off the roof. They might miss the ramp entirely. He had to be ready for anything. Besides, dramatic endings were always a good thing in America.

52

Christmas Spirit

WALTER HAD HIS cell phone. Mrs. Worthington thought her husband looked ridiculous with the phone on his belt pointed sideways. It was always going off during dinner or when they sat in the parlor. It was an invasion much like the Internet. When Megan had said she was going to announce to the world that Santa was real on YouTube, Mrs. Worthington had to ask her grandchildren what YouTube was. This world made absolutely no sense to her anymore.

And yet she couldn't stop the computer juggernaut. She had to login and put in her reports and read the requirements of *No Child Left Behind* that changed every year. So she limped through and did the minimum, pecking at the computer, feeling helpless when she had to keep asking the young teacher Melissa how to get to the proper screen and where had the cursor gone again. And now she was standing and waiting for her husband to answer his cell phone.

"Hello ... hello..." Walter had picked up. "Hello, hello ..."

"Walter!"

"Hello ... hello ..."

"WALTER!"

"Barbara—"

"Yes, it's Barbara! Where on earth are you?"

"I'm at Kronenfeldts. He just popped out the chimney. It's pretty amazing. Looks like a movie set."

"*What?*"

This was what she hated most about cellular communication. You ended up talking on top of the other person. They interrupted each other three more times until Mrs. Worthington got a sentence in.

"Come home, Walter! I will forgive you for your … outburst."

There was an airy sound and then Walter's voice.

"Nah, I'm going to watch this guy take off from the roof with his reindeer. I don't know how he's going to do that."

Mrs. Worthington felt her cheeks warm and her heart beat speed up. There was something new here in her husband. A defiance she had never seen before, and she blamed this on Megan's father as well.

"Don't be ridiculous! Are the police there?"

"Yeah. They're watching too."

Mrs. Worthington gritted her teeth and rubbed her forehead. The clock in the hallway struck the hour. The stillness of the house was suddenly oppressive. She had noticed it several times when her husband was away. She suddenly saw a life that had been lived, and she was simply waiting to die. The clock in the hallway seemed to be tolling for the years she had lived and the short years left. She wanted to see her husband. She wanted him in his chair where all would be right with the world.

"Come home this minute, Walter," she snapped, feeling a pinch of fear that made her voice sharp.

The cell phone filled with people cheering, and then Walter's voice moved in, light and uncaring. "Nope … I want to see Santa Claus. You should come, Barbara, and see him for yourself. That old bastard ruined your fantasy way too early."

The heat crawled across her skin. She stamped her heel on the linoleum floor.

"Are you referring to my father?"

"Yeah. Did you ever wonder why he told you there wasn't a Santa Claus?"

She grabbed the back of her chair. "I will not listen to this anymore," she declared firmly. "You come home this instant!"

"I'm going to tell you anyway. He told you because he had to be the big man and couldn't stand the fact you might look up to somebody else other than him … he had to be Santa for you."

"Don't be ridiculous—"

"You should come, Barbara, and get a little magic in your life—before it's too late."

And then Walter did something she couldn't believe. He hung up on her. The phone went dead, and Mrs. Worthington didn't move. She held the phone to her ear, expecting him to come back. Then she hung up the phone and stood in that awful silence. The clock ticked. Mrs. Worthington saw the pictures of her family that usually gave her such comfort. But now they stood for time lost. She blamed Kronenfeldt for all of this.

"If the police won't do their job, then I will," she declared to her overcoat, scarf, gloves, and the large woolly hat she wore that made her look like a Russian woman.

Mrs. Worthington then went outside into the strange eerie quiet. The air was very cold in her nose as she started the Lincoln she had inherited when her mother passed away. Walter had taken the Honda that he was so fond of, with the high-miles-per-gallon rating. Cars were meant to be big, and the Lincoln with its heated leather seats suited her just fine.

Mrs. Worthington began to drive toward the Kronenfeldts, where she planned out her course of action. First she would get the police to do their job and shut down the ridiculous spectacle this man had created. And then she would collect her husband, and she would do something to make him pay for getting her out on Christmas Eve. Mrs. Worthington hunched forward and concentrated on the road. She had never been a great driver, and she had to admit driving at night and in the snow had become challenging.

She turned into the subdivision that was new, with large homes on acre lots. Of course this man would live here! People living beyond their means fit Kronenfeldt perfectly. And what was Santa Claus really? A man who delivered presents for absolutely no work! A child had to do nothing to be rewarded. This in itself was reason enough to debunk the myth of a bearded white fool in a sled emerging from the North Pole to give gifts to children. She was doing the world a favor by stopping this Megan and her YouTube film, whatever that was.

Mrs. Worthington was so wrapped up in her thoughts she didn't see the large snow berm at the bottom of the hill the snowplow had left. She had not considered the car's weight and speed, and she hit the brakes too hard. The computer tried to utilize the fast pumps of the anti-breaking piston, but it was no use. Her Lincoln had become a very large, very heavy sled, headed directly for a wall of snow.

53

Engineer Santa

WHEN GEORGE BUILT the bike bridge, there was a point where he realized he had screwed up. It was the span that arced over the six-lane highway like a tribute to the early age of forged steel that made him doubt his original plan. True, the bridge would last a hundred years, and it would survive every type of stress test for pedestrians and bicyclists, and it might even be able to support a small locomotive. What worried George was that his bridge looked ridiculous.

But it was too late. He watched the ironworkers bolt the giant span in place, and he saw what every driver would notice: a giant, rust-colored girder bisecting the highway. And when it was finished, George noticed few people actually used the bridge. He took heart when he saw a lone cyclist pedal over it and stop in the middle. Maybe he was admiring the durability of such a bridge, but George couldn't help but feel the man was staring down and muttering," Who would build this in the middle of nowhere?"

And emerging from his chimney and seeing the world he had created in his backyard with Dean hovering in space and movie lights shooting all over the house with smoke machines and snow machines churning out movie snow and fog, he had a similar moment of wondering if he had overdone it once again. George shakily went down the side of the chimney with Yergen and Sven helping him, feeling the cold as something foreign after the warmth of the chimney. The wind watered his eyes and fanned the fur on his collar. Dean squawked in his ear as he descended to the snow and ice-crusted roof.

"You're looking good, mate, and the little tyke is back in her bedroom filming you, so look real Santy!"

George didn't feel *real* Santy. He felt like a fifty-year-old man who had just tumbled down a chimney then gotten hoisted up by his shoulders. His neck and back screamed out in pain. All he had to do now was get in the sled, get the reindeer moving, and follow them off the roof and down the ramp. Jeremy looked more like an elf with the movie snow clinging to his beard and hat.

"Let's see if we can get off the roof now," George said, brushing off creosote from his suit.

Jeremy grinned and remembered a day his father stayed home with him. They had gone to get some chips and soda at the hardware store and sat outside in the spring sunshine. A man walked by them and nodded, saying, "Enjoy this, because it ends before you know it." Jeremy had no idea what the man meant. *What ends before you know it?* Eating chips and drinking soda? Hanging out with his father? But when he had grown older, the man's sentence had followed him around. Everything ends before you know it. It all slips through your fingers, and then you are graduating college, and your mother has ended up with some freakoid from Florida, and your dad has become Santa Claus.

Jeremy looked at his father's soot-covered face, holding the reins now with the snow and fog swirling around them like two men lost in a snowstorm. He patted his arm and winked.

"You done good, Pops."

His father smiled.

54

Mooning Santa

MRS. WORTHINGTON WATCHED the car go by and spray snow all over her leather boots. She had kept her boots pristine, the soft brown leather and beaver fur tops never seeing a real snowfall until now. They were never meant for real snow or plowing through a berm of snow and ice that now entombed her car. Mrs. Worthington had tried to start her car again, staring at the wall of snow inches from her windshield. The tires spun and spun with the front of the car wedged tight and the back of the car digging a perfect slit trench.

That was when she murmured, "Oh, dear!" and emerged into the cold night not unlike the night those poor souls who jumped into the icy Atlantic in the book *A Night To Remember*. Gertrude Stevens had recommended the book to her, and while she didn't approve of action fiction, she enjoyed the chivalry of the first-class men who donned evening clothes and said they were prepared to die like gentlemen.

But clearly there were no gentlemen left. She had heard a car, and like the survivors in their tiny lifeboats who saw the steamship *Carpathia* the next morning, Mrs. Worthington waved and called out, "Hello ... Hello..."

The car did not slow, and Mrs. Worthington stared after the receding taillights. "I don't believe it," she declared. Mrs. Worthington viewed most adults as errant children, and this man certainly deserved to write on her blackboard a hundred times: "I will not pass up a person in need in a snowstorm." That would teach him, Mrs.

Worthington thought grimly, surveying her Lincoln Continental shipwrecked in the white wall. She turned and looked down the road of the subdivision then at the houses twinkling with Christmas lights. She had no cell phone. She had never lowered herself, but now would not be a bad time to possess such a device.

"Well, I will simply walk until I find help," she said aloud.

Imagine this kind of weather on Christmas Eve! Does God really find it necessary to turn down the temperature so low? High twenties would suffice, but this five degrees above zero is ridiculous! She pulled her scarf tight around her ears and pulled down her leather gloves. Mrs. Worthington started walking down the road in the direction of the Kronenfeldt home. She blamed Kronenfeldt for having her out in the snow and ice, walking down a badly plowed road and ruining her new boots.

She heard the crunch of her boots in the frozen snow, her own breathing filling the air. She thought of Walter and blamed him as much as Kronenfeldt. If he had not lost his senses and run out into the cold, then she would not be here risking life and limb. It would serve him right if she died of exposure. The guilt he would have to endure until his dying days gave her grim pleasure as she slipped and nearly fell to the ground.

"Shit."

Mrs. Worthington rarely cussed, and the word felt funny in her mouth, as if it didn't quite fit. But Mrs. Worthington felt like she could say far worse at this moment. She thought of Walter's comments about her father. *Absurd!* Why, she and her father would go get the Christmas tree together. They would go out and cut down the trees in the sharp air, and her father would make their own stand out of two by fours. He trimmed the tree, and her mother decorated it with antique ornaments. And on Christmas morning they had a turkey and the canned vegetables her mother had put in the fruit cellar. It was a good old-fashioned Christmas without all the commercialism and toys, and the thought that Santa should impinge on her memory of those times irritated her greatly.

Mrs. Worthington was beginning to breathe heavily. She had not exercised in many years. The doctor had told her to take walks. *Indeed!* It seemed ridiculous to walk around their neighborhood.

She and Walter had completed several constitutionals and then just stopped. First of all, there simply wasn't time and having people go jogging by was a bother. Why did everyone wear such tight black outfits? She felt she was surrounded by buttocks.

Mrs. Worthington stopped in the road and caught her breath, and that's when she saw a glow of lights. It was up around the bend, and she wondered if that was the Kronenfeldts. She began to walk again. A man putting reindeer on a roof! For what? To perpetuate the myth of overindulgence! Her father had set her straight on that one. She had wanted a bicycle when she was nine. She remembered the bicycle from the Sears catalog. It was red. She and her mother had cut out a picture of it, and she kept it in her top drawer. She had written a letter to Santa Claus and put the picture of the bicycle in the envelope. She had put *North Pole, Santa Claus* on the outside and put it in the mailbox at the end of their drive. She put up the flag so the postman would know to take the letter.

Mrs. Worthington stopped again. Her heart felt like it was fluttering, and her cheeks felt numb. The lights and sound were closer. Her feet were cold, and her fingers had no feeling. Mrs. Worthington began to feel faint. She stopped and took several deep breaths. There was something there now. Something she had felt in her home after Walter left—a dark road much like this one, without the friendly markers of her life. She was at the end of something now. This strange presence ... was it death? Was she that close now that death could swoop her in and take her? Her heart began to beat rapidly.

Then she saw Santa. He rose out of the darkness like the Hindenburg, an inflated cherub who looked at her over his shoulder in a hiss of pneumatic bliss. Then an igloo with a turret and a gun rotated toward Mrs. Worthington. It was one of those inflatables she detested. No imagination, lolling on lawns all night long in lit-up horror like globes of chicken eggs. That's what the smudged plastic looked like to Mrs. Worthington—broken eggs. They might as well put a fetus in those globes.

But the Santa is what Mrs. Worthington could not turn from. He was looking over his shoulder, holding his sack of toys with a big wink as if to say *You think you could stop me. This is what I think of you.* Mrs. Worthington, a teacher of the fourth grade for forty years, watched as Santa's pants dropped and a large pink ass revealed itself stamped with a bright MERRY CHRISTMAS!

"Oh, my!"

Mrs. Worthington gasped as the Santa pants completed their cycle and rose to cover the very large derriere. It was now that Mrs. Worthington became cognizant of the trucks and cars parked in front of the house across the street from the mooning Santa and the Panzer. She saw lights hitting the chimney, and at that moment she saw Santa emerge. It was as if the world had become an army of Santa Commandos bent on tormenting her. She stared transfixed at the man high above his roof with a hovering man farther up hunched over a camera. It was completely unreal, and Mrs. Worthington felt like one of those people who swear they have been abducted by an alien.

She turned back to Shanti's front yard, where Santa winked again and mooned her. The turret of the igloo Panzer took aim and flashed a red MERRY CHRISTMAS! Mrs. Worthington felt her grip on reality slipping away, and she felt faint. Her heart pounded queerly as she sat down in the snow on the side of the road. She felt the cold through her coat. She tried to breathe slowly. She closed her eyes and saw her father coming into the house on Christmas Eve from the barn. His face was red and his eyes watering. He took off his coat, and her letter to Santa fluttered to the wide, rough planks of their kitchen. She walked over to the letter and picked it up.

"My letter to Santa," she exclaimed.

Her father rubbed his hands and stared at her. "You don't want to be putting fake letters in the mail, Barbara," he said gruffly.

She looked up at him. "But, how will Santa know what I want?"

Her father cracked down on her innocence like a whip.

"There ain't no Santa Claus," he declared, taking the letter from her hands and putting it in the fire grate of the wood-burning stove. He stood up and faced the little girl with tears in her eyes. "There's only me and your mother, and you better get used to that."

And Mrs. Worthington felt that shock all over again now. And for the first time she questioned her father's actions. Why had he thrown her letter into the fire? Why had he not allowed her to believe in the very best of Christmas? She felt tears come to her eyes, and she murmured, "Daddy ... Daddy ... Don't burn my letter!" She was a nine-year-old girl crying for the loss of innocence.

The world flared up, and Mrs. Worthington wondered if this was the bright light everyone talked about at the end. It always seemed ridiculous to her that some light should be out there and they would all walk toward it. But this light was very bright, and she opened her eyes to a shiny brim and eyes just above the light.

"Ma'am," the policeman said, "are you alright?"

55

There Goes Santa Claus

GEORGE KNEW HE was doomed even before the bumper wheel tore the foot-long gash in the sailboat. He knew when he backed the boat up he was powerless against what the fates decreed. So much of life was like that. You are suddenly just along for the ride. And when he turned and saw Jamie on the roof clutching her shoulders in the cold, swirling smoke and snow contagion, he knew the fates had decreed once again he would go along for the ride.

He was waiting for the signal so the handlers could pull the reindeer toward the ramp and by the scrim that would block Megan's view while the digital cameras projected him flying into the sky. The handlers would guide the reindeer down the long wooden ramp, where George would alight, go around the house, slip in the back door, and take off the Santa suit, and emerge when Megan woke him to reveal she had videotaped Santa Claus.

Now here was the famous moment again where he goosed the engine and smashed *The Sally Jane* into the dock. The moment had come with his seventeen-year-old daughter shivering off camera. "Jamie! You're here!"

Dean was having none of this. "What in the hell are you doing, mate? Turn back around. You have to go down the bloody ramp! I'm going to run out of smoke and snow soon!"

And George knew all this. But there was Jamie shivering and standing there in the snow looking pathetic and abandoned. They had been very close up to the divorce. George's daughter was easier than his son. There was none of that silent shame of fathers and sons. He remembered taking her ice skating and sledding and standing in for his wife at Girl Scouts meetings. He had actually been a better dad to her than to his son.

But he had lost Jamie when he divorced. She saw his betrayal as complete when he had another daughter, supplanting her in his heart with another. George had tried to explain they were sisters, but then her mother took up with Dirk, and the Florida Christmases began, and Jamie realized there was no Santa. It broke his heart, but he didn't know what to do.

So there was now this moment.

And Jamie was freezing. She had dressed for Florida, and ever since she got out of the car she had started to get really cold. She couldn't feel her fingers or her toes, and she was starting to shiver uncontrollably. And she felt lost. She stared at her father in the sled, and she realized he had not been Santa for her. For good or bad she had lost his favor, and now she was outside of his family, standing in the cold.

"I didn't want to go," she told him.

George shook his head.

"You are freezing! You need a coat."

"I'm fine, Dad."

Jamie was crying now. George could see that. He was a man pointed to go off a roof behind nine reindeer with his son by his side and his daughter behind him.

"I think she needs help, Dad," Jeremy muttered.

He had said that many times. He had called his father over the years to tell him what was going on with his sister. And he was doing it now. Jeremy started to get out of the sled.

"I'll help her," his son muttered.

George put his hand on Jeremy's arm. This was one of those moments. *The Sally Jane* was sailing for disaster, but he wasn't going to let the fates decide this time. He turned around. "Jamie ... will you ride with us?"

"George, are you crazy? The mite will see her!" Dean screamed in his ear.

George looked around at the technicians crouching around the roof and saw Megan still at the window. He could not sacrifice one daughter for the other. They would do this thing together or not at all. He motioned with his glove. "Here." He lifted the blanket behind him. "Sneak up around the back so Megan won't see you, and get in here under the blanket in the back of the sled. You can get warm."

There was a large, thick white blanket that one of Dean's prop people had come up with to cover the sack of toys. It was fur lined on the edges and very thick.

"Come on, Jamie, ride with Santa," Jeremy called out.

She wiped her eyes.

"You sure you want me to, Dad?"

"Absolutely, honey. I never wanted anything more."

Jeremy waved her on. "Come on, sis. Let's ride with Santa."

Jamie crouched down and ran to the side of the sled then slipped under the blanket.

"Are you in?" George asked.

"Yes," came the muffled reply.

"Are you getting warmer?"

"Mmmmm ... yes. Wow, I'm in Santa's sleigh!"

George turned around and looked up at Dean cussing a blue streak in his ear. He stared into the snow and smoke and saw where the ramp fell away from the roof. Really he only had to go about twenty-five feet, then he was home free. Still he had that same feeling. He was standing behind the wheel of the boat and staring at the dock.

"Go, George! GO!" Dean screamed.

"Away, Prancer, Vixen, Comet, Cupid, Vixen ... I mean Dixon ... no, Donner ... Shit!"

He cracked the reins, and the handlers pulled on the reindeer, and Santa's sled slipped across the roof toward the snowy darkness below.

56

Santa's Tank

SHANTI KNEW IT was Kronenfeldt. He had carefully gone over the igloo Panzer and examined the knife cuts in the material. Someone had attacked his Christmas tank savagely and slashed large, gaping holes in it. He had immediately suspected the egghead across the street and went back to Menards and purchased another tank and a mooning Santa. He had it up and inflated the very next night. Then he sat vigil by the living room window, dozing in the armchair, waiting for Kronenfeldt to return.

He had sat there every night and went to work bleary eyed. He had positioned the mooning Santa's ass right at Kronenfeldt's house. Shanti took great satisfaction every time Santa dropped his pants toward his neighbor's living room. But he had not caught him in the act, and now the Kronenfeldt home had turned into a circus. There were trucks and lights and people, and now there were the cops.

Shanti had sipped his coffee behind his tank and mooning Santa and watched people walking behind his neighbor's house. He had considered it might be an elaborate diversion. Still he felt he couldn't leave his inflatables. He had been in his front yard when he saw Santa pop out of Kronenfeldt's lit-up chimney. He had scurried over then and saw the reindeer on the roof and asked an older man watching with a cell phone to his ear what was going on.

"This guy is trying to be the real Santa for his daughter," the man had declared, shaking his head. "Can you believe he's got nine reindeer on his roof?"

Shanti had stared, and he couldn't believe it, but he saw an opportunity. He had run back to his home and pulled out his cell phone and dialed the police. He had hung up, assured the cops would shut Kronenfeldt down. Then he watched the cop walk up to the front door and knock, and he saw Mary answer. Shanti had felt like he was actually commanding a tank and sending over a missile aimed right at Kronenfeldt's heart.

"Mess with me," he had muttered as the cop gestured to the backyard. "Ha! Kronenfeldt must have put out a lot of bucks, and now he's going to find out the price for screwing with me!"

But no SWAT team had appeared, and the cop had just walked back to his squad car and pulled away. Shanti couldn't believe it. *Some guy has reindeer on his roof and he doesn't get arrested?* He had dialed the police again, but they were busy. He then went back outside and continued standing guard behind his tank. He was contemplating calling the police again when he saw a cop walking by with an old lady.

"Officer," he called out. "Officer!"

The cop and the old lady turned. The woman looked familiar now, and he realized it was Julie's teacher.

"Oh ... hello, Mrs. Worthington."

She looked at him wearily, her eyes drifting to his home.

"Is that your house with those horrible things on your lawn?"

Shanti turned around slowly and felt his face warm.

"Um ... well ... yeah."

Mrs. Worthington drew herself up and stared at him.

"I can't believe someone would be crude enough to put out a man displaying his buttocks like that!"

The cop smirked as Santa's bright pink ass lit up: MERRY CHRISTMAS! Mrs. Worthington continued to melt Shanti with her glare.

"I thought it was festive," he said weakly.

"*Disgusting* is what it is, and you have grown daughters! What kind of values do you have? Only a *pervert* would put something like that on their lawn! A degenerate! There ought to be a law against cretins who put *nude men* on their lawn! Imagine a grown man buying something like that! I would think you would be more circumspect having girls in the house!"

Shanti's face was on fire, and he felt like he was nine years old again.

"I'll take it down," he mumbled, staring at the snow.

"See that you do," Mrs. Worthington commanded, staring at the mooning Santa. "Just disgusting!"

The cop looked at Shanti.

"You wanted something?"

"Uh ... yeah. I called in a disturbing the peace complaint and nobody's doing anything."

The cop breathed deeply and looked at the sled on the roof with the reindeer.

"We are shutting this down right now," Mrs. Worthington declared, staring up at Santa Claus with pure hate.

57

Rudolf with Your Nose So Bright

A LOT OF times movies hinge on programs that crash or hard drives that freeze up or digital projectors that decide a blinding snowstorm is the moment to shut down like an old tube radio. The tech running the projector had no idea what was causing the problem on this shoot, but the entire movie depended on this moment. Forget the sled was now loaded with Santa and his two kids, or that Megan was standing at the window waiting for Santa to take off; the real immediate problem was that a cop and an old lady and an old man were coming up the ramp like the cavalry.

Dean didn't need anyone to tell him this would determine the rest of his life. He remembered a story about Thalberg, the boy genius of MGM in the thirties. He had told F. Scott Fitzgerald that if a man wanted to build a bridge over a mountain, and there were three different ways to do it, then it was up to him to pick the way, even if it was the wrong way. And Dean saw that he would have to pick. His tech was saying into his ear even now, "I think snow got into it somehow ...," letting Dean know that technology had failed him, and he would have to throw the dice because the cop had just about reached the range of the shot. Dean had to pick a place to build the bridge, and he had to do it now.

He had told the tech to wait on the projector, but he had no choice. Santa had to make a getaway and how he got off the roof would reveal itself in the shot. Great filmmaking was an adventure, and this was his moment; besides, the snowstorm that had blown up out of nowhere was giving him incredible movie magic for free. Now was the time. He had to risk it all or end up with nothing.

"Go! We are good, mate!" he screamed.

"You sure?" George crackled back.

"Yes … go, mate! The cops are coming up the ramp. It's either now or never!"

"What about the projector?"

"This is it, mate. We can't worry about that now. *Go!*"

Dean watched Santa snap the reins and the handlers jerk the animals forward and the reindeer spring to life as if they had been shocked. The nine reindeer on George Kronenfeldt's roof bolted for the edge just like Santa's reindeer were supposed to do. The problem was George couldn't see the ramp anymore, and it seemed to Dean the reindeer were headed away from the exit point.

"Keep rolling!" the director shouted into the blinding snow.

58

Divorced Santa

AFTER HIS DIVORCE, George spent all his time at the Columbia Yacht Club. There he could sit in the old icebreaker moored up in Monroe Harbor and nurse Seven and Sevens with other sailors coming in for a quick burger and a beer while telling of harrowing feats out on Lake Michigan. The truth was there really were no *Moby Dick* moments in the Columbia Yacht Club. The sailing set were usually businessmen taking out their forty-five-foot boats for a quick sail. They wore expensive yellow foul-weather gear that made them feel more like adventurers.

Usually George left the bar and wandered the ship. He didn't want to return to his apartment that felt like a middle-aged man's bachelor apartment with the white walls and beige carpet. The less time spent there the better, and while the lawyers hacked it out, George preferred to be at sea. The *Columbia* had been a Canadian icebreaker and hauled railroad cars up into the Great North for excavating coal and timber. In the bowels of the ship were the railroad tracks blasted into the steel that the cars sat on. George was amazed the hold had space for a whole train.

Then he slipped up to the bridge and looked out over the city. Chicago glittered before him, and he wondered what the captain must have thought, staring out from three stories up over the Great Lakes, piloting his ship as master of his universe. George had never been master of his universe, and he wondered how men could control giant ships with cargos of locomotives and coal cars. Surely these men started out their lives that way—a declaration early on that *I will control life* and not the other way around.

He then looked into the old wireless room with the headphones and the crude technology of the early twentieth century. After that, George reached his final destination: the ship's library. It was a small library full of thick, well-thumbed books. There were several benches for men of the *Columbia* to sit on while reading after being up on deck. A single porthole with red curtains and the two sconces gave the library a Victorian sort of Captain Smith aura. George felt like he never wanted to leave, and often times he didn't.

He slept in the library more than once. His loneliness seemed far away after reading Jack London or Hemingway or Joseph Conrad. He imagined himself far out to sea, just a man reading a book in the roaring blackness of Lake Michigan. That was how he passed the year after his divorce, right up to when he met Mary and then tacked into a relationship. And George realized now—sitting in front of the sled with his two children, one beside him and one behind, with the reindeer galloping into the blurry, smoky white contagion—that while he had been lost at sea, his kids had been lost too.

Maybe it was Mrs. Worthington charging up the ramp with the police—a sight that was wholly unbelievable. And there really was only one way out and that was to put the final girder on the bridge and let the ship slam into the dock. Both moves brought unintended consequences. George tied losing his job to the bicycle bridge. He knew he had screwed up, but now there was that girder spanning the highway like a monument to George Kronenfeldt. And slamming the boat into the dock brought him back from the *Columbia* and being lost permanently at sea, the same way there would be a monument to his being Santa Claus. Every project George had worked on had this built-in epoch where the whole thing came together or didn't. The problems of the original design manifested themselves at the weakest point. George knew the flaw in his grand scheme was getting the reindeer off the roof. He had considered they might not want to go, and he had considered that they might want to go too much. Either way, the result was not going to be good.

But even as the sled headed for the edge of the roof, even as the reindeer bucked and lunged toward the edge, he was glad he had his children with him. If Megan's vision of the world was to be rescued, he was glad to be able to involve Jamie and Jeremy in it. They should all be rescued, and this time he was not going to hide in a ship's library. He was not going to let everything go to hell by just staying away. Jeremy had once told George that: "When you get uncomfortable, you just leave." And George wasn't going to do that anymore. Not now.

But the ice and the wind and the snow were blinding, and George knew they were not going to hit that ramp. They were going to go right over the edge of the roof and kill the animals, maybe his kids, and himself. He had to make the decision now—go down with the ship or save himself and his kids.

"Jump," he screamed, pushing Jeremy off the sled onto the roof.

"Dad!" Jamie yelled.

George reached behind him and grabbed his daughter. He jumped, pulling her with him, and they rolled in the snow on the hard roof as the sled and the reindeer vanished. George looked up from the roof and heard the hooves clattering down the ramp and felt a great relief. He had not killed nine reindeer. But then he felt a great sickness. He had lost his hat and was staring at a little girl in her bedroom window, holding a video camera on him.

59

Natalie Wood

THERE HAD BEEN clues over the years—the presents in the closet off her parent's bathroom, covered by the large red wool blanket that seemed to come out around Christmas; the presents in the trunk of the car that her mother said were for her cousins; the letters to Santa that mysteriously disappeared from the mailbox even before the mail truck arrived. (She had run out and checked to make sure the letters were there.) The Christmas Eve sounds that turned out to be her parents up way past midnight.

Then there was the funny look in her mother's eye when she asked if Santa was real. It was the same look when she asked where babies came from. Her cheeks turned red, and then she would say something quickly and turn away. That was how she knew her mother was lying. But still, Megan believed in Santa. It was her father who patiently explained how Santa was able to use a relativity cloud to circumvent gravity and move through time and space at ferocious speeds and essentially be everywhere at once. Megan had looked up relativity clouds on the Internet and found his explanation plausible.

But Megan had just seen Santa Claus and his two elf helpers jump out of the sled and land on the roof. What Megan couldn't reconcile was that Santa had lost his hat and there was her dad staring at her. It simply wasn't possible, but she threw up the window and jumped out onto the snowy roof before her mother could grab her. Santa had disappeared behind a veil of snow and some sort of oily fog. Small lights like airport beacons studded the roof in different spots, and there was a strange whirring sound. Megan stood in the snow in her slippers. Santa had to only be a few feet away, and if he wasn't her father, then Santa had fallen out of his sleigh on her roof.

"Santa!" Megan called out.

She heard nothing then a train horn far off. The snow blew like thick confetti all around her. From where she was standing, she thought Santa was only a few feet away.

"Santa!"

The thought that Santa might really be her parents and her parents might really be Santa or Santa might be Santa confused her. But someone had fallen out of a sled on her roof, and she was going to find out who it was. There was only one thing to do—walk to where she thought Santa had fallen out and see who was there. Megan took another step.

60

Trying to be Santa

"SHE'S ON THE roof," crackled in George's ear. "She is standing on the roof, mate! Don't bloody move!"

George was lying down in the snow. He heard Megan call out, "Santa? Santa, are you there?" Dean had aimed the movie snow and fog at him after the reindeer had found the ramp. George felt like a pilot who had ejected too early, unwilling to trust the reindeer would hit their mark.

"I think she's coming toward us, Dad," Jeremy murmured with his face just above the snow.

"Where is she?" Jamie whispered, keeping her head low to the roof.

George knew it was over then.

"Don't move a muscle, mate, don't move ... she might just go back into her room."

George saw the people in the yard, and somewhere up on the roof were the cops and Mrs. Worthington. They were waiting for him to emerge as well. And the failure hit George then. Not only would he not be the Real Santa, but he would disprove the myth by *trying to be* Santa. Megan would no longer believe in Santa after she saw it was her father who had landed on the roof. And he had no choice. No choice but to tell Megan that the world was really a place where people played with dreams that generally came to nothing at all.

"That's it. It's over," he said to Dean, standing up.

"What are you doing, mate? You can't just quit now," Dean sputtered.

"No. Enough is enough," George said, walking through the veil of snow and smoke. His vision cleared, and there was Megan with her arms crossed, shivering in the cold. She still held the video camera.

"Santa!"

George stared at her, then Megan blinked.

"Dad?"

61

Kris Kringgle

THE REINDEER GALLOPED in the backyard with people running from the crazed Santa sled. The crowd behind the barrier saw a sled catapulting down a wooden ramp, and now the sled was fishtailing in snowy arcs. Finally a man with a beard catapulted himself into the sleigh and managed to rein in the reindeer, who suddenly came to a halt and started nuzzling the snow again.

But this was after Dean had his moment. He had watched in horror as George jumped out of the sled with his kids landing in the snow. And then the little tyke had gone out the window onto the roof. He screamed at Cliff running the digital projector to get that *bloody thing* going, because that would be his salvation. Now was the time to project Santa Claus flying into the sky and keep George behind the veil of smoke and snow.

It would have worked if George had not stood up. And now Megan was staring at her father, and Dean saw his movie going down the drain. He told his cinematographer to keep rolling and barked into his headset for everyone to stay in their places. If it was going to be a reality show, then so be it!

It worked for Ozzie.

And Dean watched as George faced his daughter and realized the magnitude of his failure. He looked down and didn't know what to say. He didn't know what to say as his daughter stared at the soot-covered chemical snowman. Santa had become her father just like that, and she wasn't sure how to approach him.

"Daddy ... that was you?"

"Megan ... I am sorry honey ... I ..."

And then Dean's projector pierced the gloom, and George saw an image in the smoky cloud. A man hovered above him in Santa regalia inside a green transparent bubble. George stared up and appreciated Dean's valiant effort to bring something back from nothing, but it was over. Then the shimmering Santa spoke in a large echoing voice not unlike the Wizard of Oz.

"MEGAN! WERE YOU A GOOD GIRL THIS YEAR?"

George brought a finger across his throat.

"Cut it, Dean!"

But Dean was staring at the translucent image that warbled near then far. A light emanated from the bubble and lit up the roof and the sparkling snow. Suddenly the house was bathed in the pale bath of a light snowstorm. Megan stared at the image then looked at her father. Santa was holding the reindeer, who galloped but didn't move. The image moved like the UFOs on amateur video, darting, coming back, moving out, with a low-sonic hum emanating like the test signal from old televisions.

"MEGAN," the voice boomed again. "HAVE YOU BEEN GOOD?"

Megan stood in her pink robe and stared at Santa, who leaned over the side of the sleigh.

"I have ... but ... but you're not real ... are you?"

The image shot up over the chimney then circled back before a watch hand ticked a second.

"LET'S SEE YOUR FATHER DO THAT!"

"*You are real!*" Megan shouted, her eyes shining, her hands balled under her chin.

The shimmering Santa spread out his arms and threw down a gift to the roof. The voice came close then as Santa leaned down. "You didn't really believe that *goofball* going down the chimney was me, did you?"

Megan shrugged. "Well, maybe for just a little."

The emanating light inside the green bubble moved in close and the snow lit like fire.

"I am as real as you and all who believe, Megan. Your other gifts are under the tree, but I wanted your father to have this one."

The image then darted up and moved down the roof, and Megan saw her teacher, Mrs. Worthington.

"BARBARA ..." The green bubble floated in close. "THERE IS A BIKE FOR YOU ... I HAVE OWED YOU THAT A LONG TIME ... I THINK YOU WILL FIND IT SUITED TO YOUR NEW LIFE."

Megan saw Mrs. Worthington staring with her mouth open.

"Fathers don't know everything, Barbara ... he did the best he could."

And then the light shot above the house and started to fade. Santa's voice floated somewhere high above, becoming fainter.

"YOUR FATHER DID A GOOD JOB ... TAKING OFF HAS ALWAYS BEEN TRICKY. I TOLD HIM HE WOULD KILL HIMSELF ..."

And then Santa and his reindeer shot up and became a dot then the blue pin of a star. Dean stared with his mouth open and looked at his cameraman.

"*Did you bloody get that, mate ... did you get that?*"

Megan picked up the present and held it up.

"What is it, Megan?" her father asked.

She frowned. "It's a key and a note."

George walked over to her.

"It says, *please water the plants and feed the cats.*"

"Who signed it?" George asked.

Megan held up the key.

"Kris Kringgle."

62

Rookie

ON CHRISTMAS DAY George walked down the musty hallway to the door with Kris Kringgle on the card. He pulled out the key when a voice called out, "It's open!"

George walked in and heard a television at the far end of the hallway.

"Tell me ... is that the artist moron formerly known as *Real* Santa?"

George hesitated then walked back down the hall. Kringgle sat behind the newspapers and pizza boxes with a cigarette wicking up beside him. He looked over his glasses.

"So ... you didn't kill yourself?"

George shook his head. "No."

Kringgle opened the paper and looked up.

"Not as easy as it looks, is it?"

"No. The chimney is a real bitch."

"Oh, yes, I know," he murmured. "Everyone thinks they can be Santa Claus, and it will be really easy. Let's see someone else go all over the world giving out gifts. Ha! They couldn't do it ... wouldn't know where to begin!"

George watched his fingers on the newspaper.

"How did you know I would need help?"

Kringgle snorted and turned the page. "Please. Those ramps— they look like that bicycle bridge you built." He dropped the paper.

"That reminds me." He fished up a card. "Call this guy. He needs an engineer."

George took the card and looked at the old man in his blue sweat-suit. "You don't have to do this for me."

Kringgle picked up his cigarette and frowned.

"I'm not doing it for you, moron. I'm doing it for Megan. She asked me to get you a job."

"I think she asked me," George said, smiling.

Kringgle frowned. "Don't be as stupid as you look. She asked the real Santa, and we both know that ain't you." Kringgle yawned and shook his head. "Well, I am beat," he said, slumping back in his chair and stretching out his toes.

"Long night?"

He looked up and frowned.

"Are you a moron? I just went around the whole fricking world in one night!"

"Right … right. Sorry." George paused. "So you don't need me to feed the cats?"

"They are just fine. Mrs. Claus is going to feed them for me," he replied, closing his eyes.

"Oh. Then you are—"

"Maybe." He shrugged. "I told her I smoke and like football and eat pizza and deal with it … we'll see what happens."

"Well, I guess I will be on my way then."

Kringgle reached down.

"Take this with you."

"What is it?"

"Just take it … Jesus! Can't you accept a gift?"

George took the envelope. He paused and stood a moment.

"Was that … was that really you in that … bubble?"

"It wasn't the Easter Bunny," he murmured.

"Right."

Kringgle shut his eyes.

"Take care … *Santa*."

"You too, Kris Kringgle."

George walked back down the hallway.

"Lock it on the way out. I don't want any of those ne'er-do-well

Santas bugging me from the department stores," he called behind him. "Morons."

"Will do."

George left the apartment and went to his car. He held the envelope then opened it.

> *George,*
>
> *So, now you know the great secret of being Santa Claus. Relativity Clouds! The only way to travel! You did pretty good for a rookie. Better than any those clowns at Macy's could of done. It took a lot of balls to put nine reindeer up on a roof and have them shit everywhere. But back to the Secret of Santa, which you asked me about when we first met ... Family, George. You have family, then you have it all my friend. Not everyone can build a bicycle bridge that looks like a railroad bridge. Or sail a boat into a dock.*
>
> *My best to Jamie, Jeremy, and of course, Megan.*
>
> *Your Friend,*
>
> *Kris Kringgle ...THE REAL SANTA*

George held the letter then put it in his pocket and found the picture of his father on Christmas Eve. He stared at that harried family man for a moment. Then he started his car. His father, Mary, Megan, Jeremy, and Jamie were all waiting for him to cut the Christmas turkey. And he didn't have a second to lose.

63

Showtime

TWO YEARS LATER Dean's movie came out. People enjoyed the fact a man would try and be Real Santa. They just couldn't believe anyone would put reindeer on their roof or that the real Santa would bail out the dad. Nonbelievers saw it as justification because everyone knows there is not really a Santa Claus. The proof was that Dean had to have special effects fill in the gap in the film. None of the real Santa footage made it into the film. Even the people who saw Megan's video marveled at the dark gap. But the father going up onto the roof with the reindeer and climbing the chimney then emerging as a Black Santa got a lot of hits. Even Mrs. Worthington watched it.

You could say Barbara Worthington had a change of heart, like the people who see UFOs and are never the same. She and her husband never talked about it, but they had both seen something from another world. And Mrs. Worthington found retirement not so terrifying. She found comfort that some things were not explainable. No one was more surprised than Walter when she wrote a letter the next Christmas and placed it in their mailbox.

She rode her Schwinn bicycle every day it was nice out.

ACKNOWLEDGMENTS

Many thanks to John Koehler for bringing out *Real Santa* and to Leticia Gomez for being a great agent, once again. Thanks to my editor, Joe Coccaro, for massaging the manuscript and to my family once again for giving me one idea after another.

CPSIA information can be obtained at www.ICGtesting.com
Printed in the USA
BVOW07*1048200814

363337BV00001B/3/P